WHITEOUT

A NICK VENTNER ADVENTURE

By

ASHTON MACAULAY

WHITEOUT

Published by Aberrant Literature

Copyright © 2018 by Ashton Macaulay

www.aberrantliterature.com
www.macashton.com

Author services by Pedernales Publishing, LLC.
www.pedernalespublishing.com

Library of Congress Control Number: 2017962601

ISBN 978-0-9980211-5-7 Paperback Edition
ISBN 978-0-9980211-4-0 Hardcover Edition
ISBN 978-0-9980211-3-3 Digital Edition

Printed in the United States of America

CONTENTS

WHITEOUT

To three dudes I met on Craig's List.

To my family, who has always supported me.

CONTRIBUTOR DEDICATIONS

Helen Zbihlyj

"Ashton... don't let your dreams be dreams. —Shia LaBeouf"

Ann-Marie Blix/Kermit Macaulay

"We would like to dedicate our donation to an amazing un-published writer in the family no longer with us, Freda Blix. Mom, your purity of love that shines through your beautiful words will not be forgotten."

Rosemary and Dick Fausel

"To Grandma Macaulay (aka The Goat) who encouraged us to experience and share our adventures. She would be "proud as punch" of you, Ashton. Keep challenging yourself and provide the world with the most!"

Special thanks to **Tracy Horton** for helping to make this book happen

PROLOGUE

"So you want to know about the yeti?" said Nick, savoring the look of surprise on the man's face.

"Indeed," answered Winston, the portly man sitting opposite him. Clearly he thought there was going to be some sort of conversational foreplay before they came to that topic. Nick had never been one for small talk, and in the years since he had been back, the yeti seemed to be the only thing that interested people anymore. It also garnered the unexpected perk of free drinks, which he didn't mind.

"And why exactly is that?" Nick asked.

"The subject is fascinating," Winston breathed excitedly. "From the moment I first heard the rumors, I knew that I would have to get the real story straight from the source." He leaned forward expectantly, causing the buttons of his freshly pressed shirt to strain from the size of his girth.

Nick Ventner thought Winston looked more prepared to attend the opera than swap stories with a monster hunter. With his neatly trimmed moustache and patiently combed-over white hair, Nick doubted that he had so much as encountered a gremlin, let alone anything of substance.

Just what exactly do you want with a yeti anyway? There's nothing to be gained on that mountain apart from frostbite and blood.

Nick's concentration was broken by the appearance of an austere butler carrying a tray with a cup of steaming tea. Winston thanked the man and took the cup. Before Nick had time to ask for anything, the butler slipped away.

"Sprightly man, isn't he?"

"Yes, quite," mused Winston, taking a sip of his tea.

"Don't suppose he does drinks?" Nick raised his eyebrows hopefully.

"Oh, yes, of course he does."

Silence fell as Nick waited for an offer that never came. He grimaced at the hideous odor wafting from Winston's tea. *Smells like llama piss and probably cost more than he paid to find me.*

Winston watched Nick intently, like a toad hunting a juicy fly. "Well, then, will you tell me the story?"

"It's a long and ugly one …" Nick looked around for the butler, who remained absent.

"Yes, of course. So you'll tell it?" Winston's eyes looked eager, like a child expecting to receive sweets.

"Are you a climber?" Nick asked, moving the subject away from the yeti. "I saw a few pieces of climbing gear on the way in."

"Well, I dabble, but never anything …"

Nick stopped listening. *You look like you have trouble climbing out of bed, much less anything that even closely resembles a mountain. I bet you've never even been above 15,000 feet outside of an airplane.* Nick found himself staring at Winston's gut once more, wondering how long it would be before his shirt gave way like a bursting dam. The thought caused him to shudder.

Winston continued to talk despite the glazed look in Nick's eyes. "But Kilimanjaro really isn't that difficult if you've got the proper guide."

The conversation settled once more into awkward silence as the man waited for Nick to respond. "Oh, yes, and you must watch out for the hominids up there as well; quite dangerous when they get into a pack." Nick allowed his mind to drift to the many decorations plastered on the walls.

Every inch of the mansion they sat in agitated Nick in some way. The armchairs were too plush, artifacts from different cultures were spread around the room in a fashion that had no discernable pattern, and above all, the man was lazy, circuitous, and rich. Even the winding lane leading up to the ornate doors had been adorned with artifacts so culturally at odds with the place that Nick thought they were more apt to start a holy war than be considered tasteful. In a different time, Nick might have idolized his wealth, but recently he had been searching for more in life.

"Well, the hominids didn't really trouble us much—"

Nick grew frustrated with the lack of proffered drink and cut him off. "Look, I don't have time for this. I was told that you were interested in hiring me, but if the yeti story is all you want, then I'm out of here." Nick stood up from his chair and turned to go.

There's just no room for respectable monster hunters anymore. They all just want the spectacle.

"I can pay you," said Winston, stopping Nick in his tracks.

Nick may not have wanted to be rich, but his pockets were a tad light, trending toward empty, and the pub around the corner was not cheap. He looked back at the man's face. A wave of familiarity struck him, but vanished just as quickly as it appeared.

"Five thousand for the story," said Winston, "beginning to end. I won't publish it, I won't record it. I just want to hear it." The man sat back in his chair, hands folded across his lap. An expression of victory quickly spread across his smug face.

"Five thousand for a story? You must be some kind of bored." Nick lowered himself back into the chair.

"I've heard the tale secondhand so many times that it seems

foolish not to hear it from the man himself. I have complex interests, Mr. Ventner, and you have piqued them."

*Complex interests? Complex carbs, maybe. Your interests are
provincial at best.* The only real complexity Nick could see about
the man was the series of bands that miraculously kept his clothes
attached to his body. *A little spectacle never hurt anyone. Ah, he
would have wanted it anyway. Fortune and glory, remember?*

"Well, your money has piqued *my* interests, but there's one
final condition."

"What is that?" Winston asked eagerly.

"I'm going to need that drink."

PART I:

THE GLAMOROUS LIFE OF A MONSTER HUNTER

1.

WEREWOLVES DON'T HOWL

We should have brought matches.

The thought rang through my head clear as a bell, even after everything else had become a frozen blur. James sat beside me, panting on a rock. His boyish hair was slick with sweat, and his parka was crusted with a fresh coat of frost.

Correction, I should have brought matches and left the kid behind. I had never liked partners. More often than not, they just slowed me down or haunted me in between benders with memories of their death.

Six months prior, I ran into an eager undergrad who had drunkenly spouted off about cryptozoology. A few silver bullets and a modicum of training later, James Schaefer became my apprentice. I was amazed that even after seeing the uglier side of the world, he managed to fight off a disposition of cynicism. Despite being half-frozen in a blizzard, and likely five minutes away from a horrible fate, James managed to keep a positive, albeit sarcastic, attitude.

▼

"Hold on, where were you?" Winston inquired, taking a sip of his tea.

Nick sighed quietly, swilling ice around the bottom of his

empty glass, wondering when the butler would be by to bring refills. "If you would wait a minute, I'll tell you." Winston's interruptions were beginning to irritate him. "I've got plenty of other jobs that don't involve me rehashing painful emotional memories to old men in their parlors."

This was untrue. Even after the encounter with the yeti, very few letters had come through asking for help. While most people in the monster-hunting community had heard tell of the story, they also chose not believe it.

"Of course, I am so very sorry." Winston's words came out false, but they were accompanied by the sudden reappearance of a fresh drink on the table next to Nick.

Nick looked at the glass, astonished. "How does he manage that? Let me guess, he used to be a ninja. Got tired of the bloodshed and turned to butlery?" Nick took a sip of the fresh glass at his side and nearly gagged on some of the worst whiskey he had ever tasted.

All the money in the world and he still drinks this piss?

"Oh yes, he's quite good," said Winston, avoiding the question. Nick must have made a sour face at the drink, because Winston waved his hands apologetically. "My apologies for the drink. I like to start at the bottom and work my way up." He let out a hearty laugh. "Tastes much better in tea."

Nick laughed in spite of his suspicions about the butler. "An efficient drinker even amidst opulence. Now that I can respect."

Winston raised his cup and drained it. "One picks up a few tricks on their way to wealth." His cheeks flushed a bit with the fresh drink, and he even seemed a little friendlier. "Now, I'm terribly sorry to have interrupted you. Please, continue."

Winston's attitude had changed significantly, and it set Nick on edge. Fortunately, the feeling did not last long as the whiskey quickly made its way to his core, warming him on the inside. All traces of misgiving were temporarily erased from his mind, and his bloodstream demanded more of the deep brown alcohol.

"Yes, where was I?" He drained the highball glass and set it down on the table loudly, hoping the butler would hear.

After seeing no sign of him, he continued. "We had been tracking a werewolf through the mountains for days. Supposed to be a quick job. Silver bullet, bring back the head, in and out; simple as that. But there was one big problem: The villagers lied to us. It wasn't a damned werewolf."

— ▼ —

At midnight, the howling started. James and I had made camp in a small cave tucked into the side of the mountain. At that altitude, with the cold wind whipping through our bones, the world grew fuzzy around the edges. For the first few minutes, neither of us was sure we had actually heard howling at all. We simply sat by the glow of the flashlight, hoping that it wasn't the day we would be sent to meet the gods that our profession so strongly opposed.

"Is that it?" James asked, his teeth chattering from where he sat in a corner of the cave. Despite his best efforts to hide it, his body shivered violently, and his lips had turned slightly blue, drying out around the edges.

Should have brought matches. We could have burned our clothes. Anything to stave off the damned cold. Matches were dead useful. They started fires, created distractions, and lit my cigarettes. Unfortunately, I had left them in a pile on the bed with the rest of the accoutrements relating to my "nasty habit", as one of my many ex-girlfriends called it. I was too damned busy pouting about the cigarettes to remember the life-saving matches that had been chucked out with them. Without the heat from a fire, thinking was impossible. The cold took up every ounce of my mental capacity, rendering my mind useless.

Upon our departure, it had been a beautiful sunny day without a cloud in the sky. But the unfortunate thing about the mountains was that it only took a moment or two for things to turn sideways. What had been a distant glimmer of fog atop the mighty mountain turned into a full-blown blizzard in less than an hour.

After a few moments of silent processing, a thought broke through the icy curtain around my mind. James's question had revealed the true nature of our predicament.

Werewolves don't howl.

Movies and TV might portray it otherwise, but in the wild, it never happens. Werewolves are apex predators and lone hunters. There's no need for them to communicate. They don't reproduce, they don't have families; they just hunt. When they want to create more werewolves, they go and bite another villager. It's almost elegant in its simplicity.

Werewolves don't howl.

The statement floated through the air lazily, allowing both James and I to get a better look at it. I glanced over at James, hunkered against the side of the cave wall, and cursed myself again for forgetting the matches. *That's it, double checking for matches from now on.* Had it been the day trip I billed for, it wouldn't have been a problem. But the client had flat-out lied, and now things were getting dicey.

"We're not hunting a werewolf, are we?" James mumbled from deep within his parka.

I wished we were. Werewolves were so easy to track—big feet, lots of fur, and a swath of blood laid out behind them.

"Not anymore," I said. Then came another earsplitting howl. It was long and mournful, shaking the walls of the cave with its intensity. My already chilled blood dropped a full degree as the howl trailed off.

The animals that could have made such a noise were few. I pulled out a leather-bound tome from my satchel, which bore the scratches and scrapes of every journey I had ever been on. It had been written by the "master" that taught me the ways of monster hunting. I never left for a journey without it.

It was mostly filled with crude drawings of various hell-bound creatures that the author had tried to seduce. He may have had a coke-addled mind, but he was a damned good hunter when it came down to it. I flipped through the pages, hoping that some-where between poetry about the dismembered head of a warg and amateur comic strips detailing the mating habits of Romanian banshees, there would be useful information.

The sound came again. Like a wolf, only longer, lower, and far louder. To be heard over the fury of a snowstorm was no easy feat. Even in the cave, we could hear the roaring of the wind outside battering the mountain in nature's best attempt to bring it down. I continued to shuffle through the book until I happened upon the page I was looking for. Most people at the time thought that the upper slopes of the Himalayas were barren and uninhabited.

Most people were wrong.

2.

LOPSANG

Two days earlier, James and I had arrived in a small farming village at the base of the mountain. The scene was chaos. Goat shit in the streets, prayer flags molding and rotting in every corner. I was overcome by the powerful smell of incense mixed with cheap mountain wine. Most visitors to the town came seeking Sherpa crews. They would guide tourists up the mountain all throughout spring, but during autumn, business was slow.

Unfortunately for the small town, we weren't there to climb. A week earlier, I had received a letter at my office, a dilapidated studio apartment with a faded bronze sign bearing my name and title. It was a single scroll of parchment with a plane ticket stapled to the back. The message was a simple one:

> *We have problem. We're willing to pay you*
> *much money to fix it.*

I was less than intrigued by the destination, but the promise of receiving "much money" was enough to get me out of a bender and onto a plane.

My plan had been to use the plane ticket, go to the village, reject their offer, and get drunk in a climbing lodge. Drinking in the mountains seemed far more appealing than drinking in a dingy pub, especially one that looked like it had just recovered from an outbreak of plague. A small part of me thought the work might be interesting, but mostly I just wanted the mountain wine.

James had managed to buy his own ticket with the money we acquired from disposing of a run-of-the-mill lake monster earlier that month. Despite my attempts to evade him, the young boy was sitting on the tarmac when my cab arrived. Soon, we both found ourselves on a plane that had no right to be airborne. Corrugated metal and oval-shaped pieces of fading plastic were all that separated us from a 20,000-foot fall to the valley below. I remembered thinking that it would have only taken us around five seconds to reach the bottom. The view would have been spectacular, though.

We arrived at the town after a turbulent landing and a two-day hike. I thought it would be like a scene out of an adventure film, as when the women and children came out to kiss Indy's feet and beg for help. As it turned out, the movies weren't that far off. I'd been to Nepal twice—once to dispose of an opium-dealing necromancer, and the second to clear out an ancient curse that left villagers with no eyes and a hunger for flesh. On both occasions, the welcomes were warm—aside from those who had been infected, that is—and the parties were warmer. I found that good company was one of the few things that staved off the mountain chill.

The village itself was very basic. Two rows of medium-sized wood buildings staked out the edges, and a trampled pile of mud and shit ran between them. It was not the absolute worst I'd seen—that had been a shack built of rotten planks and the clothes of dead men who lost a fight to a bog monster in the bayou—but it still looked as though the buildings would collapse given a strong breeze. In the distance, I could see rice paddies and jungle valleys. Above them, there was nothing but the mountain.

It stuck out like a sore thumb, dominating the rest of the landscape. The mountain was the watcher, always reminding the village of who its true master was. The early snows of fall had already blanketed the lower hills, painting it white. At the top, where the winds were too strong for fresh powder to accumulate, glaciers covered the sides like angry sores. A few small clouds hung over the summit, obscuring it from view. If anyone was climbing, it meant they were going to have to come back down and wait another day to get to the top.

Echoing off the wooden planks and empty mountainside, a voice cut through the calm. "Hello, hello, you must be Dr. Ventner," a young man called out, running through the streets, waving his arms like a madman.

For some odd reason, all my clients seemed to think I was a doctor. Most people in my line of work were generally assumed to have gone through higher education, or at least some formal training, but I had a bachelor's degree in political science. My textbooks had less to do with hunting mythical creatures and more to do with getting paid for slowing down the progression of society. I often thought that a job in government might have been easier, but politicians never got to carry a crossbow.

"That's me. Who are you?"

The man standing in front of me was short, not freakishly so, but well below average height. He wore a thick fur coat and a pair of black goggles strapped to the top of a brown woolen cap. I instantly pegged him as a guide; his gear and stature were a perfect fit.

"I wrote the letter," he said, beaming excitedly. "I'm Lopsang." His eyes were wide with excitement. "I knew you'd come. Thank you so much."

"Uh, yeah, of course," I managed in an awkward tone. It was strange to see someone having so much faith in me when I possessed such little confidence in myself.

"Who is this?" Lopsang motioned to James, who was bundled in a bright orange coat. He was so heavily loaded with bags that he might have been mistaken for a very tall mule.

"My apprentice, James." I let the word "apprentice" ring in the mountain air. I knew that James hated it, and he had reminded me often that it sounded like a term for a "boyish wizard" rather than a monster-hunting companion. I often wished that James could have been more like a boyish wizard, as magical powers would have made him a bit more useful.

"Pleasure to meet the apprentice of such a famous adventurer." Lopsang bowed.

I wouldn't have considered myself very famous at the time, but word traveled quickly when you amassed more monster corpses than paychecks.

"Well, I have saved my fair share of villages"—I paused for effect—"but I'm no Manchester."

───────────────── ▼ ─────────────────

"Manchester?" asked Winston.

"You're telling me that you've never heard of *the* Manchester?" Nick was genuinely shocked.

Winston shook his head as if the name meant nothing to him.

"You're new to the hunting game, aren't you?" he asked, taking a swig from the whiskey, the flavor steadily growing on him the more he drank.

"I must confess that I am not much of a hunter. I prefer to sit back and pay people to have my curiosities satisfied, rather than risking my neck." A small grin spread across Winston's face.

Was that a joke?

"Well, if curiosity keeps refreshing my glass, then I'm keen to satisfy it." Nick thought he saw Winston make the slightest gesture, and the butler appeared again, filling Nick's glass with a smooth brown liquid. For the first time, Nick felt a certain affection for the man sitting across from him. He picked up the glass, took a drink, and felt instant pleasure as fire ran down his throat. "That's the good stuff," he spluttered, exhaling fumes.

"It only gets better for guests that can manage to keep me entertained." Winston winked and motioned for him to continue. "Tell me about this Manchester."

"Where to start." Nick thought for a moment, lost in all the negative memories he had of the man. "I had killed my fair share of beasties, but never on a scale like him. That guy took down a fully grown lake monster in less than five minutes. If you believe the stories."

"And do you believe the stories?"

"Of course not. They're full of shit. I hold the record for disposing of lake monsters at just over six minutes, but Manchester is still damned good at what he does. It may not have been five minutes, but he had nothing but a rusty old sword and a dinghy that was far from seaworthy. Didn't even have any chocolate with him."

"Chocolate?"

"They like it." Nick paused, thinking back to a cold, black lake and a boat full of chocolate boxes. "The lake monsters like it."

Winston furrowed his brow, confused. "Lake monsters like chocolate?" He laughed heartily and took another drink. "Well, I suppose we all have our vices."

Nick looked at the drink in his hand and then changed the subject. "That night, we stayed in one of the larger lodges meant for foreign climbers that pass through."

—————————————— ▼ ——————————————

Unpredictable conditions for climbing left the lodge empty in the fall. It was far too dangerous for most tourists. It only took hours for blizzards and harsh winds to pick up, and the tales of what came with them made most crews steer clear. The Sherpas said that they wouldn't go up the mountain for fear of avalanches, but the truth was that most of them were good enough to keep climbing through the winter if they wanted to.

All the surrounding communities lived in peace with the mountain. However, once the summer sun began to sink into fall, they stayed far away from the upper ridge. Old legends said it had something to do with allowing the gods a few months of peace at the top, but I didn't put much stock in superstition. If the locals were turning down coin, there was a better reason than religion.

That night, we met Lopsang down at a small bar that had been thrown together in the corner of the lodge's main room. It was more a man standing behind a tipped-over wooden sign than a bar, but they served hot wine, and plenty of it. James, Lopsang, and I sat at a table next to a thin window, looking out into the dark night sky. A light snow had begun to fall, covering the muddy streets with a layer of frost. The only light came from the fires burning in the distant temples, and even some of those had been extinguished.

Lopsang listened eagerly as I recounted tales of previous adventures. When in the profession of monster hunting, there wasn't much else to talk about. I didn't have a family and barely had a place of residence. All I had was the hunt.

Lopsang had summited the mountain earlier that spring with an American climbing team, and they soon learned that he was one of the most experienced guides in the region.

As he went on, I found myself compelled to ask about the reason for the invitation.

"I'll be honest with you, Lopsang. Things don't seem that bad around here. Why do you need us?" I was slurring my words slightly.

Lopsang's eyes grew dark and fearful, and my guts hardened. If a man who climbs glaciers for recreation was afraid, then we shouldn't have been here.

"Come on, what are we hunting up here?" I attempted to bring back a jovial note to my voice, as if I hadn't noticed the sudden pause.

Lopsang remained silent.

"Oh, come on, who died? What do they say around the campfire about what killed them?"

It might have come off as a tad insensitive, but I had seen so many people torn in half by trolls, demons, and troll-demon hybrids, that it just didn't register anymore. Or it could've been the mountain wine; I really couldn't tell. I remembered a saying about altitude and alcohol but found that the memory ended in a blackout. Which meant it couldn't have been important.

"I will show you," breathed Lopsang, his voice very low. "Come with me."

We walked to the front door and donned thick jackets. Heading out after dark meant that the temperature would have dropped well below zero.

"Should we really be going out at night?" James croaked with an embarrassing, timid squeak.

"We're not hunting vampires, kid," I said with a chuckle, amused by James's apprehension.

Lopsang gave me a sideways glance.

"Wait, we're not, are we?"

"No, we're not," he agreed.

We exited the lodge and were hit by a cold blast of night air. Lopsang continued forward to the edge of the village, where a low picket fence surrounded a small cemetery. There were four fresh graves adorned with mountain flowers quickly being covered by snow. Lopsang fumbled with a medallion on his chest and said a brief prayer.

"This one is my brother's." Lopsang motioned to the first mound of dirt. "He was guiding a group to base camp. It was a small hiking expedition. They weren't going to go higher than 17,000 feet.

"When they didn't return for a week, we went after them. By the time we got there, nothing was left but torn canvas and blood. No bodies were left whole; we found only pieces." Silence fell as we stood over the graves.

I stifled a yawn. It was a tale I'd heard a hundred times. I was more interested in how clearly Lopsang had spoken. The boyish excitement and thick accent had been left behind. A nagging feeling tugged at the back of my spine.

We might be in over our heads. I looked at James, who was wide eyed with fear. A strong breeze blew snow over the graves with an eerie whine.

— ▼ —

"After that, it was just a matter of tracking down the beast, bringing its head back, and getting our reward." Nick sighed, wishing it could have been so easy. "Are you satisfied with the background? Can I move on now?"

Winston pursed his lips as if hoping for a bit more showmanship, but eventually nodded. "I suppose so. So you went after the beast the following morning?"

"That's right, and ended up stuck in that damned ice cave for the night…"

3.

BASE CAMP

Once again, I found myself thinking about matches. It was the repetitive nature of the thought that woke me. Light was streaming through a tiny crack within a wall of snow and ice. The cave I laid in was blurry, but I was alive. What little light filtered through brought a dull warmth to my body, and as I began to move, pain shot through my limbs. My joints cracked and creaked like an ice shelf, and I lost balance at the thought of them crumbling.

Every movement was a stabbing reminder of just how close we had come to death. James lay curled in the corner, huddled against a rock for warmth. After a brief moment of panic, where I thought I had lost my apprentice, James slowly rose.

Great, still breathing. I gave him a swift kick to the ribs to wake him up.

"What the hell?" James shot up, cursing as he felt the cold creep back into his body. His anger was brief, and both of us were soon laughing at the absurdity of our survival. I guess all that crap on National Geographic about using snow caves to keep warm was real.

The moment did not last long, as I was brought back to earth by the memory of the chilling howl the night before. Somehow, through the cold, my spine still managed to prickle.

High up in the mountains, James and I dined on protein bars

and melted snow. To us, it was a bounty fit for kings. After savoring the meal, we advanced outside into the growing sunlight, finding ourselves momentarily blinded. In the early morning light, every drop of water became reflective, and bright spikes of dazzling light flew in all directions. It was enough to make me actually want to step back into the cave.

"Something tells me we're not that far from base camp," I said as my vision began to clear.

"What makes you say that?" asked James. "We could have been walking in circles all night with that blizzard." James pulled out his map and scoffed. "For all we know, we're at the base of the Vikram Wall."

It was highly unlikely that we had gained thousands of feet in elevation without noticing, but I could see that James needed to blow off some steam. After mock-listening to his complaint, I replied calmly and with as much sarcasm as I could muster. "So much anger first thing in the morning. Why don't you have a drink? Take the edge off."

I pulled a silver flask from my right pocket. I always kept it there in case of celebration or extreme danger, and surviving a blizzard fulfilled both conditions.

"Now isn't the time for drinking." James sounded like a parent scolding a spoiled child. "We could still have miles to go and who knows how much altitude to gain?"

I basked in James's pouting, then chuckled and took a swig of the liquid, motioning to the top of the cave where we had camped. A small pile of stones, topped with a set of colorful prayer flags, had been erected. It had been kept upright through the storm by a series of strings running to stakes in the rocks below.

"Well, at least we know why it didn't attack us last night. Lucky break." I took another drink.

"That's …"

"Yes, indeed," I said. "Looks like we've made it after all. Must've been pretty close when the storm hit. Let's have a look. Something tells me that 'werewolf' had quite the long night. I'm willing to bet it's crawled into some cave to rest for the day. Best for us to get the lay of the land."

I had never been to base camp. Something about the massive nature of the mountain had always managed to keep me away—I didn't like the idea of feeling powerless.

I shouldered my pack and started up the hill behind the cave we had spent the night in. In the spring, base camp was made up of a smattering of bright camping tents, hosting various parties to mourn the fallen, celebrate summiting, or numb the fear of the coming climb with drink. In the off-season, it was a barren wasteland. A low coat of frost covered the rocky ground, but it still stuck out as a large bare patch in an otherwise pristine area.

When we crested the hill, we saw what remained of a previous climbing team's camp, though if it hadn't been for the tent poles poking out of the ground, we might have walked right past it. The sun warmed our backs, giving the campsite a much happier feeling than expected. The snowsuits we wore became incredibly hot, but the sensation was misleading. If we took them off, we would be freezing within minutes.

I looked down at the torn canvas and then back at James. "Check the campsite for anything useful."

"Like what? Blood stains? There's nothing here but remains."

"Little moody today, aren't we, James?" I said, crouching in the snow and rooting through the canvas. "Everything all right?"

He crossed his arms and let out a loud sigh. "I'm at the base of the world's tallest mountain, I just spent the night hiding in a cave, and even *you* can't identify what the hell it is we're chasing. I've been better."

"Not what you expected? You know, I can have you on the next flight home if you want. I told you this wasn't always going to be glamorous. Sometimes it's bringing the head of a chupacabra to the town sheriff and partying with his entire family on a tequila-induced bender. Other times it's rooting around in the blood and snow for clues. Either way, shape up or wait in the cave."

I'd always been harsh on James, but only because I thought it did him good. In our line of work, mistakes got people killed. Taking on a partner or an apprentice was the same as taking responsibility for their life. Had it been K2 we were below, I might have cut him some slack, but we were not on a normal mountain. The air at base camp was thinner, the cold harsher, and the creatures waiting in the snow were far more dangerous than most predators in the world.

"I'm sorry," James said a little shamefully. He was quick to anger but always found his way back.

I felt satisfied as James slumped to the ground and began to dig alongside me. It's tough to admit, but having someone to question me occasionally had its benefits. Usually I get by on dumb luck, but not always. On that expedition, dumb luck would have brought me back in a wooden box.

I found a trail of crusted blood weaving away from the tents and going deeper into the mountains. It was the only remnant of what happened. Everything else had either been wiped clean by one of a few blizzards or had been taken back to the gravesite by the Sherpas.

"What could have done this?" said James, his voice becoming quiet.

"Could have been a great many things. I can see why they

thought it was a werewolf, but that doesn't explain it all. If it had been, the blood would be scattered around the entire site, and they would have found more bodies. Werewolves don't hunt out of hunger; they hunt for sport."

I picked up a chunk of gore and looked at it between my thumb and forefinger as calmly as one might examine a gemstone. James gagged.

"Their affliction slows down the metabolism. It puts them in a state similar to a bear's hibernation but without the sleep." I stood up and flicked the red mush to the ground. "They could go years without eating if they wanted to. For the most part, it's why they're so damned hard to find." I pulled out a pair of dark aviators and slid them over my eyes; the sun reflecting off the mountain was brutal in the morning light.

Just as I thought we would fail to find anything of use, a yellow flower caught my eye. Poking through the fresh snow was the torn canvas of a tent, and somehow, still blooming, a small flower.

"James, come look at this." I walked over and brushed the snow away. Beneath the powder lay a ring of similar flowers woven into a wreath.

"What is it?"

"These are yellow cobra lilies," I said, picking up the flower. "A ring of them is supposed to ward off mountain spirits and keep climbers safe."

I often found that ancient superstitions had some level of truth to them. The number of times that lines of chalk on the front of a door had saved my life were numerous, and after Latvia, I had never left home without at least one clove of garlic.

James bent down to examine the wreath. "Look at this." He pointed to a spot just below the flowers. Buds and petals had been trampled badly, but in the center of the ring was an unmistakable paw print. It was larger than the average dog, but small enough to bring a smile to my face.

"Well, hallelujah." I rose to my feet.

"What is it?"

"Well, aside from you finally being useful, we're not hunting a werewolf." I stared at James, arms outstretched in a jovial gesture. "We're hunting wargs."

4.

ON LUPINE CLASSIFICATION

"Wargs?" Winston asked while scarfing the daintiest crois-sant Nick had ever seen. He thought it a miracle that the pastry didn't crumble at the slightest touch.

"Yes, angry little buggers. Walking piles of fur that attack anything that's not another warg. Sound familiar?"

"Oh, yes, I'm quite familiar with them. I just didn't know they nested so close to the Kwiyae region."

I never said we were in the Kwiyae. Nick regarded Winston suspiciously for a minute. "How was it that you got my information again?

"I paid a lovely young man in Bangladesh who said he had a score to settle."

"Damn you, Martin." Nick's suspicion was forgotten as his hatred for shadow priests surfaced.

"Yes, Martin *was* his name. Made some very handy tonics as well."

I'm sure none of them contained snake oil, either, thought Nick, disgusted but also impressed by Martin's ability to con. *Shadow priests know nothing about potion making.*

"I throw him into one underground fighting pit with a couple of undead soldiers and he turns on me like a yellow coward." He finished his glass and set it down roughly on the table beside him. "At least it was a good bit of fun while it lasted. I'll never forget his face when one of them got hold of his ankle." Nick chuckled.

Winston laughed half-heartedly, unsure whether Nick was being serious.

"Oh, don't look so severe. He turned out fine in the end. After all, he was alive when you saw him."

If he knows Martin, that certainly doesn't bode well. Nick had not been entirely truthful about his affront to Martin. The shadow priest could have easily survived a fight with the undead, but not after being knocked out with a stolen tribal club.

"Yes, I suppose he did look well. Angry when I mentioned your name, but well."

"Well, it's good to know that he's still as loose-lipped as ever. Now, where were we?" Nick could feel the effect of his drinks taking hold and was legitimately having trouble remembering where they were in his story.

"The wargs that killed that poor Sherpa's family."

"Oh, yes." *Wish I could say it was them.* "Wargs are nasty little buggers, I'll give them that. But in the end, they're not that much worse than the common wolf. Sure, they're bigger and have a gnarly temper, but if you've got silver on you, they might as well be puppy dogs. Much easier to kill than a werewolf. Werewolves are inherently aggressive; they'll stalk prey for days given the opportunity, but wargs stick to a single area. Wargs only attack to defend their territory, and lack intelligence. Where the werewolf was once human, the warg was merely a wolf bitten by the wrong astrological fate."

———————————— ▼ ————————————

I surveyed base camp and the bright morning that had dawned.

"We're in luck. Wargs only hunt at night, and we've got all day to find their den." Autumn in the mountains meant a much shorter day, but I knew the wargs' den wouldn't be far from the attack site.

The morning was turning out to be downright pleasant. The howling from the previous night had subsided, and the ache in my bones from nearly freezing to death was beginning to wane. A pack of wargs would make for a good bit of sport, with little danger. The only real threat was from the mountain itself.

"They must be just on the edge of their winter cycle. What confuses me is why the climbers were up here in the first place. They should have known better." I thought that some questions might have been better left unanswered.

"You seem pretty chipper for someone standing atop the disemboweled remains of a climbing team," said James, returning to his moody demeanor.

"Why wouldn't I be? I'm alive and they're dead. If you want to mourn, there's a gravesite back at the village. These," I said, making a gesture to the bits of red stuck to the fresh snow, "are just the frozen remnants of nature's wrath. Likely it will serve as a reminder to the others about why they don't climb late in the year."

James stared at me with a mopey expression.

"Oh, come on, show me what you can do. Remind me why I brought you along in the first place. Where were the wargs headed?" Over the course of his apprenticeship, James had shown great aptitude for tracking. I wasn't too bad myself, but most of my cases had involved a trail of gore a mile wide, leading to a blatantly obvious cave, decorated by the skulls of unfortunate travelers and overzealous entrepreneurs.

James bent to the ground, sweeping aside snow to uncover

the tracks. Wind had scattered most of the evidence away, but the important pieces were encased in the ice. Beneath the fresh coat of powder was a tattered trail of blood and canvas, frozen solid to the ground. I thought it another stroke of good luck that hunting wargs and werewolves were similar tasks. I unstrapped my pack and laid it out on the ground, revealing a series of vials.

Each contained a different strand of pure silver. There are many books written by blacksmiths gone mad trying to find the perfect infusion, so I always carried more than one. My favorite was crafted by a crooked priest in the Vatican. The bottle swore that it was a mix of a Pope's urine and holy water, but I thought it just as likely to have originated from a vagrant. I held the bottle up to the light and then set it down. Unfortunately, wargs had no connection or devotion to gods, which made it a waste.

I opted instead for a traditional silver bullet with a thermite tracer running down the middle. The wargs would not come out until past sundown, and it was foolish to fight blind in the dark. On top of that, it left a nasty burn and made for a hell of a light show. It was going to make the Fourth of July look like a candle.

"There's only one set of tracks, leading out over that ledge and up the mountain." Base camp rested in a bowl of shattered rock fragments and snow. On one side was the steep descent to the lower valley; on the other, the mountain and all its fury. I started up the lip of the crater and felt the very air change around me.

For climbers, the upper lip of base camp signaled the beginning of their journey; it was the last safe haven on the mountain. For amateurs like James and I, it might as well have spelled death. But, I told myself, maybe when they paid us, we could use some of the money for a course on mountaineering.

Most of the climbing I'd done was on a plastic rock wall in the middle of the city. On my other excursions in the mountains,

I had been fortunate enough to stay low. Looking up at the miles of rock, I wished to go no further.

"There." James pointed to an outcropping at the base of a large glacier. It was considered one of the most dangerous areas on the lower mountain and had been dubbed a "kill zone." Climbers who walked underneath it ran the risk of falling ice crushing them in an instant. The animals of the mountain, what few of them there were, walked freely beneath it. They seemed to have a sixth sense about when the ice blocks were going to fall, and always dodged them at the last minute.

We didn't have to walk far to find the den. Only a couple of miles away, we came upon a black blemish on an otherwise pure white glacier. It was almost too easy. On any other day, I might have turned around, but the thought of a warm meal and a large paycheck pushed me forward.

"They certainly don't try to disguise themselves," said James.

"Why would they? They're the only thing up here in the winter. Those climbing Sherpas broke the cycle."

I unstrapped my bag once more and handed James a collapsible rifle that sprung out to great length. It caused him to stagger as it extended out to full size and he nearly dropped it. I chuckled and handed him a few of the thermite bullets.

"Doesn't this seem like a bit of overkill?" James stammered.

"It might seem that way, but wargs are thick skinned and far more dangerous once they've been injured. When they sense they're in mortal danger, their cells mutate. They get faster, stronger, and a hell of a lot meaner." I pulled out a second gun, much smaller, with a double barrel and loaded it with slightly larger silver thermite slugs. "When you take the shot, be sure to kill it. If you graze it, it's just going to get pissed off, and one of us will likely end up dead."

"I-I'm going to be the one that shoots them?" A slight stutter had crept into James's voice, and I took great pleasure in the idea that I was making him nervous.

"*You* are going to sit on the rocks above the cave and take the first shot. Like a baby bird, James, it's time for you to learn to fly. Besides, it's my turn to be bait."

"You're going to be bait for wargs?"

I paused for a moment, already regretting my plan. "*I* will be in a tent just on the edge of the glacier, luring them out. And for the love of God, don't shoot me, or you're going to find out that wargs are the least of your problems."

I flashed James a smile, slung the bag over my back, and started walking toward the flat expanse of ice just in front of the cave.

I finished pitching my tent right as the last rays of the sun set over the horizon. I couldn't help but feel like a matador, hiding beneath the bright red canvas. It was placed about a hundred feet away from the cave mouth, which was just enough distance to be aggravating but also gave James room to line up the shot. Wargs were very territorial, and I couldn't help but grin at the thought of them stewing at the stink of an intruder.

At four o'clock, the sun had set behind the mountain, and a bitter chill took hold. For an hour, there was still the cold blue hue of the light reflecting around the mountain's peak. The ice wall above creaked and groaned with the change in temperature. I heard the crash of a block of ice shattering on the ground, much too close for my liking. The odds are better if you sit still, so I tried not to think of the tons of ice above.

From his perch, James was enjoying what had become a clear night. Without light pollution, the sky was dotted with multicolored stars and flowing bands. I might have enjoyed it as well, had I not been playing the bait. Beneath several loose sleeping bags, I sat facing the slightly ajar zipper of the tent, shotgun held in my trembling hands. I wasn't frightened of the wargs—none of them would be standing after a face full of silver buckshot—but after two nights in the cold, I really just wanted a warm bed.

About a half hour after full dark, the howling started. It was the same as the night before. I thought it sounded oddly far away to be coming from the mouth of the cave, but then I heard lumbering footsteps. Wargs are not known to creep; they are blitzkrieg hunters who have no sense of stealth.

I had been bait dozens of times, but I still felt uneasy. James had a very small window to take his shot. One second too early, and he would only be able to kill one warg before the others were up the mountainside. One second too late, and the wargs would be in my tent. The trap required precise timing, but we had used it before. Still, I wished I had more left in the flask.

I heard a low, throaty growl outside the tent. The poles vibrated with intensity and rang my skull like a bell.

"Come on, you bastard," I muttered, resting my finger on the trigger. Years of monster movies had taught me that demeaning the enemy was key to success. It was also something I did to stop from soiling myself.

A steamy breath wafted through the tent flap. The smell of decaying climber was putrid and made my eyes water. James was taking his sweet-ass time up there. I prepared to fight my way out.

Just as I was about to move, a shot rang out in the still night air. Black liquid sprayed the outside of the tent, and I fired back.

In the enclosed canvas, the sound was deafening. There was a yelp, followed by a flaming warg crashing through the tent's opening. Bits of fur and blood hung from its mangled snout. I scrambled out from beneath the sleeping bags and pulled a knife from my belt. I slashed through the canvas just as the flaming hulk crashed into me, throwing the gun from my hands and sending me sliding on the icy ground beyond.

A warg corpse lay smoldering on the ground a few feet away. At least James hit his shot. The injured creature was grabbing wildly for my arm, and my parka had caught fire. I dove to the side and slapped at the flame until it was extinguished. Flickers of orange and red punctuated the darkness, leaving burning after-images on my retinas.

A few feet away, the warg stood and collected itself, preparing for another charge. The ground shook as it stomped its feet. Blood seeped from one eye, but it was clear in the firelight that the buckshot had only grazed him. The silver poisoning would be too slow. I cursed my inability to follow my own rules: always double tap. The other lay smoldering on the ice, missing a large chunk of its lower body.

The knife I had used to slice the canvas was sticking out of the ice a few feet away. The warg charged, and I rolled for it. Time ground to a halt as, for a brief moment, I came face-to-face with my own mortality. A common occurrence, but harrowing nonetheless. A mass of bristled fur and drool hurtled toward me like a cannonball. The fire may have gone out, but the smell of burned hair and flesh lingered.

I clasped my hand around the knife handle and wrenched it free. It glinted in the night air. And people say not to get everything made in silver. Don't listen to that rubbish. It had cost me a pretty penny, but I found that silver was sort of a cure-all when it came to evil entities. It also glinted nicely when threatening someone over a bar tab.

Time regained its usual flow, and the warg crashed into me. I drove the knife into the creature's stomach and at the same instant was blinded by a flash of orange light. Before I had the chance to realize what had happened, the top half of the warg had turned to red mist and bits of flaming gore. I fell backward on the ice, smack dab in the middle of a pool of blood that was luckily not my own.

"No laundromat is going to get this out," I said, looking at my parka. Dazed, I tried my best to brush the red goo off. The silence following the shot was deafening, but as the world came back into focus, I heard the sound of James's footsteps running toward me. "Nice shot, kid. One in a million." I laughed.

"What do you mean? I was trying to hit you." James was out of breath, but I admired his attempt at humor.

I smiled. "Now for the fun part. We get to take the other one's head back to the villagers. I'll let you do the honors." I handed James the silver knife and fell backward onto the ice, exhausted.

5.

A TROPHY

It was just past midday when we reached the village entrance, and our packs had begun to smell like rot. The cold at night did little to quell the stench of death. Blood was caked on and stained through. We were going to need new gear. Again.

I learned the hard way that clean gear was a necessity. Show up one time with a bloodstained bag and you'll get chased out of town with pitchforks. It was a fine line between appearing rough and tumble but relatively clean. I liked to think that I conveyed an image somewhere in the space between a vagrant and a businessman.

The village looked stark and barren in the midday sunlight. It took a moment for two strange men walking up the path to be noticed, but soon, people came running toward us. I could have easily gone back to the lodge and found Lopsang, but half of good monster hunting is about the spectacle. It's the cheapest advertising there is, and the only kind I could afford.

"This is my favorite part," I whispered to James as Lopsang came bursting out of one of the buildings. I opened the drawstring on the mildew-covered bag in my right hand and spilled the warg's head onto the ground. The blood had dried slightly in the cold, dampening the sickening squish I was hoping for, but the muted crunch was satisfactory enough.

Lopsang looked at the head, examined it for a moment, and

then kicked it joyously. "You did it! My brother's soul will rest in peace tonight. This is cause for celebration!" Lopsang embraced both of us in an overbearing hug.

I had found that over the years, the best parties are those that immediately follow the killing of a troublesome mythical beast. They are boisterous in nature, and in most cases involve an open bar. I sighed in relief that my flask would not be empty for long. All around us, the people were cheering. James and I followed Lopsang into the lodge to savor our victory and find some hot food.

Once inside, we were welcomed by the smell of pine and burning wood. I thought it smelled a bit like post-car-wash air freshener, but it was a rose compared to a rotting canvas sack filled with warg head. In comparison to tent canvas slathered in monster guts and cave walls that did nothing to assuage the chill, the lodge was nothing short of paradise.

Steam and smoke filled the room as the villagers prepared what little food they had to celebrate the end of terror. I grabbed a bottle of mountain wine from behind the counter and uncorked it. I wasn't going to wait for someone to start serving drinks, and at the moment, I rather felt that I had earned it.

------------------------- ▼ -------------------------

"Speaking of drinks, if you expect me to continue, I'm going to need another. Garcon?" Nick made a lazy gesture with his empty glass. The butler, who had mysteriously appeared to refill his drink before, was nowhere to be seen.

"Yes, of course. Jenkins?" The butler materialized almost out of thin air, apparently heeding only his master's call.

He's so sneaky. I wonder if his original name is Jenkins or if it's just something he picked up in the trade? Maybe they're all just named Jenkins. Nick's extremities were feeling very warm, and his mind chose to wander in nonsensical circles. Just talking about the story had brought him right back into the moment. He could actually feel himself in the village, back in the wooden lodge. Most of all, he could feel the presence of the mountain looming above him. It was a place he never wanted to visit again. It harbored nothing but death.

I should have stuck to hunting small-time beasts. James and I weren't ready for the big time.

A dull throb began to form at the back of Nick's head, and he motioned more vigorously for a drink. *Only one way to keep these thoughts out.*

"So you killed the wargs and saved the village. I don't see how this has anything to do with the yeti."

The man's voice was like tiny needles in Nick's brain. It took him a moment to recover enough to speak. "I'm getting there. What's a good story without a little buildup?"

Nick looked to his side and found a fresh glass. He drank it in one gulp and sighed as the pain began to recede. "Without the lead-in, you wouldn't understand why we had to do what we did."

"All right, yes, but if you killed the monsters plaguing the village, why did you stay? Weren't they safe?"

"Look, if I've learned anything, it's that villagers are never safe. Burn down one witch's hovel, and another will spring up one swamp over. Villagers, for whatever reason, are made to be oppressed by forces that the rest of the world doesn't think exist. It's been happening since the beginning of time, and with the upturn of cynicism in the world recently, I don't see it changing much."

"What do you mean by that?"

"Allow me to demonstrate. Jenkins?" Nick found that butlers were the epitome of cynicism, always stuck serving at the table for a master that is inexplicably richer than them. Cynicism was at its purest in the middle class. The poor have the right to be skeptical, whereas the middle class are just bored and need something to fill their time and gripe about.

Winston made a slight gesture.

"Sir?" the voice came from behind Nick, and he jumped slightly.

Crafty little bugger.

"Jenkins," said Nick, "what would you say if I told you that in the course of my employment, I have been paid to kill six vampires, two lake monsters, a herd of chupacabra, and one highly aggravated rock devil?"

Jenkins did not respond, Instead, he did the seemingly impossible by stiffening his posture further.

"Thank you, Jenkins, that will be all."

The butler slipped away behind a curtain, leaving Nick and the fat man alone once more.

The man sat with his fingers clasped across his portly stomach. "All right, I take your point. The world isn't ready for what you've got to show them. Another tale as old as time."

"No one was ready to accept Galileo, and no one is ready to accept me." Nick rather fancied the idea of the comparison to such a famous astronomer. "If I tell anyone about my work, I've got a one-way ticket to the funny farm. It's people like you, paying big bucks for nothing more than a story, that really keep me in business."

"How do you know I believe you?"

"Doesn't matter; you're paying me either way."

"Indeed I am. So, the villagers weren't safe even after the monster had been taken care of?"

"Well, that's the real problem with monsters, there's usually more than one ..."

6.

MANCHESTER

The lodge spun in circles around me, blurring the welcoming light that flickered off the lanterns. For a brief moment, I found temporary peace, high in the mountains and at the bottom of a bottle. James was standing and dancing with some of the villagers, but I kept to an uncomfortable chair in one of the darker corners. I only truly felt at ease when I was alone and blissfully ignorant of everything going on around me.

I never thought back on the beasts I had killed. It had never really bothered me. If the tables were turned, most creatures wouldn't even give it a second thought, and I never went after them unless they attacked someone first. As far as I was concerned, monster hunting was a necessity to keep the blank edges of the map in check. Without me, there'd be chaos and a series of unexplainable deaths at every full moon. I took a drink. I'd made my peace with it.

Through the haze of my drunken stupor, I felt an itch in the back of my brain. It was an omnipresent feeling that never left me. That there was more to this. Even if there was nothing left in the mountains, there would always be another job. Two dead wargs might lay on the slopes by base camp, but in a few days, maybe a few weeks if we were lucky, something else would come.

I looked back at James, who was twirling in the center of the lodge and having the time of his life. Good for him, I thought, only half sarcastically. The kid was happy; he had just killed a pair of wargs. I wasn't sure there were many apprentices in the world that could do that. I thought about running over to spoil James's good time but picked up another bottle instead. Let him have it while it lasts, I figured.

It might have been the smoky haze filling the room, or it might have been the mountain wine, but either way, I failed to notice the dark figure lingering in the shadows. He was perfectly content to stay in his corner and watch the celebration from afar. Unfortunately, he wasn't alone for long.

I was lost in reminiscence about a time I tracked down a murderer who dressed as a sasquatch when a sickly smooth voice cut through the air.

"Hello, Nick." The voice was familiar, chastising, and charismatic all at the same time. Though I wanted to loathe it, I could not.

The shadow standing before me cut an intimidating figure. He wore a long black coat with a series of silver buttons running down either side of the split. Atop his head was a wide black hat with a slightly frayed brim, only somewhat obscuring a handsome face.

"Hello, Manchester." I set the bottle down.

"Having a nice celebration?"

"Kind of you to notice. You know it's Nepalese custom to buy the celebrator a drink."

The slurring must've been evident, because a look of disgust crossed Manchester's face. He had never approved of drinking on the job, even in times of celebration. "Well, then, I suppose it's a pity we're not in Nepal."

"Aren't we?" I knew that we had crossed the border but didn't want to rise to Manchester's bait.

"You know, it's really a shame, Nick." Malice glinted in his piercing blue eyes.

I knew not to bite the hook. It wasn't worth it. Grab another bottle and just ride this out; that was the best course.

"What is?" I asked. Like I said, I'm not good at following my own rules.

Manchester's trap snapped shut, and he grinned at his caught prey. "It appears you've killed the wrong beast."

I knew the moment Manchester said it that it was true. I mulled it over for a second and let the implications set in. "Piss off," I said. "I've got two dead wargs who would say otherwise."

It wasn't the most compelling argument, but it allowed me to be angry, and I rather enjoyed being angry with Manchester.

"Did you ever take a moment to consider other possibilities? Or did you just walk up to the first warg cave you saw and kill them so you could go home?"

"What in the hell are you—"

"It's the wrong season for wargs," said Manchester, cutting me off. "The only reason they attacked you is because you sat outside their cave provoking them. What you've done is more akin to murder than good monster hunting."

I grew hot in the face. "Murder? Who's going to miss a couple of wargs?" I shouted. "Even if they didn't kill those climbers—and they *did*—they would have attacked someone else. They were nested too low on the mountain, and ..." I trailed off, my anger temporarily replaced by confusion. "Wait a minute. How did you know we waited outside the cave?"

"I'm afraid your partner has a set of loose lips."

"James, you mother—"

"Quiet down, Nick. It's not his fault. You know how persuasive I can be." Manchester gave me an infuriatingly smug wink.

"Well, I guess I don't have a partner anymore."

It was a lie. I wouldn't have gotten rid of James even if he had invited Manchester to the mountain himself. As far as apprentices went, he was pretty decent at not dying, and he wasn't the least-equipped individual for the position. Most snapped after a few months of guts and glory, but James had held on for almost a year and still seemed rather pleased with it all.

"Let's stop worrying about your partner for a moment. I want you to think about what I am saying." Manchester's tone had changed from chastising to excited. I did my best to follow. "The wargs didn't kill those people, and even you were smart enough to figure out it wasn't a werewolf."

"Yeah?" I could see there was a point to his diatribe, but most of my mental acuity had diluted along with the fermented substances in my bloodstream.

"I think you and I both know what killed them."

"Tooth Fairy," I spat, then pounded my fist on the table laughing.

"Imbecile," Manchester sneered. He unbuttoned his coat and pulled out a small leather-bound book similar to the one I carried in my satchel. I often thought it would be easier to transfer all of the information to an e-reader, but the tome looked mysterious and didn't require a charging cable. Manchester carefully flipped to an earmarked page and set it down on the table in between us.

"It's a myth," I said, and with a wide, drunken gesture, swept the book onto the floor. It was a move showing both insult and ignorance, a specialty of mine when I've been drinking.

"The yeti is no myth." As the word dripped off his tongue, I became aware of just how silent the lodge had become. No one was moving, the dancing had stopped, and James cowered in a corner as if waiting for me to yell at him.

"The last yeti was seen over two hundred years ago," I said. "They've all died out. I'd just as soon hunt a T-Rex." Some drunken part of my mind thought that a T-Rex might be a possibility.

"You're not even going to entertain the idea? All of the signs point to this. You can't just ignore it and pretend you've solved the problem. If I'm right, this isn't just going to fade away."

"Do you realize what a yeti in these mountains would mean?" My head was throbbing, and I wasn't ready to hear what Manchester had to say next.

"Yes. The gates of Shangri-La have opened."

7.

SHANGRI-LA

"You must be joking. Shangri-La?" Winston asked with an incredulous tone. "I'm not paying you for nonsense."

Nick raised his eyebrows in mock offense. "Believe me, I thought he was crazy at the time, too. We'd all heard the stories at some point or another. Explorers coming back from the mountains, dehydrated, hypothermic, and claiming they had seen a large gate carved into the side of a mountain. Most of the time, it'd come out that their o-tanks hadn't been fully opened or something of the like. The stories were good for getting new apprentices to sign up, but not much else."

"It can't possibly be real," said Winston. "Shangri-La is just something out of an old James Hilton novel."

"Well, Hilton wasn't exactly what he seemed to be." It wasn't every day Nick got to reveal the secret pasts of the famous.

"What do you mean?"

"I mean, his time at Cambridge wasn't just spent studying English literature. He took a little hiatus up in the mountains for a semester. Most say he didn't come back the same man. *Lost Horizon* sold well, but speaking from experience, I'm not sure how much of it was actually a work of fiction.

"Preposterous," scoffed Winston, taking a sip of brandy.

"Look, I'm not saying it's all sunshine and rainbows like he wrote it, but it's real."

The fat man chewed his lip, mulling over Nick's story. "Well, if it's not how he described it, what is there?"

"Beyond the gates is something more chaotic than our world. It's a constant battle between entities that don't belong on this plane. Violence reigns supreme. Gods, demons, and all manner of creatures fight for supremacy in a place that was supposed to be unending paradise. If you believe the stories, that is."

Nick sat back, pleased, and took another sip of his drink. One of his great pleasures was taking the reality that people were so comfortable in and bending it.

He wasn't entirely sure what it was that James Hilton saw, but he had definitely been close to something. Just thinking about the gates brought about dark memories he couldn't avoid. It was far too dark for the likes of *Lost Horizon*. Perhaps Hilton had thought it better to avoid such concepts and delve more into the realm of fantasies.

We all lie to ourselves in some way, Hilton's story just happened to play well with the popular media at the time.

"If such a place exists, then how is it explorers haven't found it?" Winston sat back, confident he had found a logical way out of believing in the legend.

"No one ever looks in the right place. The richest man in the world could have explorers travel all over the globe, canvas every blank area on the map, and there would still be more to find. Every living thing sees this world differently, and as such, the next explorer will always see something the last missed."

Winston looked unconvinced.

Nick sighed. "Are you familiar with the Bermuda Triangle?"

The man snorted. "Don't tell me that's real, too?"

"Oh no, of course not. Aliens aren't causing the disappearances; it's likely sea monsters. The electromagnetic disturbance is just pods of them communicating over long distances. Boring end to a fascinating mystery, if you ask me, but you're not paying me for boring tales. The point is, things aren't always as they seem."

"Yes, of course, but sea monsters?"

Nick took pleasure in the man's confusion, then continued with his story. "Where was I? Ah, yes, James and I were in the climbing lodge ..."

———————————— ▼ ————————————

"If the gates were open, your brains would spill out."

Manchester looked at me with an expression of utmost confusion.

"Because it's only in your head." I laughed hysterically and gulped down what remained in my cup. Once at the bottom of a bottle, my wit was nowhere to be found. It was a slippery slope that would eventually lead to incomprehensible gibberish and, more often than not, being thrown out of a bar.

"You didn't think werewolves were real until you saw them with your own eyes," said Manchester. "Is it really so far-fetched to believe that there is something out there? We both know that these mountains have never been properly explored. There are huge tracts of land that are considered by most to be untouchable because of the terrain."

"And what? You want to be the one to touch them?" My eyebrows raised, and I looked around the bar for laughter. No one complied. The few people left were all focused intently on the conversation, not wanting to disturb it. I sighed heavily. "Manchester, it's autumn. We know damn well why the locals don't go up the mountain in autumn. Blizzards, beasts, and boredom."

"Even the locals aren't passing up a chance to find the gates.

Why do you think the climbers you found were on the mountain so late in the year?"

I thought about that for a second. Could they really have been so stupid as to think that so few of them could have gotten to the gates alive? "It's impossible. Even the most experienced climbers have trouble."

Manchester watched me warily from beneath the brim of his hat.

"If the wargs I killed weren't the ones causing trouble, then whatever was is still out there. And if it is a yeti, we're talking about a beast that no one has ever been able to trap or kill in the history of our profession. It's a quest that no sane hunter would embark on."

"This may be the only chance for us to see something like this in our lifetimes. Hell, maybe even in the human race's."

"You know, I've never understood the motivation behind suicide missions. Clearly, the message of those action movies you watched as a kid never sunk in." I felt a brief ebb in my drunkenness and charged forward. "The hero of those movies takes on insurmountable odds and most of the time doesn't even get paid for it. As such, I never go anywhere unless the pay is guaranteed."

"How can you so blindly deny what is in front of you?" he asked.

"Life is really just a simple game of dice, and when your number is up, it's up. Why risk rolling more times than you have to?" I tried to take a drink but realized in a bitter moment that my cup was empty. "James, more wine!"

Manchester rounded on me again. "No one has ever brought back concrete evidence of the gates. We could be on the verge of a great discovery. Possibly the most important discovery of our age."

"Well, don't you have a penchant for grandeur," I slurred,

keeping an eye out for James, who suspiciously had not brought the wine yet. "I think I'll pass and go back to drinking in the safety of my flat."

Manchester let out an exasperated sigh and looked genuinely deflated.

I was satisfied I'd chipped off a piece of his armor, but despite everything, I'd started to get curious. "What makes you think the gates are even there?"

"The locals tell a story."

"Course they do. Every local has a story about some beastie unique to their home. Makes good fun for scaring the tourists." For the most part, these ended up being uneducated interpretations of monsters that had long ago been classified. As such, I never got worked up over the word of a "local tale."

Manchester continued as if I'd said nothing. "When the world is in a time of great change and turmoil, the lines that separate our world from others can become blurred. It's during these times that the gates open, letting creatures from that world into our own."

I cocked an eyebrow, my interest slightly piqued.

"Think about it. It would explain why sightings of the yeti are so few and far between. That species may only appear once every hundred years, or even millennia. Don't you see this is an opportunity to explore something completely new? Even if there's nothing up there, it's at least worth a look."

The wheels were turning for me again as the wine faded. "Back up. You said that the world has to be in extreme turmoil for the gates to open. The world may be in turmoil now, but what separates this period in history from any other?"

"Not a whole lot, as it turns out. There's still war and killing all over the world, but there is one thing different, and it's a big one. Climate change."

"Oh, get off your high horse!" I shouted, jumping up from the table. "If you wanted to peddle a political agenda, you shouldn't have come to Nepal."

"We're not in Nepal."

"You know what I meant."

"It's a fact, Nick. The glaciers are shifting. Not much up in the mountains here, but even the slightest change could have uncovered something."

"Sounds to me like you're jumping at shadows." I swept up my bag from beneath the table and prepared to head to my room. "I've got my money, and the villagers are safe. I'm going home."

A small group of villagers had gathered around to watch the argument, and I instinctually pulled the satchel of money closer to me. As far as I was concerned, the job they paid me for was done, and I'd earned my pay.

"If that's what you want to do, I can't stop you. I will be leading a team up the mountain in two days' time. I had rather hoped that you would join us. The rewards would be great for both of us." Manchester gave me one last look, but apparently decided I was too far gone. "All right, then, enjoy the mediocrity that is your *business*. I'll see you around, Nick. Have a pleasant night."

Manchester snapped his fingers, and a large group of men rose to follow him out. I hadn't even noticed them come in. A light snow blew in through the doorway as they left, sucking the remaining warmth from the room.

"James, I think it's time we retire for the evening." We made our way up the stairs fast, so as to avoid the now prying eyes of the villagers. On the second floor, the air was thick with incense. I stepped through the door to our room and began to throw everything in my bag as fast as I could.

"We have to leave at first light," I said. "There's no way we're getting down in the dark, but I'm not keen on staying here any longer than we have to. I've seen that look before, James. Those villagers want their money back." The thought terrified me. Then James said it.

"What if he's right, Nick?" he was apprehensive.

"He's not."

"Didn't it seem a little odd to you? Wargs taking down an entire climbing team?"

"I'd hardly consider three people a climbing team."

"But he's Manchester," said James, showing both his youth and his stupidity.

"And he's a bloody idiot. Just 'cause he's got a title doesn't make him right. Pack the gear, and get some sleep. It's going to be a long trip down, and you need to start thinking of reasons I shouldn't fire you."

I flopped down on top of my half-packed bag and fell into an uneasy drunken sleep.

8.

DOWN THE MOUNTAIN

The trip from the village to the airport wasn't dangerous, but it was long. The trail, if it could be called that, was merely a series of switchbacks leading down from the mountain and into a steep ravine below. As we descended, the sparse scenery of high altitude gave way to mild brush and tall grass. Water trickled down from the melting snow at the top of the ravine, feeding the plants below.

The way down passed through several villages. No one came out to greet us, but several times I thought I saw people peering out of darkened windows. Their silence was unnerving. Usually the mood was better following a successful hunt.

"Looks like word of our exploits hasn't quite reached the lower mountain yet." I laughed nervously.

James had taken on a sour look and hadn't spoken to me since we left the lodge early that morning. My voice echoed off the rocks surrounding us, the words sounding as hollow as they felt.

While the trail wasn't outright perilous, traveling with moody dead weight wasn't good for my sanity. "I'm not just going to talk to myself all the way down this mountain."

James did nothing to acknowledge that I had spoken, and stared vacantly ahead.

"Come on, we did the right thing. If we had picked up and followed Manchester we would be dead men. We'll be attending his funeral within a month." Somewhere in the distance, a bird chirped, and I found its song quite annoying. "I do suppose this is a rather lucky break for us. He just took himself out of the game. We're not going to have much competition when we get back."

James continued to trudge along.

In a last-ditch effort, I took out our small bag of gold and shook it in front of James's face. "Eh? What about this? What are you going to do with your share of this?"

"Buy a plane ticket back," James said in a firm tone.

He's cracking, I thought excitedly. "Bit boring, don't you think? Me? I've got my eye on a hundred-year-old bottle of brandy. Smooth taste, and gets you drunker than a sailor on leave."

James returned to bitter silence.

"Oh, come on, we saved the village! What's your problem?"

"Do you *really* think that?" James stopped walking. "What Manchester says adds up."

"Oh, come off it, don't tell me you're siding with—"

"We killed the wrong monster, Nick." He let the statement hang in the quiet mountain air. "You're just too stubborn to admit it. If you look at the literature on previous encounters with yetis, they all say—"

"A load of tripe and made-up bullshit. Previous encounters with the yeti are either entirely fabricated or mostly exaggerated. There hasn't been a sighting from a credited individual in over a hundred years, and even she isn't sure of what she saw anymore. For all we know, these oxygen-deprived 'explorers' might have just seen a warg covered in frost, or a particularly scary pile of snow."

"That howl at base camp wasn't a warg and you know it!" James was shouting now.

I winced, wondering just how far a voice could travel, and how sturdy the rock face next to us was. "What makes you say that?"

"Because I heard a warg call the same night."

"And that makes you qualified, does it?"

James was just about to retort when a voice yelled from behind us. "Dr. Ventner!"

They never learn. I turned around to see Lopsang running down the road toward us with an angry look in his eyes.

"Look, pal, no refunds."

Lopsang continued to run forward, then punched me squarely in the jaw. The force of the blow was enough to knock me to my knees, stunned. Stars blotted my vision, and I fell back lazily into the mud. As I stared up at the blue sky, I thought, It's really a wonder this doesn't happen more often.

"'Bout time somebody did that." James chuckled, enjoying my misery. "People always get what's coming to them."

With all the coordination I could muster, I swept my leg into the back of James's knees, bringing him down to the mud, and slapped him.

"Always pay attention, my very young apprentice." I was laughing. Keeping the pecking order almost made me forget the growing pain in my face.

Lopsang advanced forward.

I cocked an eyebrow. He must've been really mad. "Hey, back up, friend." Smooth as silk, I pulled a small gun from my jacket pocket and pointed it at Lopsang. "I understand that you're angry, but I will not hesitate." My arm was steady, despite the fact that I'd forgotten to load the pistol that morning before we left.

"Nick, what the hell?" James said, his voice cracking noticeably.

"Shut up, James. If I don't kill him, this bullet is for you. Listen, Lopsang, Manchester is telling you lies."

"No, Dr. Ventner, not lies." Even in his anger, Lopsang

persisted in calling me by my false title. "What killed my brother was no warg."

"Are you the expert now? A couple of days ago you thought it was a werewolf." I stood up from the ground, keeping the gun trained on Lopsang the whole time. "Now, if you'll excuse us, we have a plane to catch."

"No." With incredible speed, Lopsang knocked my gun into the dirt and kicked me backward into the mud.

"Is this really necessary?" I groaned, feeling the pain in my chest from where Lopsang's foot had connected. "I killed the beast, just let us go."

"No, you did not. Last night we heard it again."

"We were in the same village, and I didn't hear shit."

"Some of us weren't passed out drunk," murmured James from beside me.

I lashed out to hit him again, but Lopsang made a threatening gesture, and I thought better of it.

"The howling woke the entire village. It was so loud that I could swear it was in the lodge with us." Lopsang looked genuinely rattled. "This morning we went out to where we had displayed the wargs, and they were gone. All we found was this." He pulled a leather bag out of his backpack and tossed it to me.

I caught it and opened it. Inside was a patch of white fur. "This could be from anything," I said, casually tossing the bag to James.

"Well, would you look at this," James noted with interest. "This is far too straight to be warg fur, and look at the density of the follicles. Whatever it's from must have been huge."

I was feeling more trapped with each passing second. The evidence was piling up against me. However, it was not the idea of the yeti that bothered me the most; it was going toe to toe with

Manchester. Of all the places in the world he could have gone hunting, why did it have to be here? Wasn't there some Transylvanian village with a coven harassing its nubile virgins?

"Was there more where you found this?" James asked Lopsang. They were now huddled around the small sample while I sat in the dirt.

An unbidden voice crept into my thoughts. *What if it really is Shangri-La?* The thought still seemed absurd, but also exciting. *The treasures would be of immeasurable value.* I soon found myself transported away from the mountain and into a large mansion. I saw myself diving into pools of gold coins and drinking liquor from crystal decanters.

This image was quickly replaced by an equally powerful one of me being ripped limb from limb by an angry yeti. None of the stories I'd heard of the beast ended well. Most of the explorers who went looking for it froze to death on the side of some godforsaken mountain. They would run out of supplies, or watch their entire crew be decimated.

No one goes up that mountain in the winter. Not even the locals. Even with my ears filled with mud, I began to hear the howling. It was only in my head, but it shook me to my core. There was nothing to be gained up there but death. I turned my mind back to the problem at hand. Mainly, it was the two men arguing theories about a patch of fur that was likely from a goat.

The voice came back again. *That might be goat fur, but the rest of it adds up. This could be it, the chance for you to get your name in the book and put an ancient mystery to bed. All good monster stories start with a myth.* In fact, the field had been founded when one man had been crazy enough to follow such a tale. *Where would we be if he hadn't killed that first vampire?*

"Nick!" Both James and Lopsang were staring at me. I'd

completely checked out while working the situation out in my head. It was a common occurrence.

"What?" I said, annoyed. "I've got a splitting headache from Lopsang's right hook. Can we stop with the shouting?"

"I'm not coming back with you."

"Oh? And why is that?"

"I'm going with Lopsang. We need to catch this beast. It became our responsibility the second we took the job."

Such nobility. Self-righteous prick. Actually, I only half believed that about him. In a way, I respected James deeply. *Well, the bottles at home aren't going anywhere*, I thought, straightening up and accepting my fate. "Splendid, I think I'll come along." I jumped to my feet and began to brush the mud off my gear.

"What?" James looked utterly surprised.

"Yes, I'm coming with. While you two were arguing about that piece of goat fur, I was considering the lucrative possibilities behind this endeavor."

"Goat fur?"

"Sorry to disappoint you, James, but yes, goat fur. The warg heads were not taken by a monster. Think about it: There would be no point. Hardly any meat left on them, and the villagers would have been easier prey." I shot an angry glance at Lopsang. "The fur that you've got was taken from the back of a goat and dipped in oil to make it look sleeker. I suspect one of the angry villagers, probably the one standing next to you, brought it down to convince us to come back, and to get a refund." I said the last word with particular disgust.

"Lopsang?" James sounded hurt.

"Don't worry, James," I said, "your stupidity ended up being for a good cause."

James's face flushed.

"So why are you coming back?" demanded Lopsang.

"Well, I've come to agree with your opinion that it was not wargs that killed your brother." I let the statement sink in. "Secondly, I've got a plan, and it's going to make Manchester look like a novice. A chance I would never pass up."

Both men stared at me, dumbfounded. Frankly, I was surprised by my change of heart as well, but the thought of treasure was more than enticing enough to persuade me. I just had to be the one to make the decision.

"Just like that?" James asked, his voice tight.

"Just like that," I said. "Now, we're going to need supplies. If we have any hope of catching it, we're going to have to go high up on the mountain, and before you ask: No, we are not going with Manchester. He may be a professional, but his team is too large, and his judgment is clouded here."

I wasn't sure about the last point, but I wanted to hammer home the point that we were going on our own. "A smaller group stands a better chance than the whole convoy he's dragging up the mountain."

"You and me? Climbing a mountain by ourselves? We have no experience. It's suicide." James was obviously regretting his eagerness.

"Of course we're not going by ourselves. We're taking Lopsang."

"I did not agree to this," Lopsang said, taking a step back.

"No, but you tried to swindle me," I said, picking up my gun as a reminder. "The moment you tried to convince my partner and I to undertake a suicide mission alone, you agreed to come."

Lopsang did not speak.

"Unless you'd rather die up here on a mountain trail where no one will find you."

James turned to Lopsang. "He's got a point. You *were* going to let us die."

Lopsang sighed. "All right, fine."

"Wonderful." I clapped my hands together in delight. "Now, direct us to The Black Market. We're going to need some supplies that you can't find at the local mountaineering shop."

"Black Market?"

"Don't play dumb, Lopsang. We're in a hurry. Manchester could be leaving anytime now."

"We actually have about three days," he said. "A blizzard is coming to the mountain. Manchester will be stuck in camp until the weather clears."

"Perfect, plenty of time for us to get to The Black Market and back."

"Don't know what you are talking about," said Lopsang, shifting his gaze slightly.

"Don't lie to me." I motioned with the gun again. "I know they're hard to find, but every place has got one. Judging by that silver amulet around your neck, you've been there recently."

Lopsang tried to hide the amulet but realized that he had lost the argument. "All right, but I'm warning you, they really don't like outsiders …"

9.

THE BLACK MARKET

"This place is dangerous," I whispered to James, looking shiftily around the street corner we were on. We were waiting on Lopsang, who had gone to get us access to the market.

"I know. You've told me a thousand times," James said through a yawn, not comprehending the gravity of the situation.

"James." I grabbed him by the collar and shook him, half because I was serious, and half because I just felt James could use a good shake. "These people will kidnap you and sell you as a slave to a lecherous, vampiric imp without even batting an eye."

Before he could answer back, I released him, sending him sprawling backward. There was a moment when I thought he would fall into the mud-strewn street, but luckily he regained his balance.

"Yeah, I get it. It's dangerous."

"They will take you into a back alley for a game of dice, steal your liver, and then let the cannibal orphans eat it in front of you." There were no cannibal orphans in The Black Market because of the age limit, but I wanted James to grasp the severity of the place we were heading into. I had only been to a few black markets, and each time had ended poorly. Whether it was losing a limb or losing a high-stakes chess game with a shaman, I always ended up in trouble.

"Jesus, man, can't we just go in?"

I sighed. "No, we need Lopsang to get us the code. If we don't, golden idols recessed in the entrances will cut our genitals off with laser beams and then burn us alive." This I was unsure of, but it was entirely possible. Maybe.

Either way, it shut James up. We waited on the street corner, watching as people hurried about their days, passing us by. The buildings were much taller than I expected, made from colorful brick, and strung in between them were rows of prayer flags blowing gently in the afternoon breeze. The air was cool, but it might as well have been the tropics compared to the mountain. Just over the tops of the buildings, I could see the crest looming. I was not looking forward to heading back up there.

Just in time to interrupt my thoughts of freezing to death on the mountainside, Lopsang appeared. He was carrying a pair of thin black hoods and a bamboo scroll. "Put these on," he said, handing the hoods to us.

"What for?" James sniffed at the fabric with a questioning expression.

"It's customary for all visitors to The Black Market to cover their faces," I said. "This way, all the deals are truly anonymous, and no one can carry out assassinations inside." I tugged the fabric over my head, trying to ignore the overpowering stench within. Though dark, the fabric in front of his eyes was thin enough to see through. "God, something definitely died in here, and I don't think it was recent." I gagged and did my best to hold back the vomit behind it.

"The man who wore it before you was decapitated for not giving a fair price." Lopsang spoke with not so much as a hint of remorse. It was just the way things were. James looked horror-struck.

It was more than enough to lighten my mood and allow me

to forget that I was wearing a gore-soaked rag. "Come on, James, put it on. Wouldn't want a merchant to cut off that precious face of yours."

James obliged, but he did not look happy about it.

"All right, follow me, and do exactly as I do." Lopsang led them down the street through a series of twisting alleyways filled with shops. As they passed, a man with few teeth held out a plate full of hot buns that issued a green smoke. His eyes were misty and swirled with the same green color. He mumbled a short in-cantation, and the green smoke took the form of a dragon, which dove back into the bun.

"You ain't seen nothing yet," I said, masking my own surprise. I wasn't sure whether to be terrified or hungry.

We continued walking until we came to a pair of black doors recessed in an alley wall.

"Is this it?" A noticeable tremor had crept into James's voice.

"Shh," hissed Lopsang. "Only I speak until we are safely in the market."

The building itself was easy to miss. It looked much like the others surrounding it, and the black doors hardly stood out.

Lopsang approached the doors and tapped lightly. On the left side of the building, one of the bricks gave way and exposed a small deposit box. The lid snapped open, clanging against the stone above it, and Lopsang lowered the bamboo scroll into it. Even as he did so, the box began to shut again, narrowly missing Lopsang's fingers.

I got the impression that those who weren't quick enough would leave a few digits short. I grimaced at the thought. We'd see soon enough whether or not that code was worth the price we paid. It had not come cheap, and we were already running low on funds. What was left of the money we had earned from the wargs would likely go to supplies, and I felt miserable at the thought that we wouldn't have enough to buy a drink. I told myself if Lopsang cheated us, I'd sell him to the circus for beer money.

From behind the doors there came the loud grinding sound of stone moving across stone. I braced myself for a rock guardian to rise from the ground, but it never did. The doors swung open, revealing a dark hallway that swallowed all light from the outside.

Lopsang walked forward and motioned for us to do the same. Together, we stepped over the threshold and into complete darkness. Behind us, the doors swung shut with a heavy groan, and for a moment, there was only silence. Then, with a gut-wrenching jerk, the floor dropped out from beneath us.

James and I stumbled to keep our balance, but Lopsang was prepared and stood comfortably in the darkness as though none of it bothered him. The room shook and shuddered as we descended deep into the ground, the sound of metal scraping against metal drowning everything else out.

Then, just as abruptly as it had started, the motion stopped, and a thin white line began to spread out before us. Doors were opening, and beyond them I heard the alacritous din that came from the mass purchase of illegal products.

The compartment filled with light. James was struggling to get to his feet.

Lopsang laughed and exited through the widening gap. We followed, stepping out into a city street lined with stands and shops. Above was a vaulted ceiling that had been decorated to look like the night sky. It shifted and swirled like an impressionist painting. People in black masks bustled around on the street, trading and carrying various goods.

"Welcome to The Black Market, James."

As soon as we entered the street, a group of people moved past us to leave.

"Lopsang, this is incredible." I felt genuine awe. I'd been to a few black markets, but none of them were nearly as big. Most consisted of a twisting network of back alleys, barely shielded from the sun by tattered canopies and filled with the worst kind of people.

This black market, in my mind, was exquisite. I never expected it to be lurking beneath the dilapidated city above.

"It is impressive," said Lopsang with the casual air of someone who had seen the same sight many times over. "Now, where do you want to go?"

Despite our surroundings, Lopsang's nervous tone told me he was not keen on staying very long.

"Where does one go for information?" I was trying to seem coy, but really I had no plan past entering the market.

"Information?" repeated Lopsang.

"Yes, information," I said dryly, feigning confidence a little too desperately. "There's got to be some old-timer with information about the creature."

Lopsang stared at me blankly.

"Oh, come on. You mean to tell me there're no survivors of the creature's wrath here?"

Lopsang looked uncomfortable. "There is one, but trust me, you don't want to go to him." Lopsang's tone was dark. There was a brief silence between us, punctuated by the general murmur of people going about their business.

"Why is that?"

"Most people say he's crazy, and he's not very friendly."

"Neither are you," I pointed out cheerfully, "but we're getting along just fine." I flashed him the grin of someone who was sure they were about to gain the upper hand.

Lopsang said nothing.

"Would he know anything about the yeti?" I asked, softening a little.

"Almost certainly." Lopsang was tense, knowing he had been backed into a corner.

"Then he's our best chance of getting out of this alive. Anything he knows is more than we know now, and hell, he might even know a way to get rid of the damned thing."

It was a long shot, but every creature had a weakness, or at least, every creature I had met so far.

"All right, fine, but we'll need to be quick about it."

"Excellent. Now, we're also going to need some mountaineering supplies." I turned to James with a used-car salesman smile. "James, I'm going to delegate that task to you. Find us everything we need to get up and down that mountain safely."

James began to protest, but I cut him off.

"And make it quick. As always, time is short." I shooed James away to his task.

It was difficult to tell what his emotions were through the hood, but I'm sure James was fuming.

"I want to learn about the—"

"Listen, James, I didn't want to come along on this little excursion to hunt a non-existent beast, but now that I'm here, we're going to do things my way." I turned very serious, impressing even myself with the authority in my voice. "If we're going to get up the mountain and not die, we're going to need gear. We'll get out of this potentially dangerous situation faster if we split up. I've got a better chance at reasoning with this 'crazy' friend of Lopsang's, and frankly, I want to test your bargaining skills. Now quit your whining and go find us some pitons."

James stared at me through the black mesh of his hood for a few seconds and then trudged off.

James was unlikely to find climbing gear in a black market, but I enjoyed testing him.

"Shall we?" I asked Lopsang.

Lopsang shook his head and led me into the crowd.

10.

LITTLE SHOP OF HORRORS

After what felt like miles of winding through haphazard stands, dark buildings, alleyways, and tightly packed streets, we arrived at a shop nestled in one of the market's corners. While the rest of The Black Market was well-lit to attract customers, this building was not. A solitary oil lamp lit the rickety porch, barely illuminating the entrance. The shop itself was more of a crooked shack that had begun to list to one side. The boards looked like they had been pieced together from several other projects that were never completed. The main door was nearly diagonal, and the shutters that covered the front windows were broken, hanging by threads. I got the impression that it was not often visited.

Lopsang waited, looking at the shop for a minute with hesitancy. "Are you sure we want to?"

"Yes," I answered clearly. "If we want to live through this expedition, then we're going to need all the help we can get."

Lopsang sighed and walked up to the front porch. There was a dull tinkling as I brushed by a wind chime made of obscure creatures jarred in formaldehyde. A faded wooden sign read "Jim's Oddities, Curiosities, and Necessities", underneath which a plaque had been nailed that said "Thieves leave empty-handed." The small severed hand beneath it made me grimace.

Together, we stepped through the creaking door and entered the shop. Dense smoke hung in the air, making it nearly impossible to see anything, and gave the small space the illusion of being much larger. Shelves were lined with various amulets, trophies, and weapons. One corner of the store held what appeared to be a mummy in a glass case, still clutching the sacrificial dagger it had been buried with in its brittle hands.

At the back of the shop stood an elderly man behind a stained black counter, smoking from a long-stemmed pipe. The smoke he exhaled was a dull, acrid, red color. He was dressed in a tattered robe adorned with circular gold discs that shone in the dim shop light.

I turned to Lopsang. "Jim, I presume?"

Lopsang did not speak and motioned for me to move to the counter, which I obliged, but the man did nothing to acknowledge our presence.

I looked around at the various ornaments and tried to find one to strike up a conversation about. I settled on a row of heads mounted above the counter, each the remains of brutal creatures with spiked horns that curled out in front of them.

"You kill these yourself?" I asked.

The man straightened his newspaper and continued reading as if I was nothing more than an irksome fly. I looked to Lopsang for help, but he just shrugged and mouthed "I told you so."

It was a boring conversation anyway, so I got right to it. "We're here about the yeti."

In one swift motion, the man put down the newspaper, picked up a menacing sword from behind the counter, extinguished his pipe, and leapt over the counter. Before I could blink, cold steel was pressed to my throat. Up close, the old man's face was far more wrinkled than it looked from a distance; it reminded me of an ancient temple. His beard was long and white, hanging almost to his waist. Scars crisscrossed his face, intersecting each other at odd angles, making it impossible to tell where one ended and another began. He stared at me with mean eyes beneath bushy white eyebrows.

"If I offended you—" But my words were cut off by the blade being pressed closer to my throat, until a tiny bead of blood dribbled down my neck. Obviously I should have sent James to do this.

The old man sniffed like a dog, assessing me, and then took the sword off my throat. I relaxed, but then the man brought the sword back in a wide arc and swung at my neck with what was intended as a killing blow.

Lopsang jumped in front of me at the last second, the blade stopping inches from my neck. He began babbling in a language that I did not understand, clearly trying to explain why we should not be killed. The man's blade lowered slowly with every word that Lopsang spoke.

The old man muttered something gruffly and pointed at me. Lopsang turned to look at me, and then both men started laughing and pointing to areas I wished they wouldn't have.

"What's he saying?" I asked, growing angry.

"That you talk too much and lack respect."

"I know a few ex-flames who might agree with him," I muttered.

"Don't worry, I'm working on him." Lopsang turned back to the man, who quickly ushered him into a back room.

The old man glanced back at me with dangerous eyes. "Don't touch anything," he said in gravelly English, then disappeared with Lopsang behind a curtain.

I waited for what felt like the better part of an hour. Occasionally, I heard laughter from the back of the shop and saw plumes of smoke wafting out from behind the curtain. Not wanting to see the man's sword again, I did as I was told and touched nothing.

Instead I wandered through the aisles of the shop, looking at the wares the man was selling. As it turned out, not touching anything was a difficult task. Buried beneath layers of dust and hidden behind assorted shrunken animal parts, I occasionally caught glimpses of sparkling gold and glittering diamonds.

As I paced, an amulet on one of the dusty shelves caught my eye. It was painfully obvious that the object was cursed, but still I felt drawn to it. It was solid gold, bearing carved Aztec symbols. In the middle was a blood-red gem that stuck out like a sore thumb. I knew that rubies had been difficult to obtain for the Aztecs, and if they put them in an object, it usually denoted something of high importance or great danger. Either way, I could not help staring at it. I jumped when Lopsang and the man reappeared in a haze of smoke, laughing like a couple of teenagers who'd discovered their first joint. For a moment, they just stood there, whispering to each other.

"Well? Is he going to help us?" I had grown tired of waiting for answers.

"Yes, I will," grumbled the old man, flexing his hand uncomfortably close to the sword at his side.

"*Fan*-tastic." I made no effort to hide my sarcasm.

The man's voice grew grave. "But know that what you are setting out to do is a fool's errand. That valley contains nothing but suffering and death. You will all surely perish on the mountain."

The shop was unnervingly quiet.

I almost reconsidered the journey in the absolute silence, but as always, overconfidence carried me through. "We're all right with long odds." I gave Lopsang a friendly smile. "Now, can you help us kill it?"

The man stiffened, as if he had been expecting to scare me away. "That is no easy task."

"Oh, come on, you've already told me it's not going to be easy."

The man's hand shot out, faster than lightning, and slapped my mouth shut. "You are very disrespectful."

"So I've been told," I mumbled, rubbing my jaw.

"Right now, I wager that I'm the only person who can help you. I'd suggest finding some humility. If there is any left within you."

Lopsang remained off to the side, silent and looking at me with disapproval.

I sighed. "I'm sorry. It's just … we're running out of time. There's another team moving up the mountain as we speak, and they will be in grave danger if we do not find a way to help them." The false worry rolled off my tongue like water. I impressed even myself with my ability to feign amity with Manchester. It was a technique that had earned me free entry into many secret societies, and it never stopped coming in handy.

The thought of others in danger changed the old man's tune. "If your heart is set on this, I will help you, but know that I do not encourage it. You will die on that mountain. Maybe with my knowledge you'll be able to last a few hours longer, but there are reasons why no one has ever come back. If the creature could simply be killed, he would be on my wall." The man was speaking painfully slow, as if the contents of his pipe had just started to kick in.

"We just need to know how to kill it." I tried to remain respectful, but I knew with every passing second that Manchester was getting closer to claiming his prize.

"Of course, the simple question." The old man rolled his eyes, eventually settling them back on me. "There is only one way to kill a yeti."

I knew this, of course. Throughout my travels, I had found that most mythical creatures have one severe deficit. It was as if the gods had sat around after the battle of Troy and thought, "You know, I think that Achilles fellow was really on to something." The occasions where just shooting a monster to kill it were few and far between.

I had tried this approach a few times before and knew it was folly. For example, when I blew apart the King of Resurrection with my shotgun, he had come back as two equally powerful kings, who luckily quarreled over power long enough for me to escape. The lesson was essentially that research was key before embarking on a job. Unfortunately, when looking in the large tome written by my master, I found nothing about yetis other than a long list of obituaries for those who had gone after them.

"The yeti is a solitary creature and the apex predator of these mountains," said the old man. "It hunts everything and is hunted by nothing. Luckily for you, this makes it less cautious. The moment you set foot on the mountain, it will begin stalking you with extreme prejudice, but will never perceive you as a threat."

"Good, so it's going to come to us."

"Yes, you can use this to your advantage. The only way to kill it is to get up close. Its hide is thick and not easy to pierce." The man was growing excited, as if the prospect of hunting the creature would be great fun.

I just wanted him to get to the point. I was bored with legends and wanted to retire to someplace where I could lose myself in a stiff drink. My many years of experience with mythical beasts told me that most of what the man was saying was guesswork. Creatures in the mountains were generally very tough—they needed to be to survive—and made formidable opponents. Even a yak might give me a run for my money, if it had something to live for.

I don't like yaks, as I feel that they are far too strong for their own good and might possess more intelligence than they let on about.

"You will need a rare potion brewed from the Cobra Lilies that grow upon the mountain," continued the man, either unfazed or unaware of the tired look on my face. "It will slow blood coagulation, reducing the creature's unnatural healing rate."

"Will the potion slow the creature at all?"

"No, but it will aggravate it." The man was smiling, clearly enjoying the dismay on my face.

"Great …" I gave Lopsang an angry look. So far our detour had been about as useful as holy water in a mummy's tomb. "So, where's the weak spot? There's always a weak spot, right?"

"Not one weak spot," said the old man, wringing his hands together. "Three spots in total that you'll have to cut." As he said it, he thrust three bony fingers into my face, their papery texture making me cringe. "One shot to the neck," he whispered, making a motion across my jugular, "and one shot to the back of both its knees."

I had to back away to avoid getting knocked over with the man's sword as he gestured. Crazy old goat.

"I'd suggest doing the knees first. Makes it easier to hit the neck." The man leaned back against the shop counter, pleased with himself.

"I don't suppose you have any of this potion on hand?" I looked around the shop, figuring there had to be a few vials hidden in there somewhere.

The man stared vacantly into space for some time. "Yes," he finally answered. Then, he quickly hopped away from the counter and ran through the shelves that lined his shop, grazing his fingers over jars and bottles as he went. Loose items went flying, and one glass vial shattered, sending a foul-smelling liquid splashing across the floor. The man paid it no mind and continued searching.

"Why doesn't he wear a mask?" I whispered to Lopsang.

Lopsang did not have time to respond, as the old man yelled from between the shelves: "Because no one is stupid enough to try and come after me." He laughed maniacally as he tipped over a large pile of old books. The shop was chaos, and he thrived in it. "The one man who tried never got the chance to do so again. His thieving hand made a lovely ornament to light my counter."

I looked at the counter and saw a blackened hand haphazardly tacked to a wooden board, fingers clasped around a wax candle. The preservation process seemed to have shrunk it—or the man had been very small—but it got the point across. No one was going to be stealing from that shop. I admired the man's ingenuity for keeping the criminals at bay.

"Got it!" shouted the old man. He came hobbling back toward us with three vials of bright purple liquid. "These should be enough to get the creature to bleed. If you can get close enough, that is." The man was laughing again, and my annoyance grew stronger.

"How much?" Hopefully Lopsang's money was enough.

The man laughed even louder. "How much you got?"

11.

A KNIFE IN THE DARK

"All of that gold for three bottles of miserable purple goop," I moaned as we stepped back out into the lit streets. "This stuff better work, or I'm coming back to haunt that old man."

As I spoke, I noticed a faded line of white chalk across the entryway. That nixed that idea. Once invited inside, the undead could go just about anywhere they wanted, but until then, the chalk might as well be a brick wall.

"It'll work, don't worry," Lopsang said serenely. "Jim is many things, but a liar isn't one of them." He was starting to come down from whatever he had smoked with the old man in the back room. We walked away from the shack and back into the more populated streets of The Black Market.

Once we reentered the main thoroughfare, I noticed that the night sky had shifted to become a canvas of multicolored stars and a moon that appeared to be melting toward the horizon. In the middle of the street, a circle of hooded figures moved rhythmically, and I could hear the sound of fists on flesh. Shopkeeps were yelling from behind their stalls and cursing in various languages, but none dared stop the fight.

"Looks like someone's in trouble," said Lopsang.

"We might be in for a bit of fun," I said, cracking my knuckles in what I hoped was a menacing gesture.

Lopsang only laughed and moved forward.

Fights at black markets are always interesting, so long as I'm not the one participating. A benefit of being surrounded by thieves, magicians, and trained assassins is that when brawls break out, it's often spectacular. Shops would be broken to pieces, items from fruit stalls would be transmogrified into deadly weapons. In short, I was excited.

"Let's get in there, I don't want to miss this." I pushed my way through the throng of hooded figures to the center of the commotion. Once we broke through the outer layer, I saw two men throwing punches and grappling with each other. Scattered around the circle's edges were pitons, ropes, and other climbing gear. I let out a loud sigh.

"You've got to be kidding me. James?" I called into the vortex of fists and blood.

It was hard to distinguish who was speaking in between blows.

"He didn't want to sell the gear," James said. Then, his mouth was filled with an elbow.

I craned my neck out in an exaggerated gesture. "I'm sorry, James, I can't hear you. What was that?" I fully intended to stand on the edge of the ring and watch, but Lopsang had already moved in to assist. It only took a moment for the outer circle to notice the intrusion, and then all hell broke loose.

Well, here goes nothing, I thought, and I stepped into the brawl, aiming a blow at the hooded figure I half-hoped wasn't James.

Interfering with a fight in a black market is strictly forbidden, and carried with it the highest penalty. The man who had not been hit stood up and tried to remove his hood. I immediately moved to shove it back on his head.

"Idiot," I hissed. "We've already broken one of the sacred

rules. Show your face now and they'll hunt you down for the rest of your days."

The man lowered his hands. Behind us, Lopsang had picked up two men by the scruff and was swinging them in wide circles to hold back the crowd. "We need to get out of here, now!" he shouted.

"I'm thinking!" I yelled back, picking up a climbing axe just in time to beat away a hooded figure with his hands around James's neck. There was a resounding clang as the flat end of the axe collided with the man's head, and he crumpled to the ground.

"Thanks for that," murmured the hooded figure I was now mostly sure was James.

"Gratitude can wait. We need to get out of here. Grab the climbing supplies," I said, spinning the axe in my hand and pointing it at the growing din around us. I don't know how in the hell he managed to find climbing gear, but I was impressed. I was also overwhelmed by the seemingly hopeless situation. Any minute now, some assassin sitting on a rooftop was going to end the whole thing. I scanned the buildings around us, knowing full well that if there were people there, I likely wouldn't be able to see them.

Lopsang and James scrambled to pick up the climbing gear. In the end, I settled on the only logical thing to do when presented with insurmountable odds. I brandished the pickaxe in front of me like a battering ram, let out a loud yell, and then started running toward the exit. Lopsang and James did not hesitate, joined their yells to mine, and followed me through the crowd.

Most of the people standing around were confused, and they parted to let us madmen pass. This led to a momentary calm on the street, while everyone stood puzzled, wondering what to do next. A few men behind us were still exchanging blows, not realizing that one of the two parties involved in the original fight had departed. The crowd remained still for only a few seconds, and then they quickly coalesced into the easiest shape for a large group of people to form: an angry mob.

A group of people were exiting the elevator atop the stone steps before us. We were almost up the first step when I felt a *thunk* on my right shoulder. At first it was just an odd heavy feeling, but then the sensation rocketed from my arm to my brain. I cried out in pain and looked just briefly enough to see an arrow sticking out of my shoulder, thankfully having the foresight to dodge the archer's next attempt.

"Haven't these people ever heard of a god-damned bullet?" I grimaced just thinking about the agony of having to pull the arrow out.

Seeing my injury, James picked up the pace. Together, the three of us pushed aside the crowd that had just exited the elevator and dove into its inky black carriage. The door snapped shut quickly, but not before several arrows and knives flew through the gap. There were dull thuds as they hit the back wall, but no one was hit. With a jolt, the elevator started moving swiftly upward, taking us out of harm's way.

A sudden pain shot through my arm as Lopsang reached over in the darkness and pulled the arrow out.

"What was that for?" I screamed. Liquid poured over my arm and the strong scent of mountain wine filled my nostrils. Hot fire raced through the wound, and I yelled out in pain once more. "Jesus, Lopsang, do you bring that everywhere? Give me a drink."

Lopsang obliged and passed me the bottle. "You know, for a seasoned hunter, you're a bit of a baby."

I grunted in response and drained Lopsang's flask.

Lopsang cursed in a foreign language and took it back. "What? Never been shot before?" he asked sarcastically.

"Not when I can help it." My temper rose now that we were temporarily out of harm's way. I'd been shot only once before, after running afoul of a remnant of the Knights Templar in London. At least those bastards had the courtesy not to use barbed arrows. It had still been incredibly painful, but afterward we had all gone to a pub to celebrate our differences with a drink. Something told me that the assassins of The Black Market would not feel the same sense of comradery.

The elevator doors snapped open and revealed red-lit streets. Through the tops of the buildings we could see the evening sun setting over the mountain, its silhouette drawing longer, sending the street into a half twilight. Ignoring the pain in my arm, I got to my feet, stepped out of the elevator, and threw my hood in a basket next to the door. By the laws of The Black Market, anyone who escaped with their anonymity intact was free to go. The assassins would not hunt us unless we tried to reenter.

James removed his hood as well, and I felt a wave of relief that I'd hit the right person.

After taking a moment to catch my breath, I turned to him. "How exactly did you manage to find climbing gear?"

"Well," started James, cheeks reddening a little. "This guy just happened to be walking by with it."

"How did you get the gear?"

"Well, I had no money, see, and I took some judo classes in college."

"You've got to be kidding me," I said in disbelief.

Lopsang started to laugh hysterically.

"I offered to fight him for his gear."

I joined in Lopsang's laughter. I could hardly contain myself.

"I had it completely under control until you two showed up," he countered defensively.

"Wonderful, not only have we broken the laws of The Black Market, we've stolen from it as well. Thank God for the amnesty law." I sighed loudly. "Banned from the nicest market I've ever been in. I really can't take you anywhere, James, can I?"

"At least I got the gear." James was annoyed and in pain.

I stopped to give him a stern look but couldn't hold it for long, and soon the three of us were laughing together. "You thought you could fight a member of The Black Market for climbing gear? You must have really wanted to impress me." I laughed a bit more.

"Don't flatter yourself," he said. "I thought I could take him."

I could tell he meant it, but I was still a little dismayed by the extent of James's pride. On the mountain, ego would lead him to nowhere but a snowy grave. "Well, let's be thankful we never had to find out." I looked up at the darkening sky. "We'd better get a move on." I picked up my bag and started walking in the direction we had come from earlier that morning.

As we passed a bar, I considered stopping in for a drink and slipping James a sleeping tonic. Lopsang and I could ditch him in the middle of the night, and the apprentice would be out of harm's way. I scrapped this plan almost immediately, though, knowing it would be pointless. James would pick up our trail and be caught up by nightfall. He had proved himself incredibly useful, and I admit, the thought of no longer having a target for constant berating saddened me.

Consigned to the fact that we would all travel together, I struck up a conversation. "What do you think of all this, Lopsang?" I gestured to the climbing gear and the looming silhouette of the mountain in front of us. "Heading up the mountain with a couple of adventurers who swindled you, that is." I kept my distance in case Lopsang had regained his thirst for violence.

He did not respond for a while and instead gazed off at the

mountain. Was that longing in his eyes, despite the many dangers that lay on the mountain's slopes? We walked up the emptying streets in silence as he pondered. A chill began to set in the evening air, cutting through even my thickest layers.

"I suppose I could have done with having my money back," started Lopsang slowly, "but this is certainly more interesting." He favored the two of us with a smile.

Oddly enough, I was beginning to like Lopsang, despite having held him at gunpoint earlier that day.

"That's the spirit!" I said. "You could ferry people up the mountain the rest of your life, servicing their glory, but coming with us? Now there's a story worth telling." I was lost in the grandeur of it. "In a few weeks, we could be entering the gates of Shangri-La." I let the sentence sink in. "Or we'll be a bloodstain on the side of a massive mountain, but either way, we're in for a bit of fun." I laughed and clapped Lopsang on the back.

The three of us continued toward the mountain, determined not to lose any time. The second brush with death James and I encountered since entering the country had left us invigorated. We were eager to start our journey, but for different reasons. James was excited to get more experience and potentially discover the unknown. I felt like a man possessed. And full of what might have been hope.

More accurately, I was full of the suicidal urge to beat Manchester to the top, no matter what it took.

PART II:

THE MOUNTAIN

1.

EMPTY SLOPES

"So that's it, then? You all just escaped death at The Black Market and went on your merry way?" Winston took a sip of tea, pursed his lips, and then dumped what looked like the entirety of the sugar bowl into his cup.

Nick could not help but grimace, once again offended by the man's lack of taste. A part of him wanted to slap the teacup out of Winston's hand, but then he remembered he was being paid. "Well, there was quite a bit more bickering, but as far as the story is concerned, yes, that's all." Nick had left out the game of Russian roulette for a bottle of brandy, but that part of the story was too fuzzy to accurately recall anyway.

"I will warn you only once not to skate around the facts, Mr. Ventner." Winston's tone had turned oddly threatening. "I have a keen interest in this story, but only if it is the truth, and only if I can hear all of it."

Nick was taken aback, unable to find the right words to respond with. He had not expected to be challenged. "Of course. I didn't mean to imply you weren't getting the whole story," he amended, quickly trying to backtrack. "I only meant that I didn't want to waste your valuable time recounting pointless chatter."

Winston sat back in his chair, and Nick did the same, trying to look confident. Winston's sudden desire for the truth made him uncomfortable. *Something about him doesn't quite feel right,* he thought. He took another look around the room as if hoping for a clue of some sort, but found nothing but the confusing decor of the room. The conversation fell into an awkward silence.

To Nick's relief, Winston smiled once again. "Of course, my boy, only trying to chap your hide a bit," he joked, taking another drink of his disgusting sugar tea. "What's the point in paying for a story if you can't get your money's worth, eh?" He gave Nick a wink and motioned for him to continue.

Nick picked up his glass for a drink but realized with dismay that once more, it was empty. The more he told of the story, the more painful memories came back, and there was nothing to cure them but strong drink. He had always believed nothing good came of rehashing the past. That was, unless someone was paying him to do it.

As if sensing Nick's need, Winston snapped his fingers, and the mysterious butler appeared at Nick's side with a full glass.

"Cheers." Nick took a big gulp of the strong liquid. The butler was gone before the glass left his lips. Warmth spread through his body once more, albeit a little more dully than at the beginning of the night. *That'll do,* he thought, and then he prepared himself to tell the rest of the story.

"The three of us were headed up the mountain …"

▼

It was around midnight that I really began to feel the cold. The light of the moon shone down through a cloudless sky, just barely illuminating the massive mountain before us. Higher up on the slopes, I recognized the outlines of storm clouds. The blizzard could hold for a few more days or be gone in a matter of hours. Either way, it was likely not long before Manchester and his experienced team would begin their ascent. It was also likely that the storm would move down the mountain, meaning they would need to find shelter for the night soon.

The only sound was the crunch of boots on the frost, echoing off the empty mountain slopes. I almost found it pleasant, until Lopsang stopped dead in his tracks, refusing to move.

"Oh my," breathed Lopsang. He looked far off into the distance. I could see nothing around for miles but hillside and rocky trail.

"What? Did you leave the kettle on before you left?" James and I snickered, but the sound died in our throats as Lopsang clarified.

"We are in danger." He raised his hands above his head and sank down to his knees in a gesture of surrender. His voice was calm but very serious.

"Lopsang, this is no time for jokes," I said, hoping that he had suddenly developed a sense of humor. "Manchester is going to be moving up the mountain any minute." As I said this, I looked up the trail, and my heart stopped dead. "Well, shit."

I followed Lopsang's lead, put my hands on my head, and knelt on the ground. The day just kept getting better and better.

Emerging from the darkness ahead of us were three men, like pale warriors, holding AK-47s. From their stance, I guessed that they weren't friendly militia. Allies tended to point their barrels in the air when patrolling, rather than at weary travelers' heads. I muttered a prayer to a god that I never put much faith in and only contacted when it was convenient.

"What are you two doing?" demanded James, thinking we were making some joke he did not understand.

"Get on your knees, idiot," I seethed, not wanting to lose James over a matter of pride.

James looked aggravated until he, too, noticed the men and joined us on the ground.

As the gunmen approached, their shapes became clearer. They wore silver masks over the lower halves of their faces that glinted in the moonlight, carved into expressions of great pain and suffering that were clearly meant to intimidate and unnerve. They were also wearing heavy climbing gear and moved silently.

"We might be in trouble," I whispered. My mind raced through possible escape plans. Out of the corner of my eye, I saw the large gear bag James had been carrying. When that idiot knelt, he'd dropped the bag behind us, out of reach. There were enough weapons to kill an armada, but we couldn't use any of them without getting shot.

We should have been carrying them. In hindsight, it was idiotic to think that we were going ascend the mountain without harassment. It was always the parts of the map that were "uninhabited" that played host to cannibals, killers, and cults. I'd even made a point the last time, when I was being spit-roasted by an island king, to always travel with my thumb on the safety.

As the gunmen got closer, I heard a deep chant coming from behind their masks. It was thick, sonorous, and made the mountains feel as if they were shaking. They rumbled onward, distracting me until I felt the cold metal barrel of an AK-47 pressed against my face. The man in the lead had barely begun to give orders when I stifled a laugh.

If they were going to kill us, they would have done it already. We were going to be taken prisoner. I always prefer being taken prisoner to the alternative. Being stuck in a cell holds many possibilities, whereas execution holds only one. Out of the countless times I've been a hostage or a prisoner, I've only been harmed once. In short, the odds were turning in our favor.

"Listen closely. I will only tell you once," snarled the taller masked man with a red patch emblazoned on his arm. "You will stand, you will walk, and you will not say a word."

His voice was foreign, but I couldn't quite place it.

"What if we don't?" said James in an utterly stupid show of defiance. Whether it was because he heard my laugh or because he wanted to impress Lopsang, the outcome was the same. The masked man slammed his rifle butt into James's jaw and sent him sprawling backward into the snow. Never argue with a man who has a rifle to your head.

I winced as James sat up, dripping blood from his mouth. All the same, I couldn't help a small smile. More shows of non-lethal force meant they weren't planning on killing any of us.

"Do what he says, James, or you won't have many teeth left."

"Yes," said the masked man. "This will be much easier if you cooperate. Now stand."

I did as the man said, standing, keeping my hands on my head. While they hadn't shown lethal force yet, I didn't want to give them an excuse to. Hostage situations, while better than executions, were still quite dangerous. James had never even been held for a night in the drunk tank, and I probably should have explained the process of captivity better to him.

When James was reluctant to stand, the man made a threatening gesture with his rifle again. Head still spinning from the first hit, James stood as well. He was shaky on his feet but otherwise looked all right.

Lopsang remained silent and regarded their captors with cautious eyes.

"Walk, now." The man's voice was firm and left no room for argument.

I was still confused by the slightest hint of an accent. Maybe some kind of Russian? I thought back to just how many Russians had been sent to kill me. The idea of some hit squad being sent high up into the mountains just for me was flattering, but also terrifying.

The masked man moved behind us, and the other two flanked our sides. There were no escape routes. We resumed trudging up the mountain path, only this time at gunpoint. This made the entire act of climbing the mountain far less tiring. The mundane walk through the dark seemed a lot less so when there was the potential to die at any moment. Each step was another tiny opportunity to keep on living. In a way, the highwaymen had done us a favor by picking up our pace.

Snow began to fall, and the storm was getting closer. Rather than worry, I busied myself by trying to figure out more about the masked men. Silver masks probably meant they were in some kind of cult or secret society. This would not have been all that out of the ordinary for me, as I had tangled with cults before.

Watching the masks of our captors shine in the moonlight, I had the nagging feeling that they looked familiar. Where had I seen it before? None of it fit together. Their accents sounded Russian, but the masks looked like they were from somewhere farther east. They contained both elements of samurai and Mongol war masks. My head ached the more I thought about it, and so I decided to focus my thoughts elsewhere.

Snow continued to fall around us, growing heavier as the storm moved down the mountain. Hopefully they could get us to their hideout before we all froze to death. I secretly hoped that they would be the type of kidnappers who shared drink with their hostages. We had all bundled up tightly with the gear that James stole, but being caught in a blizzard wouldn't bode well for any of us. It would be disorienting, and I didn't want to contend with hypothermia for a second time in the same week.

We walked for about an hour, winding our way up the mountain path and eventually leveling off at a rocky ravine. The moonlight threw long shadows off the rocks, adding to the already impenetrable darkness. I had a feeling, like we were being watched by thousands of eyes. Every so often, chittering sounds echoed off the rock walls, but our captors did not seem bothered by them. After a few minutes of walking through the ravine, small fires began to illuminate deep pits in the rocks, casting long lines of orange light across the path ahead.

The path ended abruptly in a towering cliff face. Carved into the massive slab of rock was a tall stone door. Symbols from cultures around the world had been etched onto its surface. I could make out hieroglyphics, kanji, Sanskrit, and several languages that I did not recognize. The door was open just a crack, and bright red light shone from within.

As we approached, fire shot up incrementally across the wall of the cliff, illuminating large holes that seemed to run its entire length. From within these holes, more men with silver masks stared down at us. Out of nowhere, drums started up, and I began to question my assessment of our danger. It was a combination of the onlookers and the fact that I could feel an uncomfortable warmth spreading out from the crack in the open door. It felt unnatural in the cold mountain air.

"We're definitely in trouble," I said to Lopsang and James. As if they hadn't come to the same conclusion already. Their weapons were carried by the man on the right, who also happened to be the bulkiest of the three. I fancied myself a fighter when I needed to be, but I did not engage in fruitless exercises. With everyone in the line packing an assault rifle, and with the men on the cliffs also potentially being armed, trying to make a break for it was suicide.

Meanwhile, James was shaking beneath his parka despite the warmth coming from the door. Chills wracked his body, as if he had the sense that he was about to face his own death. I myself wasn't bothered, as I experience this feeling several times daily. All the same, the men on either side of us might as well have been pale riders carrying scythes, at least in James's eyes. He let out a mumbled prayer for safety, probably hoping I wouldn't hear.

Lopsang, in contrast, looked perfectly at ease with the situation. The Sherpa looked more like a man taking an evening stroll than a captive. His calmness infuriated me, and I could only assume that there was some sort of double cross involved.

Thoughts of treachery were wiped from my mind as the door in front of us swung slowly open, accompanied by the creaking sound of the impossibly large iron hinges. Red light spilled out from the twenty-foot doorway, and where it hit, the fresh snow melted. Heat rocketed toward us, and I smelled the stench of sulfur. I began to sweat instantly. Who would have thought the hot breath of Hell had been hiding in the Himalayas the whole time? I wanted to take off my outer layers but wasn't sure I could without being shot.

Beyond the door was a hallway, flanked on both sides by deep troughs filled with crackling flames. One misstep and we would become nothing but a crispy reminder of what used to be a human being. I had no desire to share the same fate as a piece of bacon, so I watched my step. The drums grew louder as we moved farther away from the door.

At the end of the hallway was a series of much shorter passages. Our captors took us down the middle one, and before long, I was hopelessly lost. A vaulted ceiling quickly lowered to where

I felt like I might scrape the top. Each offshoot looked exactly the same as the last, except for the few that I swear were filled with flames.

Eventually the passage we were in began to widen once more, and we found ourselves outside of a large iron gate. On the other side was another nondescript passageway. The line of men stopped. One of them walked up to the gate nervously, knelt, and prayed. For a moment, there was nothing but the sound of distant drums, echoing faintly from behind. A set of dark pools below the gate's twisted structure rippled with each beat.

The kneeling man finished his prayer, pulled out a large knife, and ran it methodically across his wrist. He did not flinch, and I thought I saw the faintest grin on the man's face. The cut was deep, and blood spilled fast into the pools below. The man waited, allowing the blood to drain until he was satisfied with the sacrifice. He then wrapped his bleeding arm and stood. Only then did the other men move forward to push the gates open.

Definitely a cult, then, I thought, trying to ignore how queasy the blood sacrifice made me. Half of it came from the sight of a man slitting his own wrist, and the other came from the implications it had for me and my companions. Maybe we could convince them that we had tainted blood?

We were led through the gate and down another series of winding passageways. After what felt like an hour, we emerged in a cavernous chamber lit with dim red light. In the center of the room was a large stone dais, propped up by several statues that I could not identify. They all depicted the hulking form of a beast, but the darkness obscured their features. Similar statues were set around the room, ranging in size from knee height to towering upwards just below the top of the high ceiling.

Suddenly, the sound of drums returned, and flames began

to shoot up from recesses in the side of the room. In the harsh light, I could make out the statues in detail. They were all slightly different but depicted the same creature: a yeti. At the base of each was a small pile of bones. Some of the skulls littered across the floor were far too small to be adults.

"Good day, Dr. Ventner," boomed a threatening voice from atop the dais. "We've been expecting you."

2.

THE HIGH PRIEST

A man stood high on a pedestal at the center of the room, dressed in flowing black robes and wearing a gold helmet wrought to look like the snarling face of a yeti. He looked down at us through black slits in the helmet's pupils. The mask's thin, pointed teeth gleamed in the light of the fires crackling at the edges of the room.

"My scouts tell me that you were on your way up the mountain. Is this true?" His voice was deep and sounded calm, but it still made me uncomfortable.

The three of us looked at each other and, in silent agreement, said nothing. Ordinarily I would have liked to run my mouth, but I still couldn't put my finger on exactly why we had been taken in the first place. It was the same path we took down the mountain, so we couldn't have been trespassing. No, if it was sacred ground there'd be thousands of dead mountaineers each year. The bigger expeditions used the path on the way to Everest as well, which ruled out the possibility of it being a common occurrence. Missing mountaineers tended to make headlines.

Usually when I trespassed or made some rude error, I knew exactly what it was. Half the time this was because it was intentional, but the fact stood. Had he somehow figured out we were there for Shangri-La? The thought seemed even more likely as I considered it. Every damn guide in the lodge probably heard Manchester talking about searching for the gate. It didn't explain how anyone would have known we were turning back to try ourselves, but it did mean they might have been on guard.

The man on the altar made a tsk sound from within his helmet. It was a hollow, sarcastic click, and echoed off the chamber walls only to be swallowed by the drumbeat. "Your silence will not help you here, my friends." He made a sweeping gesture, as if he were showing a group of guests his living room. "Speak the truth, and your death may be quick and painless. This is how the Almighty would want it. However, if you refuse, we have ways of making you suffer for days in the Chamber of the Beast."

I did not have time to think through my response, so I just started talking. The longer I had to think about our captors, the more I believed that something truly terrible was in store for us. In a rare moment of honesty, I decided to come clean. Given the situation, it seemed the most likely thing to help me survive.

"I am here to hunt the yeti. These two were not privy to my plan and were only necessary to get me up the mountain." The last sentence made James grimace, which made me curse him. You gotta pick your battles, and this was definitely not the time.

The man laughed, loud and long, before speaking again. "Why would you engage in such a fool's errand?"

For a moment, I swore I could see a red glow coming from behind the helmet's dark eye slits. "Fortune and glory, same reason I do everything."

The man remained silent for a minute as if contemplating this, and I charged on.

"This is a nice place you've got here. Very Temple of Doom. To whom do I have the pleasure of addressing?" I was beginning to gain a little confidence back until a rifle butt caught me in the stomach. I doubled over in pain and tried not to vomit on the floor. I doubt he wanted his trophies mixed with refuse.

"This one talks too much," grunted the man who hit me.

If I had a nickel for every time I've heard that, well ... Anyway, I slowly got to my feet.

"Leave him be. If he is willing to talk, then we shall allow his tongue to be loose. It will be the last chance he gets." This sentence had a tone of finality to it that brought panic into my heart. "I am the leader of the Herukas. Welcome to my palace." His tone was grand, as if we were standing in a room ordained with marble and gold rather than idols and bones.

Where had I heard that name before? I *knew* I'd heard that name before. "Lopsang? A little help here?" I implored, hoping that if I could get them talking, I might have a chance to figure out an escape.

"Wrathful Gods," seethed Lopsang quietly. "They are nothing but a ghost story." The way he said it was fierce, as though even when faced with the truth, he still believed it to be false.

"Yes, nothing but a ghost story," I muttered sarcastically, looking up at the Heruka leader. Men who think themselves incarnations of a vengeful god; things just kept getting better. "Ah, yes, I remember now." I had been wracking my brain for where I had heard the name, and I finally remembered a page in my tome dedicated to this particular group. "You are the blood drinkers. Consumers of flesh."

The man on the altar swelled with pride. "You are correct, Dr. Ventner."

"Yes, that would explain all the pools, skeletons, and scary idols. Yes, yes, it's all coming together now. But I still don't understand. Why does that put you in conflict with us? We seem to be low-hanging fruit as it were. On a quest doomed for certain death and all that."

"For thousands of years we have kept watch over the sacred valley and those who attempt to enter it."

"No, they haven't," Lopsang spat angrily. "They're just a crazy cult that came here uninvited." He barely got the last word out before he too was doubled over, struck by a rifle butt.

I looked at Lopsang with annoyance. The idiot was just angering our captors. I willed Lopsang to hear my thoughts, but the Sherpa just looked up, slightly bloodied, and smiled. He was still completely unconcerned with our situation. James, on the other hand, was trembling, looking paler by the minute. At least he knew when to keep his mouth shut.

"I'm sorry about my friend. One too many blows to the head, sadly," I apologized, attempting to ingratiate myself with the cult leader.

"It is not often someone has the bravery or foolishness to insult me while in my own palace." The man turned to face Lopsang directly. "You will die slowly, but know that you will have much honor in doing so."

Lopsang didn't seem to be bothered by this, but I jumped in all the same. "You know, there's a bigger party heading up the mountain as we speak. They'll be starting their ascent in the morning, when the storm clears." I tried to say it nonchalantly, but the man on the altar merely waved his hand dismissively. My heart sunk a little.

"You are referring to 'The Great Manchester,'" mocked the man.

That annoyed me, but I was willing to bet Manchester loved that title, and I was a little disgruntled at not being referred to as "The Great Dr. Ventner."

"His team will never make it past base camp. As soon as we have disposed of you, we will assure that their party goes no farther." The man let his hands fall to his sides as if this had ended the conversation.

At least we were all going down together. If I could only manage to outlive him by a few minutes. I tried to think quickly of arcane loopholes and tricks that had gotten me out of cult sacrifices before. There was always something, I just had to find it. The guard to my right smacked his lips in a way that made me uncomfortable. Knowing that they were likely blood drinkers and cannibals made the situation doubly unpleasant.

"So what do you want with us, then?" I was stalling, hoping to keep the leader talking.

"You were a threat. There was a chance, however slim, that you would discover the valley, and that cannot be allowed." The man paused, looking wistful. "Really is a pity, though. I thought you'd have a bit more fight in you. The three men we sent after you were nothing more than a scouting party."

The men said nothing in response to this slight, but the flames at the corners of the room lowered, casting them once more into a deep red gloom. My heartbeat began hammering again. The lights turning down never meant anything good, and I hadn't had a chance to come up with a plan yet.

"I don't suppose there's a chance we can just walk away?" I asked, grasping for anything.

"I'm afraid, Dr. Ventner, that the hour grows late." The fires dipped even further into the floor, until the man was nothing but a shadow against the stone backdrop. "As much as I am enjoying it, our chat is at an end. It is time for the three of you to face the gods."

3.

BLOOD SACRIFICE

We were led out of the chamber at gunpoint. I regretted the casual tone I had taken with the negotiations for our lives, if they could have been called negotiations at all. The unnerving scent of burning flesh wafted through the air, and I was sure that the tunnel we walked down was growing hotter with every step. The floor sloped downward, giving the feeling that we were heading toward the mountain's core.

The room we were led to was even more frightening than the last, which was a feat, considering it had been filled with human remains and yeti idols. Pots of liquid fire glowed around the edges of a smaller, perfectly square room. Through the dim glowing light, I could make out humanoid statues carved into the room's four corners.

Rather than the beastly depictions of the main chamber, the statues in the Chamber of the Beast were faceless and muscular. Their hands stretched upward to make it look as though they were supporting the ceiling. Above them was a mosaic with a large white yeti in the center. It was depicted as feasting on the flesh of lesser beings. If I hadn't thought I was about to be sacrificed in its honor, I might have admired the artist's attention to detail.

Directly in the center of the room was a stone table, approximately ten feet in length, with spikes jutting off the edges. The floor around it was etched with crisscrossing grooves that led to reservoirs beneath the feet of each of the four statues. They had been stained black from what I could only guess to be the blood of the unlucky soul who had entered the chamber before us.

"Now would be a pretty hot time for that plan of yours," muttered James, only half hiding the apprehensive tone in his voice.

I couldn't be mad. Sarcasm in the face of danger was a habit I had as well. While it didn't always solve my problems, it kept me calm.

"Don't worry, James, I've got it under control." I tensed for a hit from one of our captors, but they had apparently lost interest.

Instead, they began to chant once more, deeply, and with slow rhythm. Shit, I thought. The mix of the chanting, the smell of burning flesh, and the heat of the room did not bode well for us. The situation was now dire, and our escape routes were growing fewer by the minute. Our weapons were long gone, and none of our captors had shown a propensity for long speeches or mistakes of any kind. Just our luck to catch them on a busy day. I had been hoping for a much longer pre-execution speech from the cult leader and was left feeling slighted.

Upon examination, the room appeared to be inescapable. The chamber was surrounded by stone walls, presenting no exit strategy other than the door we had come through. That was not an option, as it was currently blocked by muscular men holding rifles. In short, we were up a certain creek without a paddle.

The only thing left to do was think, and we were running out of time to do so. Maybe I'd get killed last? Maybe they'd already sent the team to kill Manchester and I could manage to outlive him by a few seconds? A petty goal, yes, but it gave me a little hope in what was otherwise a futile situation. The three of us were pushed to our knees in front of the stone table.

The omnipresent drums in the background stopped and were replaced by the clicking of military boots on stone from the tunnel behind us. The guards parted and a soldier appeared, dressed in a mix of traditional kabuto helmet and samurai armor with strange wooden carvings dedicated to the yeti that hung all around. Each step he took was followed by the hollow clacking of these carvings against his armor.

Just like the man on the altar, he wore a mask that covered most of his face. The only difference was an opening at the mouth, where his unpleasant smile could be seen. I couldn't tell which was scarier, the sharp teeth of the mask or the rotted grin that lay beneath it.

An executioner that needed war armor? Usually they just go with the black hood and are done with it. Through the terror that gripped me, I felt a hint of flattery. Most of the cults that had held me captive had not been nearly as thorough. As a rule, their plans were porous, leaving multiple avenues for escape. I suppose that by virtue of being "ancient," the Herukas had used that time to hone their techniques and learn from past mistakes. If only we'd gotten there a few hundred years earlier, we might have been able to trick them.

The masked man followed in the tradition of the rest of their captors and began to chant. He walked around the table in meticulous circles, brushing his hands over the surface and muttering incantations.

James whimpered beside me while Lopsang continued to sit silently.

In a moment of either bravery or stupidity, no longer able to stand the anticipation of death, I spoke. "Get on with it, then; we haven't got all night." The guard behind me kicked me in the back, but the pain didn't make it past the adrenaline beginning to pump through my veins. The immediate threat of death had made me desperate and willing to do anything to keep breathing, even for a single moment longer.

Time slowed down, and the chanting of the man somehow grew deeper. First thing, I had to piss off the executioner. Enraged people make mistakes; calm ones don't.

"Why do they have you chanting in the basement instead of in the main hall? Couldn't make choir?" It was a feeble attempt at an insult, but it seemed to sting at least a little.

Just as I thought the executioner might slip, a second kick caught me in the back, knocking me face-first onto the ground. My head hit the stone and I saw stars. What was the next part of the plan again? My mind was moving slowly, but not wanting to lose my edge, I struggled back to a kneeling position.

The executioner stopped chanting and walked over to me, drawing a long blade. It ran nearly the length of my entire body. At the top half were several jagged points that eventually ran down to a smooth edge. It glinted in the dim light, as if it had been meticulously polished for precisely that moment.

To me, it seemed a weapon that was meant for pain. "Too late for last requests?"

The executioner laughed and brought the blade to my throat, drawing a single bead of blood.

The feeling of cold metal on my neck brought a fresh wave of adrenaline, emboldening me. "Oh, come on, then, it's a big enough blade, you're bound to hit at least part of me." It may not have been the best idea to taunt my executioner, but I was out of ideas. "I've got nothing to fear, so just get on with it."

The executioner stopped and lowered the blade for a moment, staring dully into my eyes.

I'll admit, I was surprised that's all it took.

After what felt like an eternity of silence, the executioner laughed again. "You die last."

Hallelujah, I thought, savoring what few extra minutes life would hold for me. Every second I was spared was a second for me to be proven wrong about the presence of divine intervention. Some minutes more are better than no minutes, after all.

"Don't worry, Lopsang, we're going to be fine," I lied, purposefully ignoring James in an effort to set the execution order. Who was going to carry my gear if the kid died? I really didn't want to have to start the interview process all over again.

Lopsang shot me a nasty look, and James continued to shake silently.

"He goes first," barked the executioner, pointing to Lopsang. "You will watch your friend suffer. I will make his death slow, until in the end, you beg for your own." His voice was gravelly, like he was speaking through sandpaper.

Not a bright bunch. I noted the awkward phrasing of the executioner's threat. I could have done better. All the same, I tried to appear frightened.

The executioner walked over and grabbed Lopsang, hoisting him onto the table. Lopsang did not struggle and allowed them to tie him down. His neck fell just off the edge of the slab. He almost seemed relaxed, as if the event were nothing more than a Sunday drive. The executioner held the blade to Lopsang's stomach and drew it slowly across, taunting him. Where the blade passed, his jacket split open smoothly, as if it were nothing but paper.

"You will regret this," Lopsang whispered. He closed his eyes and waited for the executioner to make his move.

I could only sit and wish I'd be that cool when the executioner came to me. In that one moment, Lopsang had managed more grace in the face of death than I had ever seen, and I hated him for it. Bastard thought he was so cool. Well, it's tough to stay collected when your head is rolling around the floor. It was petty and irrational, but I just couldn't help myself.

"I don't think I will," said the executioner, raising the blade high above his head and positioning it over Lopsang's arm. "Right or left?"

"Your blade won't touch me." Lopsang kept his eyes closed, never flinching.

"Both, then."

Spoken like a true henchman.

Lopsang continued to lay on the slab, waiting.

I wanted to scream at him, tell him not to pull that Obi-Wan bullshit. He had to have a plan, right? It appeared that he didn't, for the blade came down swift and strong. I winced and shut my eyes, but then, a strong voice whispered, "It's a fine swing, but I think it's my turn."

I opened my eyes. The blade had hit Lopsang's forearm but could go no further. Lopsang was just lying there, completely unperturbed by the situation, staring at the executioner. The next few seconds were chaotic and difficult for me to comprehend. The room flashed green and red, temporarily blinding me. A light blue powder exploded from where Lopsang had been sitting a moment earlier. I couldn't see an inch in front of my face.

The fine blue powder swirled with movement, and I saw shadows shoot around the room. Then came what sounded like the cries of a wounded animal. They were abruptly silenced. More flashes of light followed and were accompanied by a few stray gunshots. Next came the harsh thuds of bodies hitting stone. Two swords collided next to my face, shooting sparks into the gloom and filling my ears with the ringing sound of combat.

Then, just as quickly as it began, the commotion stopped. The powder began to settle and coat the entire surface of the room. When it cleared, Lopsang was sitting, unscathed, upon the floor. He brushed the blue powder from his skin languidly and smiled.

"What the …" was all I could muster.

James couldn't say anything and simply sat with his mouth open, unable to even make a sarcastic remark.

"It's a long story," admitted Lopsang. "Why don't I tell you once we get out of here?"

"Fine by me. Lead the way, murderous powder magician." The name didn't feel right, but it was the only way I could describe what I'd seen. The bodies on the floor were contorted at odd angles, and their helmets had fallen off to reveal shocked faces full of pain. I hopped up, ignoring them, thankful to have my life, and motioned for Lopsang to lead us.

James remained on the floor, sitting in silence with the same look of confusion.

"Oh, come on, James, it's not the first time you've seen a little magic. It was a good trick, I'll admit that, but we need to get moving." I thought it was much more than a "good trick" but wanted to save that conversation for another time. The guards were dead, but there would be more on the way.

"I … almost … died …" muttered James, sounding oddly like the living dead I encountered years back.

Christ, what a ham he could be. "You almost died a few days ago. What makes this any different?" I sounded annoyed, but I softened a bit. "You didn't come as close as he did." I motioned to Lopsang. "He was nearly decapitated!"

James was not moving.

"James, get off the floor, there will be more of them soon."

"They almost killed me," he repeated, his voice monotone.

While James had been close to death on more than a few occasions, this had clearly been the closest.

"Well, it's not going to be 'almost' if you just sit around waiting with your mouth lolling open like a trout." I shivered at the thought. I've always harbored an unnatural hatred for fish, and felt they were the vilest creatures that inhabited the planet next to yaks.

James seemed to finally get the message and stood to follow. He was dazed but seemed steady enough to walk.

"Which way, pal?" I asked Lopsang, not wanting to chance our good fortune by outstaying our luck. Ordinarily, I would want to be the one calling the shots, but given that Lopsang appeared to be some sort of ninja magician, I was content to follow.

"Well, there's only one door." Lopsang took off at a run. James and I followed without question.

The temple seemed to have a different feel once I was unbound. In the brief flashes as we ran past, I noticed the masterful architecture and the various carvings along its long, narrow hallways. That was, until the bullets started flying.

Ahead, the path split in three directions. From the left, a group of men with guns ran out and started firing. I don't know whether it was Lopsang guiding us through the fire, or just sheer dumb luck, but none of the bullets touched us. We came so close to the men as we ran past that I swear I could smell their rancid breath. I nearly gagged, but was thankful that I didn't have another hole in me; the arrow wound from The Black Market was still throbbing.

"Hey, can you do something about them?" I gestured to the men behind us.

Lopsang didn't even turn around, and from behind us, a cloud of blue smoke erupted. The gunfire stopped.

I wanted to stop and gawk in amazement, but Lopsang continued to run forward, and I didn't want to fall behind. We wove
through the temple's labyrinthine structure, past dead ends and
great statues of the yeti. Just as I thought we were horribly lost,
we skidded around a corner and into the open space that was the
temple's entryway. I froze.

A veritable army of men stood in front of the entrance, all
dressed in black and wearing the same silver masks, pointing
guns at our party of intruders. As if more menace were somehow
needed, they simultaneously cocked their guns in preparation.
Standing behind them, raised on a stone dais that had not been
there when we entered, was the leader.

Did he bring a pedestal out there for intimidation? It was
ridiculous. I hoped that Lopsang had more tricks to help us out of
our predicament.

"Well, Dr. Ventner, it looks like you've managed to extend
our talk just a little longer," admired the leader. It was clear he'd
been surprised by our escape but was prepared all the same.

"Actually, I didn't do—"

"Modesty does not become you, Dr. Ventner. Humble or not,
it does not change your fate. This is the end of the line. You aren't
getting past my soldiers, and I don't see any reason that I should
allow you to live."

The wall of soldiers was menacing, but the longer their leader
talked, the longer I had to figure a way out of it. I started wondering about miracle bullet scenarios where a deft dodge could
somehow send a stray shot through the ranks. To pass through
… forty men … the caliber would have to be … I counted the
soldiers quickly.

"No last words, then?" boomed the leader, interrupting my
mental math. "Fine. Ready! Aim …"

Something told me he wasn't going to make it to fire, as I saw the mischievous glint in Lopsang's eyes.

There was another flash of blue powder, and Lopsang was no longer beside us. Instead, there was just a thin cloud of dust. The room was momentarily eclipsed but cleared quickly. When I was able to see once more, all forty men were lying on the ground in various states of dismemberment. My jaw dropped. The gods would be pleased after all. It was quite a blood sacrifice.

Lopsang appeared out of the mist, carrying one of the men's rifles and walking calmly toward the only one still standing: the leader.

"Impossible. We are the guardians of—" He never finished the sentence. Lopsang shot from the hip and hit the leader square in the chest. He fell to the floor, clutching at the wound and gasping for air. "How … How could you?" The words were interrupted by a horrible choking.

"I'm not one for long speeches." Lopsang looked down at him with fiery eyes. "You filth have polluted this mountain for too long. We'll see how pleased the gods are when you meet them." He fired the gun again, hitting the leader in the head.

James and I stood dumbstruck, still unable to believe the carnage. Staring at Lopsang's handiwork, I had no true way of comprehending it. A magician taking down a few guards and an executioner? Sure, I could buy that. Even the bullet dodges were plausible. But a squadron of trained fighters before they even got a shot off? That put more than a few questions in my head.

Lopsang ran off to a side room and returned a few moments later with our gear and a pair of rifles.

"Well, I guess it couldn't hurt." I spoke in a daze, lost for words. "How did you—"

"That is a story for later. For now, let's get out of here and find shelter for the night. The storm is worsening." Lopsang picked up his bag and walked into the snowy night air, as if what he had done were completely normal.

I looked at James. We both followed, unable to speak.

4.

RETURN TO BASE CAMP

What had been a flurry when we entered the temple had turned into a full-on blizzard, making it nearly impossible to see anything as we trekked back up the mountain. Even the narrow canyon walls were obscured from view, leaving me and James to trust Lopsang's direction. Neither of us objected to leaving the valley before making camp for the night. The chill felt even worse after exiting the oppressive heat of the temple, and I found myself shivering.

▼

"Now wait just a minute. You mean to tell me that you saw a man produce godlike powers, and you just kept following him, without question?" Winston's eyes were bulging, as if the very idea of it was preposterous.

Nick supposed it was a bit preposterous. "Well, I certainly questioned him later."

"And? What did he say?"

"I'm getting there, but if you must know the gist, he was sort of a ... demigod" Nick threw the term out nonchalantly, knowing perfectly well the reaction it would get.

Winston did not disappoint and spluttered as he tried to take a sip of his tea. "A what?"

"A demigod."

"How did he get his powers?" Winston spoke quickly and with great excitement. "Where did he come from? Was he actually a god?"

"No idea. Somewhere in those godforsaken"—Nick paused at the term and corrected himself considering the circumstances—"er, cursed mountains. And I did not say a god, I said a demigod."

"What on earth is a demigod?"

Winston's stupidity was annoying Nick as it always seemed to. "Demi, for half, god, for god. It means half god."

Winston looked bothered by this and was about to speak when Nick cut him off. "Look, this isn't a superhero or a demigod origin story, so if you don't mind, I'd like to get on to the part about the yeti. We're burning up a perfectly good night, and I've got a bar to visit when we're done here."

"I think the demigod is quite interesting," noted Winston matter-of-factly.

"Well, the yeti is more interesting, trust me, and that's what I'm here for, right?" He paused to look Winston hard in the eyes. It was true—Lopsang's story was no more interesting than a two-bit fairy tale, but Nick also didn't want to reveal too much. Something about Winston told him to stay on his guard, despite his non-threatening appearance.

Winston squirmed in his chair, clearly wanting to hear both tales. "Yes, all right, let's finish the story, but I want to hear about this demigod another time."

You couldn't pay me enough to tell you that story. There was a lot more to Lopsang's origin than his godly parentage, but it was long, and in Nick's opinion, not very compelling. He had said something along the lines of "real evil in the world" and "power overwhelming." Nick couldn't be bothered to remember most of it, only that there were parts he wasn't supposed to tell, and those were the only interesting bits.

The thought fled from his mind as he found himself once more distracted by the room's furnishings. Dead center above Winston was a large oil canvas of a duke or some other portly man of power. Nick could not help but stare at it, as it felt slightly off. The frame was crooked, but only slightly. Ordinarily, it would not have been enough to make him take notice.

Who are you? You must be of some importance if this slob is willing to hang you in his living room. But not so important as to hang you straight.

Nick's concentration was shattered by Winston's voice. "Please continue. I am sorry for the interruption."

Nick tried to regain his train of thought, but it was lost somewhere between the booze-addled part of his brain and consciousness. Either way, he had the creeping feeling that something was not right about the place and tried to keep himself ready.

"Right, we were headed up the mountain once more, only this time, in a blizzard ..."

———————— ▼ ————————

The storm was full well down the mountain, but Lopsang continued to hike on as if it were nothing. It was night and the clouds above had blotted out the moon. The beams of our flashlights illuminated only a few feet in front of us. In short, we were traveling blind.

"Shouldn't we wait for this to blow over?" I asked, my teeth chattering from the cold.

Lopsang had not stopped walking since we left the temple.

Sure, we all wanted to get out of the valley, but I assumed we would be camping soon thereafter. If he was a demon, we were going to be in even more trouble. I clutched at my bag and thought about how we were much lower on silver bullets than I would have liked.

"Come on! Even blind, I could find my way through these mountains," shouted Lopsang over the sound of the storm. "If we want to beat Manchester, we must move fast. Don't worry, I know a shortcut that will lead us to a crag just below base camp. We'll camp there for the night."

Famous last words. I turned to James. "And what about you? How do the miraculously undead feel about this?"

James had pulled his coat far up around his face and was looking at me through a small slit in his hood. "You did say you wanted to beat Manchester." It was muffled, but I got the gist.

Exhausted, I shrugged and trudged on through the snow after Lopsang. Before long, we were at the bottom of a large rock face. Even without the snow, I wasn't sure if we would have been able to see the top, but in the blizzard it was impossible. Looking up, the rock seemed to extend forever into the sky.

Lopsang turned around to face us. "How are your climbing skills?"

James let out a snort, but his humor died when he saw Lopsang's expression. "I did some rock climbing in college," he claimed. "I can hold my own." He tried to insert a bit of false confidence into the words.

Lopsang seemed to believe it, or at least didn't care enough to press the matter, and turned to me. "And you?"

I had never climbed more than a steep hill in my life. There had been a few times where I'd chased monsters into the mountains, but that was mostly along trails. Or with a proper guide who could do the climbing for me and serve as bait. "Can't say I have any," I admitted with the asinine confidence of a man who had agreed to climb a dangerous mountain with no prior experience.

Lopsang shook his head. "How exactly were you planning to get up the mountain?"

Confidence usually gets me pretty far, but I didn't say that. Our plan had plenty of holes, but when Manchester was involved, I tended to get a little blind.

"That's where you come in." I clapped Lopsang on the shoulder. "You're a professional guide, right?"

Lopsang made a sour expression.

"Well, guide us up." I gestured toward mountain, emphasizing the point. It wasn't a strong case, but it was all I had.

James seemed none too excited by the idea, but Lopsang shrugged it off and started pulling supplies out of the gear bag. "If you want to meet Death, he will welcome you," he stated.

He walked over to start hammering pitons into the rock face. The process was much faster than I anticipated, and within a few minutes, Lopsang had strung a rope up the face and was out of sight. After a while, even the clanging of his hammer on stone was inaudible over the growing wind.

Every time I began to feel cold, I tried to think of the warming image of the riches and splendor lying in Shangri-La. In reality, I had no idea what I would do with the money, only that it would be lavish and unnecessary. The thought of a solid gold boat came briefly to mind before a rope fell from above and hit me on the head.

"Tie yourself to the rope and follow my trail," Lopsang yelled. "Take it slow. Nice and easy."

Some guide, right? "All right, James, you're up first."

James muttered something that was likely offensive and tied the rope around his waist. Whether his hands were shaking from cold or from fear was impossible to tell. Luckily, Lopsang had placed the handholds very close to each other, and James ascended easily.

As James climbed, I put my back to the rock wall and pointed my rifle toward the blinding darkness. If any of those bastards lived and decided to make the same mistake twice, I'd be ready for them. Around twenty minutes after James started the climb, the rope fell back down, and it was my turn. I tied the rope around myself and felt tension as someone up top acted as the counterweight.

The rock itself was cold and ugly, and as I started to ascend, I realized the benefit of having Lopsang around. Despite the frigid and windy conditions, the path he had chosen made the climb feel almost recreational, if still physically challenging. I had to cling to the rock face a couple of times to avoid being blown off by a strong wind, but such was the nature of climbing at night in a blizzard.

Just as I was starting to feel good about our progress, the sharp howl of an animal cut through the wind. It echoed off the mountainside, and carried with it a deep resonance that shook the very rock I clung to. Even through the freezing cold, I felt a chill creep up on me.

"Climb quickly, Dr. Ventner!" I heard from above.

I did not have to be told twice. I gripped the handholds and began pulling myself up as fast as I could, not stopping for anything. When I reached the top, I scrambled over the edge, arms still moving in a climbing motion from habit. My entire body ached, but when a white-faced Lopsang pulled me to my feet, they went numb with adrenaline.

James had taken on his usual green quality that accompanied mortal danger, and Lopsang looked rattled.

"How far?" I asked.

"Very close," Lopsang said gravely.

"All right, James, get the poison; we may not get a better shot." I had not expected us to find the beast so quickly, but I am not one to waste golden opportunities. Despite the blizzard and the lack of preparation, there was a foolhardy drive that pushed me forward.

A cold slap from Lopsang cleared my vision. "If you go after the beast tonight, you will die. I will not be able to help us out of this one."

I thought about it and looked to the bag containing our gear. Dangerous or not, we could end it tonight …

"This blizzard"—Lopsang swept an arm through the air in case I hadn't noticed—"is the beast's doing. It's hunting, and we need to hide fast, or we're going to be the prey."

I was about to argue when an earsplitting roar tore through the snow, followed by the deep vibration of massive footfalls. "Right, grab the gear, let's go!" I slung the rifle on my back to firing position. "How far to base camp, Lopsang?"

"Not far, but I don't think Manchester's team will help us." The thundering footsteps grew louder.

My heartrate quickened with each booming footfall. If we didn't do something soon, we were going to die. "There's a cave protected by a holy marker where we escaped last time. Might be buried by the snow, but it's our best shot. It's right off the main trail." Our only other option was to find an outcropping in the rocks and pray that the beast didn't have a very good sense of smell. Based on what I had read of other mythical apex predators, I was not willing to bet on it.

There was a loud boom as a huge sheet of ice crashed down the mountain not far off.

"It's getting closer. We need to move now!" shouted Lopsang.

Without any more questions, we all took off at a run. Lopsang took the lead, guiding us through the blizzard so that we didn't run straight off a cliff. The howling of the wind was occasionally interrupted by the roar of the beast, blocking out all thought that wasn't dedicated to propelling us forward.

It must have been busy or it would have come for us already. I was feeling good about our chances, despite not knowing how close we were to the cave. My heart was hammering so hard that I thought it might burst out of my chest.

The footsteps came again. *BOOM, BOOM, BOOM.* The very surface of the mountain felt like it was about to crack. Then another roar, accompanied by the unmistakable scent of a fresh kill. I thought I could feel the snow melt around us as the beast's hot breath blew through the night air.

The cave was nowhere to be seen, not that we could really see that much. James screamed from behind, quickened his pace, and overtook me. Smart kid, really. Didn't have to outrun the beast, just had to outrun me.

"James, look for the cave," I called through the din.

"No shit, Sherlock," called James through his panting breath.

Ever the energy to be sarcastic. I tried to avoid the thought of massive jaws closing around me from behind.

The yeti continued to gain on us, dropping large sections of snow pack with every footfall. Every few seconds, debris would come sweeping through the path we were on and cascade over the edge. I dared not turn back for fear of what I would see, and that it would be my last vision.

Just as I thought my legs would give out, I saw it. Barely protruding from the snow, just ahead of us, was a red prayer flag. It was half buried, but I could see the entrance to the cave below it. It was nothing more than a black hole in an otherwise white wall of snow, but it was our only shot. Neither James nor Lopsang had seen the cave and were running past it.

"James, Lopsang, over here!" I yelled desperately. They spotted me and doubled back. I ran full force toward the hole and threw myself into it. For a moment, I was suspended in space, and then I hit the snow with a loud thud and broke through. Darkness enveloped me as I hurtled into the cave and shot straight into the back wall. The wind knocked out of me, I scrambled out of the way just in time for Lopsang and James to come skidding in.

I hustled to my feet as the other two came running through the cave entrance, and raised my flashlight to the opening of the cave. Moments before a drift of snow sealed us in, I saw it. Twelve feet of matted white fur towered just outside the cave mouth. The face was obscured through the thick snow, but the shape was unmistakable. I tried to get a better look, but a fierce roar nearly knocked me over, and I retreated quickly to the back of the cave, stumbling over James and Lopsang in the process. I fell flat on my back but felt only a distant pain as the cave walls rumbled, sending a cascade of snow over the entrance, sealing us in for the night.

The three of us lay on the cave floor, panting with exhaustion. Lopsang got up and quickly rooted around in one of the bags, producing and expanding a collapsible metal tube. With a swift strike, he punched it through the snow that covered the cave's opening.

"Don't want to escape the yeti only to die of asphyxiation," I said with a laugh. It was a strange feeling in the moment, but mostly I just couldn't believe we were still alive. The tube would assure that we got at least some fresh air over the course of the night. I raised myself to a sitting position. "Unless there's another cult on the mountain, I think we might have this in the bag."

I began laughing again, and this time I couldn't stop. At first, James just looked at me, but the overwhelming joy of survival overtook him as well. Soon, even Lopsang couldn't help it, and the cave was filled with the joyous sound that could only be produced by those who had just cheated death. When we had finished reveling in our unlikely escape, I went through our bags and pulled out the small camping stove James had obtained to make heat.

Lopsang scooped up snow from the entrance to the cave and boiled water. After, he brought out a few rations of salted jerky and passed them out. To me, it tasted better than anything I had eaten in my entire life. The hot, savory flavors warmed me, despite the tons of ice surrounding us. Soon I found myself leaning against the cave wall, drifting off. The cave was surprisingly warm, and for a moment, my mind was at peace.

5.

YAKS, THE WORST CREATURES

I awoke to the crunch of hard snow beneath boot heels, punctuated by the loud grunting of yaks. We were in trouble. It sounded like there were twenty or thirty men, at least. My estimate ended up being wildly inaccurate, but it made me feel smarter in the moment.

Slowly, cautiously, I opened my eyes. A tiny shaft of light illuminated the cavern from the end of the metal tube we had used to puncture the snow. The cave was warmed by our breath and a fine dew had built up on our gear. While the temperature was still uncomfortably cold, it was better than I could have hoped for on the mountain.

Lopsang was sitting upright, wide awake, listening carefully.

James, on the other hand, lay across the cave, sleeping surprisingly soundly for someone who had been chased by a yeti the night before, though maybe the little guy was simply all tuckered out.

"What is that?" I whispered.

Lopsang merely raised his hands in confusion. Whoever was out there continued to pass by. The marching of feet and hooves was endless. For all we knew, an army could have been passing by the cave entrance.

More gently than usual, I kicked James in the ribs, assuring that he would wake, but also that he wouldn't yelp in pain. In the ice cave, we were camouflaged from the outside world. With any luck, whoever was passing by would see nothing more than fresh snow pack.

James rustled to life and tried to speak, only to find his mouth covered by Lopsang. Sarcasm and vitriol was briefly stayed as the predicament dawned on him.

"Who are they?" he whispered.

"No ide—" I was cut off by loud squishing sounds coming from the mouth of the cave. I stood up and walked over to the pipe and was blasted with an awful stink that smelled like a mix of stale grain and slop. I recognized it immediately. *Wonderful, it looks like we've made a new friend.* Looking out of the tube, I saw the thick tongue of a yak, one of my least favorite creatures, undulating in a most unpleasant fashion.

Every minute or so it would take a break from licking the tube to make filthy yak calls and fill the cave with its stench. It continued for what felt like an eternity, turning the cave into my own personal hell.

"If it doesn't move soon, someone will find us," I mouthed. I would have liked nothing more than to point the barrel of my revolver up the tube and send the yak to wherever beasts of burden went, but that would only exacerbate the problem. As it was, we could do nothing but sit and wait, hoping that eventually the creature would tire and leave.

After what seemed like an eternity, the squishing noises stopped, but not on the yak's accord. A pair of heavy boots could be heard trudging up to the animal, and it snorted as it was dragged away. I was sure they'd found us. Any minute there would be the sound of shoveling, and we would be discovered. I sat, trying not to move, and listened in surprise as the footsteps and the grunting yak moved away.

We waited for twenty minutes in silence and heard nothing outside. The group had passed, and I once again felt we had skated by on luck alone.

"I think we've waited long enough," I said cheerfully. I stood up and began to put away our camping supplies. "Let's get a move on. We need to climb while there's still daylight."

I reached into the bag, pulled out a small snow shovel and tossed it to James.

"What's this for?" James looked like a petulant child.

I smiled. "That snow isn't going to shovel itself. That's what I have an apprentice for."

James grimaced, stood up, and moved to the mouth of the cave. While he despised the term apprentice, he still felt the need to do what I said. Luckily for him, only about two feet of snow had accumulated, and the digging was quick. Soon the small shaft of light had turned into a bright opening, showing clear skies and brilliant sunshine.

We all squeezed through the small blue tunnel and stumbled out into dazzling white light. All around us, mountain ranges shone like beacons, reflecting the rising sun. I stretched in the open space, shaking the last of sleep and frost from my body.

"I guess we didn't burn that much daylight after all. Good, we can start catching Manchester's trail."

"Oh, I think you've caught it," called a cold voice from behind me.

I whirled around to find the bright light of the sun obscured by a commanding shadow. He wore all black climbing gear and sported his characteristic wide-brimmed black hat. It couldn't have been convenient attire for mountain climbing. One should never compromise functionality for fashion. Still, silhouetted with a cadre of men behind him, I could not help but feel that

Manchester looked almost like a god. Somewhere in the distance, I heard the yak call again. Son of a bitch yak. I knew what we were eating for dinner.

"Hello, Harvey," I said slyly. I knew that Manchester hated the use of his first name and had gone through great lengths to hide it from the world. Luckily for me, it had only taken a few cheap drinks and a silver tongue to get it out of Manchester's old nanny.

The look in Manchester's eyes was murderous.

"Fine day for an expedition, is it not?" I beamed, easing the tension and gesturing to the mountains surrounding us.

"And here I thought you had decided not to come. I must say, I was surprised to see your little lights heading up the mountain last night." Manchester tut-tutted at us like a mildly disappointed, but not surprised, parent. "In the middle of a blizzard, too. Very brave, some might say."

I may have disliked Manchester, but I couldn't help it—my chest swelled at the compliment.

"But others, specifically anyone who knows what it means to climb this mountain, would have called it stupid."

That deflated me, and I returned to my passive disposition of sarcastic judgment.

"Stupidity aside," Manchester continued, "I do applaud your decision to step down from your tower of indifference to chase the unknown." He proceeded to make a half-hearted clap. Some of his men attempted to join in, but he silenced them by raising a finger and looking up at the sky. "Now that we have the formalities out of the way, I'd say it's time we get a move on. We've got a lot of ground to cover while the trail is still fresh."

I felt a fearsome defiance at being commanded. "I'm sorry to have to repeat myself, Harvey, but we will not be joining your tawdry expedition." I gave a derisive snort in the direction of the yellow-bellied yak that had exposed us in the first place. "I've made plans of my own, and I'm only half sorry to report that they don't involve you or your army."

I looked over the massive group of climbing guides, Sherpas, and what looked like guns for hire. How they'd get up the mountain at all was a mystery. Most climbing teams tried to keep their numbers small to avoid getting jammed up in the narrower areas, and I couldn't help but feel Manchester had made a critical misstep.

"Oh, I see," replied Manchester with a tone of little surprise. "Good luck, then." He waved us off and turned to leave, but as he began to walk away, he turned back once more. "I should mention that the rear guard has been ever so trigger happy lately and, well, with all the snow, they'd be hard pressed to tell you from a yeti. Best you don't follow our trail. For your own safety."

A group of three men and one woman who looked like they had just stepped out of a war zone waved at me. One even went as far as to check the magazine on the unwieldy machine gun he was carrying.

He couldn't possibly be planning on hauling it the whole way up the mountain, could he? "Glad to see you've graduated from vague insinuations to threats, Harvey. Not like you, but an improvement nonetheless."

"Not threatening," Manchester mused idly, "just protecting my investment. I would hate to find the gates only to have some charlatan with delusions of grandeur and a hand cannon coming to steal it out from under me." He paused to let the words sink in. "You wouldn't know anyone like that, would you?" A grin spread across his face that sent white hot anger coursing through my veins.

I had to keep my cool. I couldn't let him win this. "I trust you will show us the same professional courtesy? There's plenty of mountain for the both of us. No need to step on each other's toes." I surprised even myself with my calm tone.

Manchester let out a cold, high laugh with too much superiority for my liking. All the same, I couldn't blame him. It must have seemed ridiculous for a three-man team to be taking an unorthodox route up such a dangerous mountain. Even if Manchester had known about our demigod guide, we were only three men, and I had barely been able to climb out of bed that morning, much less a mountain.

We stared at each other, stiff in the morning cold.

"Of course, Nick," he said in a placating tone. "But I think we both know there's no second path up the mountain. I wish you luck."

It was an entire god-damned mountain. There had to be plenty of routes up, right? The short answer was no. There were not many paths for us to take. After years of failed attempts all over the mountain, it had been widely accepted that there was only one safe way up.

"We've got our own way, don't worry about that. Consider how a team of thirty or so men are going to do on the face." I wasn't sure how our team of three men would do on the face, or if there was a face, for that matter, but it sounded like something a mountaineer would have said, and so I stuck with it.

"Splendid," said Manchester icily. "We wish you a safe journey." He tipped the brim of his wide black hat and resumed his way up the mountain. "Move out," he yelled to the team. The mountain air was filled with the cacophony of his team getting into motion.

It almost seemed like a great engine of war marching out to battle. As the group started to move, I could see that there were around fifty of them. Most were Sherpas, carrying large bags and guiding yaks up the mountain. I took solace in the fact that soon the wretched yaks would have to be sent back down, as the trail would become too steep. Manchester led at the front, flanked by the four mercenaries as his personal guard.

"I gave a long whistle. "Well, that was pleasant."

"You're an idiot." Lopsang looked furious. "That was our only way up the mountain. How are we supposed to find the sacred valley if we can't even get past ten thousand feet?" Lopsang was panting in his fury.

"Are we sure the valley is that high on the mountain?" I knew that it likely was but didn't want to seem like a complete fool.

"The valley is said to be in the most inhospitable environment on Earth. Well hidden from the prying eyes of man. So yes, I would imagine it to be very high." Lopsang's frustration was growing, and I had no intention of stopping it.

"Where exactly is the valley?" I inquired casually.

"How should I know?" Lopsang shouted.

"I mean, you *are* the demigod among us. If anyone was to know, it would be you."

"Surprisingly, my supernatural powers don't create maps that lead us wherever *you* want to go!"

"All right, all right, calm down." I held my hands out like I was calming an angry steer. "We can figure this out." I looked up at the mountain. Stones that had been barren only a week ago were now covered in snow, giving everything a rounded appearance. It would have looked friendlier had the glaciers above not remained ever jagged. They cut the sky like a razor, sharp and barren. I found it hard to believe that lurking within the icy crags was the hiding place of one of the world's most reclusive creatures.

Out of nowhere, I was struck with dismay. I didn't have the faintest idea where to start.

In despair, I looked up at the dregs of Manchester's team, growing smaller in the distance. They were moving sluggishly into the valley ahead, burdened by their yaks and the size of their team. The valley would lead them to the bottom of a great ice fall, where they would have to ascend and leave behind anything that wasn't necessary. Thinking back to the yaks, it seemed strange that Manchester would have brought them so far up the mountain. Unless he didn't know where the valley was either. I considered this possibility for a moment, then began to laugh out loud.

"Why so jolly?" snapped James, testy as ever.

I positively beamed at him in my joy. "Because, my dear apprentice, it appears that Manchester has no idea where the valley is either." I laughed again and could not stop. The fool made the same mistake we did, and he'd had more time to prepare.

"What makes you so sure?" Lopsang looked at the team, trying to understand.

"They're moving slowly, and their team is too big." More and more, it began to click in my head. "Think about it. Manchester is smarter than to move a whole team up the mountain at once. They saw us coming up last night. We forced their hand. At their current pace, they'll barely be above us by nightfall. He has no idea where he's going!" My voice echoed off the mountains.

Lopsang and James were still staring at me as if I was evangelizing cannibalism.

"Don't you see? He's waiting for us to make our move. He bought our bluff." Excitement pulsed through me once more. Not only were we no longer behind, I was beginning to think that we almost had an advantage.

"That's all well and good," said James, "but we still have the problem of not knowing where *we're* going."

"Glad to see you're feeling good enough to criticize again, James. I have a plan." It may have been half-baked, but it was more than nothing. "Lopsang, can we take these prayer flags with us?"

Lopsang looked at me, disgusted. "No, we can't just move them. It doesn't work that way. Not only is it disrespectful to those who put them there, moving them would take away the protection from this spot and from the items themselves. They have to be placed by a shaman, most of whom are dead or live too far down the mountain in fear."

It was worth a try. It wouldn't have been the first sacred artifact I had disturbed to save my own skin. There were still a few angry Italians that thought I had stolen the sword that stabbed Christ. It had been a fake, but I'd been up against a corner with no weapon. For a supposed holy relic, it had worked pretty well. Maybe I should have told them it was a fake.

"Okay, so if the shamans are too afraid to go up the mountain, then there's no more hiding past this point?"

"That's not entirely true," said Lopsang. "There are holy sites like this all along the mountain, but there's a slight problem."

"What's that?" I knew I wasn't going to like the answer.

"The shamans were excellent climbers and did not want their holy sites to be found. They will be safe from the creature but very dangerous to reach."

I looked up at Manchester's party. The valley they were moving up was flanked on both sides by high, rocky ridges.

"What about up there?" I asked, pointing up, just east of where Manchester was headed.

"That path has only been traversed once." Lopsang's tone was grave.

"So who traversed it?"

Lopsang sighed. "A shaman, but he did not make it back."

My interest was piqued.

"There are fissures and chasms everywhere," he said. "It would be slow to get there and incredibly dangerous."

"Do we have the proper gear?"

"Yes, but not the proper skill. One of you would almost certainly die."

I thought about it. The ridge seemed to be our best bet, and I had rolled the dice with my life a few times already. If anything, I was worried about James more than myself, a fact that made me uneasy. "Here's hoping it ain't me."

James just shrugged and shouldered his pack. "We might as well get going while it's still light. There's no talking him out of it now."

After months of traveling with me, James had learned when my mind was set. Occasionally he put up a fight, but most of the time he just saved his efforts.

"We don't even know that the shaman left anything up there," said Lopsang, growing angry. "If we climb up there and find nothing, we will be sitting ducks."

"Looks like a good enough place for a shaman to leave a holy relic."

"Looks like a gamble," said Lopsang.

I was happy that he was fighting back again, but we were also past arguing the point.

"Come on, Lopsang, live a little." I turned away and began to hike up the mountain.

The rocks would provide good cover once we were on top, and it would confuse the hell out of Manchester. I grinned at the thought of him scratching his head as he watched us climb. It could stump him for days.

My reverie was interrupted by Lopsang stepping in front of me and planting a hand on my chest. His face was hard, and he was staring coldly into my eyes. "If we are going to do this, I will take the lead. You will not question me, and you will do what I say."

"Glad to see you're with the progra—"

"I will not have either of your deaths on my head. This is one of the most technical sections of climbing on the mountain, and most would not attempt it."

He was really selling the plan, so much that I was beginning to have misgivings. "All right, Lopsang, you're the boss. Lead on." I was not one for taking orders from anyone, but I also had no intention of ending up dead in a crevasse. Freezing to death at some unfathomable depth beneath the mountain was not the blaze of glory I envisioned for myself.

"All right, up we go," said Lopsang, and he turned to walk up the mountain. In a low voice, he began to hum what could have been either a drinking song or a battle hymn.

I thought both might be appropriate, and in the end, it inspired me to move. Together, we began the climb.

6.

THE SPINE

By midday we had reached the base of what the locals collo-quially called Merudanda, or the Spine. It jutted out of the middle of the mountain like a crooked fin, running along the valley. The Spine led up to a glacier, ending a fair distance below the mountain's summit.

"No one comes near this place for a reason," said Lopsang, staring upward. He looked both reverent and terrified. "Meru-danda is known for shifting ice. Large blocks fall off into the valley below and will sweep past faster than you can avoid them."

"Piece of cake," I said, noting the potential irony of a block of ice knocking me down to Manchester's camp. Aside from the like-ly painful death, I couldn't stand the idea of Manchester standing over my body and speaking the words: "I told you so."

Lopsang ignored my comment. "When at all possible, keep your body close to the mountain. If you do that, there's a chance the ice will fall over you. Keep the mountain as your friend, and maybe we will pass unharmed."

"Anyone think we should turn back?" James's voice was calm and rational. "We could easily go back to the cave and wait to see what Manchester's next move is."

He was a voice of reason, but I'd gone farther on worse plans. Besides, we'd come too far to turn back.

"Sorry, James, we don't have time for your special brand of

cowardice." I let the last word drip off like venom. "No, today, we climb." I struck a pose that was meant to look confident. In truth, it was all I could do to stop my legs from falling out beneath me.

"If the mountain wills it, we will pass safely." Lopsang pulled out the gear and began to hammer the first of our climbing holds.

"Hell of a motivational speaker, Lopsang."

James walked off a distance to look down at the valley, and I joined him. Manchester's team was still in full view, progressing at a consistent, sluggish pace. I could not make out their faces, but James swore that two of the guards were watching us as we prepared to ascend.

"Looks like we have their attention," he said.

I looked at the guards and held up a middle finger. "Let's give them a show, then, shall we?"

The climbing route to the top of the Spine was essentially a series of steps made of brittle rock and ice. Lopsang was halfway up, but with each smack of the hammer, tiny spiderweb cracks would fan out. If it bothered him, Lopsang didn't show it. He moved carefully and quickly. In less than ten minutes, he had crested the first step and called for us to climb up after.

James and I followed, tying ourselves to the guard rope Lopsang left behind. The ascent was not perfectly vertical, but it was close. Each section of the climb took more time than I would have liked, and by the time we were halfway up, the sunlight had already begun to decay in the mountain sky.

My arms burned with exhaustion and shook as I grabbed each handhold. Every time we crested a step to start the next leg, the slope was even steeper than the last. As we neared the top, I didn't think I would be able to continue much longer. Despite the freezing air surrounding us, I was sweating profusely and craved water. It was only the sheer will to beat Manchester that kept me placing one hand after the other. Before I knew it, I was scrambling over the top, and it was nearly full dark.

The top of the Spine was no glorious summit like the mountain proper, but it did provide an open view of the valley below. The lights of Manchester's team could be seen moving about as they made camp in the growing darkness. I looked around and found that the terrain was no more hospitable than the climb had been. The ground was a jungle of jutting rock and ice that necessitated constant vigilance and careful steps.

In the growing darkness, we picked our way through the rocks without speaking to one another. While exhaustion was plain on James's face, and probably mine, Lopsang showed no sign of tiring. Instead he moved ahead, sure-footed and watchful. The setting sun only meant one thing, and we all wanted to focus on finding the marker before it was too late.

"What exactly are we looking for?" panted James, exhausted from the climb.

"Small piles of rocks with flags strewn about them. Shouldn't be hard to spot," said Lopsang.

James turned on his flashlight and squinted into the growing darkness. I did the same. A pile of rocks among a forest of rocks. Needle in a Haystack: Mountain Edition. As we followed the ridge up the mountain, the footing became more stable, the air thinner. Each step was more laborious than the last. Ideally, we would have spent some time acclimatizing, but our expedition was rushed.

I scrambled over the rocks, doing my best to keep my balance. On a particularly steep incline, I lost my footing and began to slide. Survival instincts took over, and I turned onto my stomach, trying to grab for anything to slow myself down. *This is it,* I thought, *I'm going to slide right down to that smug bastard's camp.*

"Help!" I yelled, more scared than I prefer to admit. The ice rocketed past me as I picked up speed. The loud thump of my heart coalesced with the grating of my gear on the ice, and I knew the end was near.

Then it stopped, and I found myself at the bottom of a small gully, Lopsang and James laughing at me from only ten feet above.

"Careful, Nick, people might think you're in danger," teased James, barely able to contain himself. In hindsight, it's possible I may have overreacted.

I groaned, turned around, and immediately jumped backward with a yelp. Once more, gales of laughter could be heard from above. I ignored them and shined my light on a large stone statue of a yeti. Red wax spilled out from the corners of its jaw, and I could see the remnant of the last candle that had been placed there. The eyes possessed a lifelike quality, with more red wax running down from their sockets. At the base of the statue was a small basin that had been stained black. Bells that had been hung on either side chimed mournfully with the slightest gust of wind.

I crawled forward to examine it. Along the contours of the creature's body were characters I was unfamiliar with. They twisted and curved in a flow that didn't match any language I had ever seen.

I looked above. "If you two are done up there, come take a look at this."

Lopsang slid down the small hill with grace and landed upright, as if it had taken no effort at all. James, on the other hand, tried to follow suit, but instead tumbled down like an incompetent circus performer. Had I been paying more attention, I would have seen it fit to mock him, but my mind was too focused on the statue. I reached out to feel the grooves, but Lopsang quickly slapped my hand away.

"We have nothing to offer. Do not touch it or you will doom our whole expedition."

"What's the worst that could happen? Will the gods send a yeti after us?"

"This is no joking matter, Dr. Ventner. This statue was made by the earliest of my people to protect against the evil spirits that dwell upon this mountain. After what you have seen the past few days, you should understand the severity." Lopsang was dead serious and kept his hand out, ready to stop me if I tried again. "We must move past it quickly, lest the gods think us greedy and send their wrath."

"Sure, whatever you say." I tried to sound sarcastic, but at that moment I was willing to take just about anything Lopsang said on faith. A few days earlier, I would have sent someone who believed in the yeti packing, but I knew better now. The idea of finding the creature again both excited and terrified me.

We crept away from the statue, careful not to disturb it, and climbed back up the hill. It didn't take much longer for us to find a marker—a small oblong stone poking out of the ice upon a plateau overlooking the valley. A few prayer flags remained encased in the glacier, but the others had blown away long ago. If Lopsang hadn't seen it, I was sure we would have passed right by.

"Seems like as good a place as any to make camp for the night," I said with a yawn. I was ready to rest, my entire body burning with the exhaustion of the day.

"Yes, we will be safe here." Lopsang's voice was distant, as if he were thinking about something far away.

"Fine by me," said James, still panting. He threw the gear he had been carrying onto the ground. There was a shatter as something within broke, and he braced himself for my expected fury.

Lucky for him, I was too tired to care, and I turned to stare out at the valley, once more picturing fortune and glory.

Thankful for his escape, James began removing our tents and

setting up camp without complaint. Our supplies consisted of two winterized tents, a camping stove, and enough dried food to keep an astronaut happy. There were also a few bottles that I'd insisted on packing in James's bag. While one of them had shattered, it was bottom shelf, so I felt okay with it.

As James set up the tents, I watched Manchester's camp miles to the west. They were some ways below, but had still made more progress than I liked. The lights from the camp made strange halos in the fine mist that accompanied the nighttime cold on the mountain.

James pitched the tent so that we had a clear view of Manchester's camp and secured it to a few of the many rocks sticking up behind us. On Lopsang's advice, he anchored another cord to the sacred stone as a secondary precaution. I wasn't sure that the ward would transfer through the rope, but it was worth a shot.

As the last, dim ring of light around the dark mountain faded, Lopsang brewed a hot liquid that approximated chicken soup. The blue glow that had hung over the edge of the sky was replaced by inky blackness, and one by one the stars winked into life, giving way to a dazzling array that left me speechless.

Bands of color leapt across the sky, revealing the true nature of the space that surrounded us. Tiny motes of red and green popped in as well, providing us with a sense of security, even where there was none. Ever since I had started the profession of monster hunting, I had gained a profound respect for the stars. *If there's so much we haven't discovered down here, imagine what's happening up there.*

As we gulped down the hot soup, thankful for the warmth and the water within it, we began to tell stories. It was like the first night back in the lodge all over again. I told more stories about long-lost castles in Romania, the terrifying people of the

American Midwest, and even a little bit about the legend of Manchester. We laughed at some of our near-death experiences, but as the night grew on, we turned to more serious matters.

"Lopsang, why was your brother up at base camp that night?" I hadn't intended to ask him about it, but it just seemed appropriate. "You both knew about the yeti. Why would he risk it?"

"That is a sad story." Lopsang sighed.

I pulled a flask from my bag. "Well, we've got some time on our hands."

I passed the container to Lopsang.

7.

THE FALL EXPEDITION

"Manish was always a willful child. He was the more active of the two of us, and that led to some altercations that most would have rather avoided." Lopsang trailed off and took a drink from my flask.

"He got in a few fights, eh?" I grinned. "Man after my own heart."

Lopsang smiled a little but turned grim as he continued. "Yes, quite a few fights. No matter how many cuts and bruises he came back with, he never stopped. That's just the way he was; the only opinion that mattered was his, and to some lesser extent, mine."

A tear might have brimmed at the corner of Lopsang's eye, but he blinked it away and replaced it with a stoic stare into the blue flame of the camp stove.

"We were both mountain guides, but he always took more risks. It's no secret that our village does not provide guides for expeditions in the fall. Mountaineers will tell you that it's the unpredictability of the weather, which is true, but that's not the whole truth. There's the occasional rogue blizzard, but for the most part, they're nothing but an inconvenience. It's what roams the mountain in the dead of winter that strikes fear into our hearts.

"During the spring, the mountain is barren; nothing there

but snow and ice. During the winter, it's a completely different place. Creatures come out of hiding in the worst of ways, and even expeditions to base camp become dangerous.

"When we were children, the elders would tell us stories of the creatures that dwelled on the mountain during the winter months. Some would talk about frost wolves, stalking prey on the slopes, but they were always considered the lesser of evils. The worst was a singular beast that only roamed once the first snow had fallen. From the time the winter chill took over the mountain to the first melt in spring, the mountain became its domain. Every year, with the first blizzard of winter, we would hear the howling and know it was time to stop climbing. They called it *Mirka,* the wild man of the mountain. An omen of death.

"It was for this reason, and not the weather, that at the first sign of snow, our village would stop guiding expeditions. We put out notices, closed the shops, and waited for spring to come. But despite all the warnings, some would still try." Lopsang shook his head slowly, and I could sense a great weight upon him.

"When my brother and I were children, there was a Norwegian climbing team determined to summit before the winter snows came. It was already September, and most crews had given up and gone home. They went to every door in the village, offering money, fame, you name it, but every family gave the same answer: No expeditions until spring.

"Just as they were about to give up hope and leave the village, one man stepped forward and was foolish enough to offer his services."

"Your brother?" asked James.

Lopsang shook his head. "My father. He never paid much heed to the tales of the beast. He wrote them off as ghost stories, told only to frighten children and caution foreigners. Besides, the first snows had not yet fallen, and he was convinced he could get the team to the top before the weather turned."

"I bet they offered a lot of coin, too," I said, thinking that anyone who paid to go up the mountain was insane. Why not holiday on a beach somewhere? Who in their right mind would come to this frigid wasteland and then pay to go closer to danger? Even with the thought of considerable pay, I was regretting my decision. The whole idea of recreational mountain climbing seemed asinine to me, and I resolved that once I had found the yeti, I would never do it again.

"Yes, lots of coin." Lopsang sighed. "We were not a rich family, and any chance at prosperity in our village was to be treasured, not ignored. Of course, there was an exception to this rule for fall expeditions, but my father didn't see the difference. Prosperity was prosperity."

Which wasn't a bad motto, but I didn't think Lopsang would appreciate hearing that. As the story wound on, I found myself identifying with Lopsang's father. However, judging by Lopsang's tone, his hubris had not served him well.

"They packed up for what was to be the most ambitious summit attempt in years. The shaman said that the snows were no more than a few weeks away, and so my father set out to reach the summit in a week."

"A *week*?" said James. "What about altitude acclimatization?"

"You're right." Lopsang smiled. "There are several stages of altitude acclimatization that one has to go through on the mountain. It usually takes weeks to summit, but the well trained, or the foolhardy"—he motioned to me—"can do it much quicker.

"My father had previously made the trip from base camp to the summit in only ten hours, just short of the village record. So he was the best they could have asked for. They were one of the strongest climbing teams we had ever seen, and they came fully prepared for harsh conditions. Just a month earlier they had completed two of the seven deadly summits without so much as a slip. Overall, the bid seemed safe so long as they were able to maintain their timetable.

"They set out early in the morning. One of the village elders turned up and begged my father not to go, but he waved him off. He told them that they would have a good laugh about the 'omens' when he returned. With that, they started up the mountain. I remember watching in the darkness just before sunrise as their lights moved slowly up the slopes. There was something about the air that day; a chill that ran heavier than usual and bit straight to the core.

"To ease our worries, my brother and I made trips to the highest temple and spun prayer wheels for their safety three times a day. For the first two days, it appeared to be working; the skies were clear and the wind was low. On the third day, however, we woke to find dark storm clouds blotting out the horizon. Two hours after first light, the worst blizzard in twenty years struck the mountain, blocking everything from view.

"That night, the howling of the wind was different. The very walls shook around our heads. No one in the village slept. All I could do was look up at the fearsome clouds billowing around the mountain and pray. Around midnight, we started to hear screaming, distant at first, but then coming right into the village itself. Everyone ran into the streets, wanting to help, but by the time we got there, it was too late.

"As I opened the door to the raging blizzard, I was greeted by the ragged silhouette of a man, slumping through the street. I approached him, and in the dim light saw the pale face of my father. Sweat beaded on his brow, despite the frigid cold. He was as white as the snow around him. Half of his arm had been torn away, and he bore three gashes across his chest." Lopsang drew his fingers across his breast, showing where the cuts had been.

"As he stumbled through the door, mortally wounded, his eyes were wide with fear. I had never seen my father look like that. His parka was soaked red and dripped onto the ground, staining the floorboards. Not two steps after entering the house, he collapsed. His breathing was shallow, and he could not speak.

"All I could do was sit and watch as life left him in those last few moments. His body tensed and seized, as if he were still trying to run away. Even in his final moments, he kept looking toward the mountain with horror. When he closed his eyes for the last time, his face relaxed, and a great relief spread over him. In that final sleep, he could escape whatever had hunted him on the mountain. The man who had never feared anything was once more at peace."

The three of us sat in silence for a minute, listening to the flapping of the tent canvas in the gently blowing wind. I had found a profound respect for Lopsang, and a great fear of what we had come on the mountain to hunt. We may have made a terrible mistake. I tried not to show my misgivings, but the fear was plain on James's face as well. The danger we were facing was real, and the odds of facing it and coming out alive seemed to grow slimmer by the minute.

When Lopsang resumed speaking, it was with a measured calm, accompanied by a deep sadness. "The other members of the village said the wolves of winter had come early, and that the team had not been properly equipped. At the time, it made sense. My father never put much stock in the stories of creatures on the mountain. The expedition had carried no weapons with them and were not prepared for such an outcome. Eventually, everyone repeated the story, and for the longest time, I believed it. It wasn't until two weeks ago that I changed my mind."

"That's when you wrote to us." I was beginning to understand more and more.

Lopsang nodded. "My brother didn't even want to summit. A small group of travelers came into town looking to go to base camp, no higher. It was to be a scouting expedition to get the lay of the land for the following spring. Said they wanted to see the mountain for themselves and 'feel the chill.' At the time there was no mention of Shangri-La, but looking back, it seems obvious why they were so desperate to climb. No other Sherpa would take them, remembering the fate of my father. However, over the years, my brother had come to believe the story of winter wolves. He trained day and night so that he would not meet the same fate, understanding their hunting patterns and even killing a few on his expeditions.

"He agreed to take them but vowed that it would be a quick journey and that they would go heavily armed, just in case. They would make the trip to base camp, stay there for one night, then immediately come back down. They left before first light, just as my father had, and did not return. Three days passed, and that's when I wrote to you."

"Why did you come to us for help? Surely with your powers, you could have done more." I felt genuinely confused. This guy could probably tear a few winter wolves apart with his *mind*. All we had were a few thermite bullets and a lot of misplaced confidence.

"The nature of my powers makes me unable to affect the beasts of the mountain. A part of them is not of this world, same as me. We sort of cancel each other out." The way he said it was simple, and matter-of-fact. Lopsang hesitated. "And I couldn't afford Manchester. You were the next best."

This was added as an afterthought, but it stung. "And yet somehow he ended up here anyway… That bastard has eyes everywhere. Flattering that we were second best, I suppose."

Lopsang continued, giving me an apologetic look. "I knew what we were dealing with wasn't wolves, and so I baited you with a much smaller case." He almost seemed sheepish.

Clever. I would never have gone if I knew the true stakes. But what anger I felt toward Lopsang for tricking me was replaced quickly by the admiration of his ability to deceive.

"In the end, it worked, didn't it?"

"I suppose it did. A few days ago you would have never got me to talk about the yeti with a straight face, but here I am, believing in myths I have long thought to be folly and hunting a monster that will likely kill me. It all worked out." I tried to take a swig from the flask but realized it had been emptied over the course of our talk. Thinking about the insurmountable odds and the dwindling alcohol supply made my head hurt. It was all so foolish, and yet something pushed me forward, toward the danger, further into the unknown. "I suppose there could be worse company for a suicide mission."

After Lopsang's story, none of us had anything to say; we all just sat, watching Manchester's camp until one by one, sleep crept upon us. I crawled into the canvas tent and lay back in my sleeping bag. Above me, the wind whipped loudly at the canvas. In spite of this, I found myself drifting off. The exhaustion of the day had taken its toll. Within moments, the cold mountain was a fuzzy memory, and I was asleep.

8.

RUDE AWAKENINGS

I bolted upright from my sleeping bag. My spine prickled as I came back to full awareness. Lopsang was shaking me back and forth, shouting, "Listen!" The tent flaps were whipping violently, and outside, the howling was back, louder than ever.

"I doubt I could hear much else," I muttered. Still half asleep, I crawled forward to the open flap of the tent, hoping that the beast would not be staring straight back at me. Luckily, I saw nothing but the cloudless sky. I stepped out of the tent and shivered in the biting cold. Below us, Manchester's camp was illuminated by the ghostly white light of the moon.

"What is it?" I asked. Other than the howling, everything seemed to be fine. We knew the beast would hunt at night. It was no surprise as far as I was concerned.

"Look," whispered Lopsang, and he turned my head toward the top of the mountain.

A large storm had formed around the summit, and cascades of white clouds and snow were rolling down the mountain as we spoke.

"We have to warn them, Dr. Ventner." A pleading note had crept into Lopsang's voice.

"We certainly do not," I scoffed, ready to kick back and watch the carnage.

"If we don't, they'll die."

"That leaves one less team on the mountain for us to compete with."

Lopsang glared at me.

James, who I hadn't even noticed, was doing the same. "We are not just going to sit here and watch them die," James stated, with more incredulity than I thought an apprentice could possess.

"Even if I did want to help them, how could we do it?" I sighed, exasperated. "In case you haven't noticed, it took us all day to get up here, and they're at the bottom of the valley. I'm not going to risk my life to climb haphazardly down a mountain, at night, in a storm, for someone I'm not that fond of." I crossed my arms to let them know that settled the matter.

James was ignoring me and instead began rooting through our climbing supplies.

"Don't be an idiot," I said. "You're going to throw your life away over some prat like Manchester?"

James had pulled out a flare gun. "Don't be thick; we're going to signal them."

Before I had time to move to a safe distance, James fired it in one quick pull and ended the conversation.

The flare shot just over my shoulder, close enough that it nearly singed my skin.

"You're scrubbing our gear when we get back," I seethed. I turned around and watched the red halo of the flare descend into the valley, landing squarely in the middle of Manchester's tents. It was a nice shot. "You want to save them by lighting tents on fire?" I may have thought James's decision to be a smart one, but I was not about to let him get a big head about it.

"Give me the binoculars," I said, making a curt gesture toward the gear.

James, satisfied with his act of rebellion, returned to obedience and rooted through the bags again. He found the binoculars and handed them to me.

The lights of Manchester's camp were still on, but weren't moving at all. Men bustled around within the tents, their silhouettes plain against the canvas, but no one was on guard duty. It was difficult to find people willing to stand outside in subzero weather, especially when it often meant minor frostbite, but given the omnipresent danger of the mountain, it seemed to be a large oversight.

"Well, they weren't paying attention, guess all we can do is watch," I said, feigning sadness.

James, however, was not so easily deterred. He began rooting through the gear once more and returned with three road flares.

"Were we in a highway accident?" I said, knowing perfectly well we needed flares that didn't fire out of a gun, but I was also enjoying the frantic look on James's face.

James thrust one of the flares into my hand and gave the other to Lopsang. "Nick, you stay there. I'll go to the left, Lopsang to the right."

Lopsang followed James's instructions, striking up his flare and sending hot sparks onto the ice below.

Not wanting to be left out, I did the same. We were all yelling, even though we knew it wouldn't make a damned bit of difference over the howling of the coming storm. I wasn't sure whether it was the flare catching one of their tents on fire or the ridiculous men waving at the top of the valley, but either way, Manchester's team was soon out of their tents, confused by the commotion.

I tried to direct their attention to the storm like an air-traffic controller, but found that I just looked stupid. The men were already acutely aware of the danger they were in and moving frantically to try to avoid it. The scene below was chaos as tents were broken down and people trained their rifles on the oncoming storm.

No idea why they thought that was going to going to help. From deep within the swirling mass of snow and ice there came an inhuman howl, followed by a roar that shook the mountains around them. High above the valley, a shelf of ice broke loose and tumbled down into the camp below. Most got out of the way, but I winced as one man was hit by the full force of the debris and swept away. The light from his gun spiraled away down the mountain and off a cliff.

"Poor bastard."

"There's nothing we can do now," said Lopsang. "The storm is too close." He was calm as ever, a dispassionate observer to the oncoming disaster.

The storm moved like a wall, thundering toward the camp with the speed of an avalanche. The valley was known for its sudden and unpredictable weather, but I had never imagined it would look like this. From the top of the Spine, it all seemed almost unreal. Forty or so tiny lights scrambled for cover while the storm carried onward toward them.

"What do we do now?" James asked, teeth chattering as he shook from both cold and fear.

"You believe in God?" I was surprised I hadn't broached the subject before.

"Not really, no," James answered sheepishly.

"Then we wait."

The line of snow collided with the camp, and chaos ensued. The whiteout obscured our vision, and soon the roars of the beast were punctuated by brief bursts of gunfire. I thought I heard screaming a couple of times, but it was impossible to be certain from such a distance. A bright orange flash momentarily illuminated the entire storm. It was just enough time to see a massive silhouette moving at inhuman speed through the camp.

The wind continued to whip across the surface of the Spine as the storm raged below. After the first five or so minutes passed, we heard nothing but the storm. Then, one by one, the lights extinguished. Scared of what the morning would bring, the three of us crawled back to our tents in silence. There was no point in watching and risking our own limbs to frostbite.

James did his best to shut out the roars, pulling his sleeping bag tight around his head. We slept uneasily, unable to stop images of the yeti from flooding our thoughts. James could not help but repeat the mantra *"One of us is going to be next"* over and over again until I was ready to throttle him.

I, on the other hand, had dreams where I repeatedly returned to base camp, only to find the entire ground soaked in red. Large slashes ran the length of a high ice wall where the yeti had struck. A terrible feeling stayed in my gut, unmoving and heavy. It was the resolute notion that no matter what we did, mortal danger was near.

It was nothing compared to what we found in the stark light of the morning.

9.

AFTERMATH

"Are you sure you want to hear this part? I could just skip past, tell you the camp was massacred, and move past it," offered Nick, hoping Winston would accept. As pleasant as making him squirm was, the memory of what happened to Manchester's camp was one he kept locked away for a reason.

Winston paused, thinking it over. "While I am sure it's a painful memory—"

"It is."

"Yes, while it is painful"—Winston paused in a weak effort to show empathy—"I would still like to hear the whole story."

He stopped, and they sat in silence for a moment.

They always want the grisly details. It's fascinating when it didn't happen to you. Pain and suffering can be observed, but not endured. It's the same as the fifteen seconds after a man collapses at a party where the others just look on in morbid curiosity. Nick felt a wave of nausea come over him. It might have been the story, or the alcohol, but either way, he pushed the feeling back down.

Human nature drives them to the grotesque and the macabre, right up until the moment it becomes real, then they're all running for the doors.

"If it is more drink you require ..." said Winston, misinterpreting Nick's reluctance.

"No," he answered firmly. "That's all right. I'll tell you, but don't say I didn't warn you."

Nick looked at the soft velvet cushion of Winston's chair. *He has no idea what he's in for,* he thought with mild disgust. "We awoke to another bright and clear day, just like the previous. A passerby wouldn't have even known there was a storm. Unless, of course, he entered the valley ..."

—————————— ▼ ——————————

When we stepped out of our tent, we were surprised by the clarity of the morning sky. There was not a trace of the storm that had besieged us the night before. If we had not known better, it might have seemed like spring. I stretched the sleep from my bones and tried to ignore the tiredness hiding just behind my eyes.

James emerged a moment later, and without a word, walked over to the edge of the plateau to see what had become of Manchester's camp.

I grabbed the binoculars and observed as well. There was movement, but considerably less than the night before. Where the ground should have been stark white from the fresh snow, it was instead a light pink color. Sickening lumps dotted the landscape where presumably there had once been men. Torn canvas and broken tent poles littered the valley like tiny markers on a mass grave.

I saw a man, frozen mid-crawl, trying to drag another man back to his tent. It took me a minute to realize that it wasn't another man being dragged, but the same man's lower half. I fought back the urge to vomit and continued to look around. The bodies that the snow hadn't covered were all hideously deformed. It was hunting for sport. Most of the bodies had been left rather than eaten, just like base camp.

I was about to turn away when I spotted Manchester among the sea of wreckage. He'd made it out. The black, wide-brimmed hat was easily spotted from a distance. Manchester stood, peering down at a particularly bloody lump in deep thought.

"Looks like our friend survived." I handed the binoculars to James.

James scanned the landscape and stifled a gag. There are just some things that cannot be unseen.

"On the bright side, that will set them back," I admitted, trying to cover my own revulsion. "We should get moving while they're busy recuperating."

I sounded more confident than I felt. In truth, I was surprised that the words came out of my mouth. Most of my thoughts were about turning tail and running home, but the others, arguably the asinine ones, wanted to carry forth and not let the loss be in vain.

"Shouldn't we do something?" asked James, eyes glued to the binoculars, unable to look away. "They might need our help."

"I'll bet they do," I said flatly. "But by the time we get to them, it will be nightfall. Correct me if I'm wrong, Lopsang, but there don't appear to be any holy sites in that valley."

Lopsang put a hand on James's shoulder. "He's right. Any relics that were left there got destroyed long ago. There would be no shelter there." His tone was sorrowful. It was obvious that he wanted to help but knew that there was no way we could. "We need to keep moving if we are to reach another haven by dark. Perhaps they will learn from their mistakes and leave."

"Something tells me this isn't going to inspire cowardice in Manchester." Looking down at him, Manchester's posture looked more curious than disgusted. There was still a sizeable chunk of his crew left, and Manchester would not stop. I knew this because we were alike in more ways than I cared to admit. "He brought a big crew for a reason. Told you he was a bastard."

"You don't think this was on purpose, do you?" James's tone was one of disbelief.

I grabbed the binoculars back and looked around the wreckage. It did not take me long to notice the oddities.

"All of the crew that are still alive look unharmed. Their gear is perfectly intact and they even look well rested." That was low, even for Harvey. "He didn't camp with them last night. The creature just killed the bait."

Lopsang cursed under his breath. "That man will get more people killed before he even gets close enough to take a good look at the yeti. He's a coward." Lopsang spat on the ground.

"A coward he might seem, but he is tactical." I looked back through the binoculars at the camp. "Ah, and now we see the true nature of the man. I'll say it again, I did tell you both."

Below, Manchester was on bended knee, examining the carnage for any traces of the yeti. At the same time, he was yelling at his workers. No rest for the wicked.

"Manchester will stop at nothing to get what he wants, and he doesn't care who gets killed on the way." I handed the binoculars back to James and then began to pack up my gear.

James wore an expression somewhere between anger and disgust.

Poor kid was already losing another hero. Only about a year prior, James had witnessed the true nature of one of his favorite TV personalities while they had been hunting for a sasquatch. As it turned out, most people who claimed to be cryptozoologists for money were either frauds, assholes, or both.

After the tents were packed up, we moved out. In the fresh light of day, the top of the Spine seemed much closer. The steep initial incline tapered off to a gradual slope, leading to the top of the valley. For a while we didn't say much, each of us lost in thought for different reasons. I relished in Manchester's mistakes, Lopsang thought about ways to honor the dead, and James questioned his place in the world. The morning dragged on, and we continued to walk.

Eventually James broke the silence. "How exactly are we planning on finding the beast?"

"I've been trying to tackle that problem myself," I said, which was a lie. It was the first time that day I'd given it any thought. "From what we've seen, it only comes accompanied by snowstorms. So far that means two things: One, that beast is a meteorologist's wet dream, and two, we won't be able to find any tracks as the snow covers them up."

"So we have no way of tracking it?" asked James.

"Oh, we've got a host of tracking devices, but we're going to have to get very close to use them." I thought about the creature's putrid breath and shivered at the idea of having to come face-to-face with it again.

Lopsang chose that moment to end his silence. "And what's your plan for that?"

"It's a good one, but he"—I motioned to James—"isn't going to like it." A devilish grin spread across my face.

James's eyes turned to daggers. "No," he answered flatly.

"No what?" I acted surprised, as if nothing had been implied.

"No, I'm not going to be bait for a yeti!" He stopped in his tracks and turned to face me. "Do you really think after how close things got with that lake monster that I'm going to play the bait again?"

"James, it's your turn." My tone was firm but calm. Being bait for two wargs didn't seem all that bad now.

"This does not fall into the category of *turns*, you psychopath!"

I put my bag down, looked through it, and pulled out a small leather-bound notebook.

"Oh, come on. Don't bring that up, man, it's not fair." James moaned, his resolve dwindling.

"What's that?" asked Lopsang.

"A handbook that this young man signed," I said, holding the book out to Lopsang. "I believe it's on page three, line ten. You were so eager that you signed in blood." I was being smug, but I couldn't help myself. From the first day of James's apprenticeship, we had sworn to take turns as bait, no matter what we faced. I had wanted James to always play the bait but had eventually yielded to negotiation.

Lopsang turned to page three and read it. "He's right. You did sign." He held the book out to James as if somehow it would help.

"God damn it," cursed James.

"God had nothing to do with it," I said. "It was just plain, youthful stupidity." I snagged the notebook from Lopsang before he had a chance to read any more and tucked it safely away in my breast pocket. I didn't want to lose it with the gear. The notebook had turned out to be one of my greatest assets. "Don't worry, I'm not going to let you get hurt."

Lopsang laughed a little.

"You're doing wonders for his confidence, Lopsang," I said. "We have to give him some hope that he's not going to get brutally mauled by the creature while tied to a post." I said it matter-of-factly, but in truth, I was a little nervous. The whole situation gave me a bad feeling.

James was looking green again. It was likely a mix of mild altitude sickness and fear. I did have a plan. It was only half-baked, but it was a plan nonetheless.

I was the one to break the silence "Well, we've still got a day of trekking ahead of us. Let's put our evening plans aside and get moving." I motioned for Lopsang to lead the way, and we began the day's journey.

We only ended up hiking until a little after midday before we found the next marker. An hour after leaving the edge of the Spine, we came across a narrow canyon at the edge of a large snow field. Lopsang went ahead to scout and returned with the first good news of the day. Nestled into the canyon wall was a small crag, crisscrossed with prayer flags and covered in paintings in the shaman style. Not wanting to risk being caught out in the open, we opted to stay there for the night.

As we stepped out of the sun and into the much cooler air of the canyon, I saw paintings on the canyon walls of massive beasts that I did not recognize.

"Why don't they ever paint sunrises?" I wondered if we would ever find a non-cursed camping spot again.

"I suppose there are worse places to die," James added morosely.

"Oh, don't be like that. You're not going to die. I have a plan, remember?" It still wasn't firmed up, but it was getting there. It consisted of luring the yeti into the canyon using James as bait, and then shooting it at close range with a tracker. The part I hadn't yet worked out was how exactly I was going to get the yeti to leave once it appeared. The canyon was only twenty feet at its widest, which made it ideal for close-quarters combat but also impossible to escape.

After we dropped our gear in the alcove, I walked around the entrance to the canyon, trying to find a way out. Only a thin sliver of light could be seen above. The walls were so high that at the top, they almost appeared to touch. Icicles hung on them, thick and white. Taking it all in, I had a flash of inspiration.

"Okay, I've got a plan."

"Fantastic. What is it?" James summoned as much enthusiasm as he could muster, which wasn't a whole lot.

"Stay with me on this one, it's going to get a little complicated. First, we remove all the elastic from our bungee cords. Then, you and Lopsang will sew our backpacks together into a sort of seat." I was talking with great rapidity, inventing on the fly. "Meanwhile, I will scale the canyon and tie elastic to the top on both sides. You"—I pointed to James—"will sit in the makeshift seat right in the middle of the canyon, held in place by a series of sharpened sticks I will obtain from the local fauna."

"Local *fauna*?" moaned James, continuing to turn ever paler.

I continued, incredibly pleased with myself. "We wait until nightfall, the yeti comes in to eat you, and I"—I mimed holding a large rifle—"shoot him right in the backside, planting the tracker. Then you release the switch which we've made from a recycled radio antenna and catapult out of the canyon to safety." I stopped, out of breath, and struck a pose, trying to look proud.

"Really?" James's voice quivered with both rage and fear.

"No, not really," I said, resuming my sarcastic air.

"Oh God, I'm going to die," James said, for what felt like the hundredth time on our short trip. Although, people who say that often do. "Come now, I was just having a bit of fun." Our impossible situation had most definitely called for it. "Now, for the real plan."

I set down the bag and pulled out a second notebook I carried to document my adventures. To date, it was mostly filled with foreign recipes for strong drinks and crude doodles of monsters I had seen, but I hoped that one day I would find the inspiration to contribute something of value.

I found an empty page and began to draw. "We'll erect a small tent here, right in the middle of the canyon." I marked the center of two squiggly lines with an X. "James, you'll sit in the tent, poised to strike in case you get the chance, just like with the wargs. Meanwhile, Lopsang and I will wait in the protected area here. I will run out, dart the beast, and once the tracker is in, I'll signal to you.

"Lopsang will then run out behind the yeti with one of our *sorely depleted* flare stock"—I paused to glare at James—"and will distract it while you scramble to safety. Once you are within the hollow, I will run out behind the yeti and distract it with another road flare, while Lopsang—"

"Let me stop you there," said James. "How long does this continue for?" He had no sense of humor about the matter.

"Until we run out of road flares. Odd man out needs to run fast." I smiled slyly.

Neither James nor Lopsang looked to be in a joking mood.

"All right, fine, we tie the remaining road flares to a bag of holy powder, throw that out, and blind the beast while you scuttle back to safety."

"Holy powder?" asked Lopsang.

"It's my own recipe, made from the bones of Christ himself. When mixed with fire, it creates a powerful flash that blinds all enemies, mortal or otherwise."

James rolled his eyes. "It's what he calls flash powder mixed with holy water."

"You're just no fun today," I grumbled. "Yes, in this case, it's likely just flash powder. I doubt the yeti puts stock in any laws of Catholic mysticism, so we're just going to have to hope that flash powder blinds it like anything else."

"Well, that's comforting."

I grabbed James by the shoulders in a rare moment of sincerity. "It's going to be fine, James." For the most part, I believed it. The biggest area for failure would be the tracking dart not seating correctly. "This is not where you die. I'm a good shot, remember?" I stared straight into James's eyes and saw a great deal of fear. "And hey, if I miss, we're all going to die together."

"You should have been a motivational speaker." We stared at each other in silence for a minute. "All right, fine, but if I die here, I'm coming back to haunt you. That's a promise."

Not if the chalk line on my doorframe had anything to say about it.

"If it comes to that, I'll rescue you from the Land of the Dead myself." At the time, I didn't think there was such a place, but it sounded like a nice sentiment.

A chill settled over our camp, indicating that the sun had begun to pass behind the mountain. In the eternal twilight of the canyon, it was difficult to tell what time it was. Snow began to fall through the top of the canyon and stuck to the walls.

"We may not have much time. We need to set everything up now."

10.

CANYETI

"It's freezing out here, Nick," James said, his teeth chattering again. He had begun complaining the moment we set the trap. Snow continued to fall steadily through the top of the canyon, but it had not yet reached the same level as the blizzard the previous evening. So far, there had been no howling and no sign of the yeti. The canyon itself was eerily quiet. The only sounds were the occasional gust of whistling wind and James's whimpering.

"We're all in the same canyon, pal. It's cold here, too." Lopsang and I sat safely in the alcove, watching. I took a sip of the hot spiced tea that Lopsang had brewed for us. The sound echoed off the canyon walls.

"Do you guys have tea in there?" James fumed incredulously.

I tried to take a quieter sip.

"You do have tea in there! I'm out here freezing my ass off, waiting to die, and you're drinking tea?"

"James," I said, trying to sound like a reasonable parent, "there's no reason all of us have to suffer." It was true, and the same thing would have happened if I had been the bait. It was the way of things.

"Bastards," muttered James. "Can you at least roll me a thermos?"

"Too dangerous, James. You're going to have to wait until after." I took a louder sip.

James cursed from within his tent, and the sound of a shotgun cocking loudly echoed off the canyon walls.

I couldn't help but laugh at him. "That does make for a thrilling show of displeasure, but you do realize that you've wasted a shell, right?" I'd prepped the gun myself before sending James out.

There was more cursing and the sound of hasty reloading.

So many action heroes waste bullets by needlessly cocking guns. I could make a fortune selling their wasted shells. The thought of a simple life as a gun runner sounded nice. Anything other than freezing on a mountaintop. I wondered if maybe The Black Market would reinstate me if I brought them a yeti head.

These thoughts were interrupted by a loud, ominous crunching from the far end of the canyon, followed by a strong gust of wind. I brought the rifle to bear upon the tent.

"Get ready, James," I said, my voice calm, unflinching. "I think it's here."

Lopsang set down his tea cup and picked up a shotgun that I'd loaded with pyramid shells, so named because I had mixed the buckshot with stone fragments gathered from beneath ancient Egyptian relics. They had worked wonders on the mummy I intended them for, and I figured we might as well try everything while we had the chance.

"Are you sure that thing has enough power to pierce its hide?" Lopsang asked, motioning to my rifle.

"It doesn't have to. The tracker has a barb that's covered in micro serrations so that if nothing else, it'll get caught in the creature's fur. As long as it doesn't start shedding anytime soon, we should be all right."

I also had to hope the merchant who sold me the darts wasn't a liar. The man had one eye and fewer teeth than most, but had replaced what was missing with gold. I figured if he could afford gold teeth, he probably did well for himself. Selling fake gear didn't make for many repeat customers.

The noise grew closer, and with it, the cave began to illuminate slightly.

"Photoluminescence," I marveled, "amazing, truly amazing. I'd never thought of the yeti as a creature that glowed. That's how it sees so well in the dark," I said to Lopsang in an excited whisper. "The glowing helps guide it through snowstorms. It also probably serves as a show of strength to other animals, keeping them out of its territory." Jane Goodall ain't got shit on me.

"Mr. Ventner? Is that you in there?" called a high and superior voice.

Son of a bitch, I thought. Strike one for being a naturalist.

"Hey, Nick, I don't think that's the yeti," said James, not even trying to stifle his laughter. "But if by photoluminescence you meant flashlight, you were correct."

Lopsang was also laughing, and my face turned bright red. I walked out cautiously from behind our hollow, and sure enough, in the mouth of the tunnel was no yeti, but Manchester, holding a flashlight and looking as smug as ever. Behind him stood a much smaller team than the last time we'd met.

Despite the air of superiority and annoying grin plastered on his face, Manchester looked the worse for wear. There were bags under his eyes, and the outfit that had been carefully manicured a day earlier looked disheveled.

"Well, hello there, Harvey," I seethed without missing a beat. "Where's the rest of your team?" I instantly regretted saying it; it was too soon. I may have hated Manchester, but there was a time and place to mock the dead, and standing in a chilled canyon with friends of the departed was not it.

Manchester did not miss a beat and continued as if he had not noticed the insult. "We saw you on the ridge last night. That was a bold route to take. I half expected that we would never see you again." His tone implied that they would have been better for it. "Still, you seem to be unscathed, and that is another small miracle."

"I guess I'm just lucky."

Manchester smiled back at me venomously. "I don't believe in miracles. What allowed you to evade the beast last night?"

I was getting frustrated. The longer Manchester stayed in the canyon questioning us, the greater the chance our entire plan would be shot. We needed to get rid of him quick.

"It's a simple rule of predator and prey. The predator will always go after the bigger target if it feels it's able. We remained unscathed simply because your group was too big."

"Splendid. Then we shall all be a bigger target tonight." Manchester motioned to his team, and they began walking into the canyon.

I motioned to Lopsang, who aimed his shotgun at Manchester's chest. I was surprised he did it. There was a clicking as a dozen or so rifles were aimed back at us.

"What is going on out there?" James called from within the small tent.

"Shut up, James, I'm handling it," I hissed angrily. "There is no way in hell your team is staying here tonight. I told you, try to follow us, and I will extend the same courtesy you extended me. Now, if you don't leave, I'm going to let Lopsang shoot you."

Manchester considered that. "No, I don't think you will."

Just as I was about to prove I would, a sudden wind kicked up and blew through the canyon. It was followed by an earth-shattering roar that had become all too familiar. I looked over Manchester's shoulder and saw a white wall of snow just outside the canyon entrance.

"James, get out of the damn tent!" I yelled. "Plan B! Plan B!"

Luckily, Manchester's team had lowered their rifles and turned around to quiver at the sight of the oncoming storm. James scrambled out of the tent with his shotgun and made it to the safety of the alcove. Lopsang and I followed suit. The alcove didn't have much room, but we all packed in around the shrine anyway.

Manchester followed hot on our heels. "Just where the hell do you think you're going? What've you got back there?" He rushed through the small opening to the alcove and was quickly packed in by several members of his team.

"You imbecile," I spat. "James, do you have a problem with shooting him? If you do, just hand me the gun and I'll do it." I aimed a kick at Manchester, but Manchester caught my leg, twisting it in a most painful manner. The dart rifle went clattering onto the stone as I fell backward. "Shoot him, James," I said, gritting my teeth in discomfort .

Manchester squeezed tighter on my leg, increasing the pain to levels I had not thought possible. "Pipe down, Mr. Ventner. We wouldn't want the yeti stomping in here, would we?"

The booming of heavy footsteps interrupted his chiding. The ground shook as the yeti entered the canyon. The creature let out another roar, and I fell to the ground, clutching my ears. I would have been embarrassed, but after a cursory glance it was clear everyone else was doing the same. Even Manchester looked like the sound had staggered him.

As my senses returned, one thing became abundantly clear: we weren't all going to fit. Manchester, with true cowardice in his eyes, had dove in first, leaving the rest of his team to fend for themselves.

Everyone has a survival instinct; it's only the coward's that puts everyone else at risk. Manchester's body blocked the entry-way so that his men could not get in.

"Let them through, idiot!" I shouted. On one hand, I wanted to get a clear shot, but on the other, leaving men out in the canyon was a death sentence.

"Tell me your plan and I might," said Manchester, panting and struggling to stem the tide of those trying to avoid death.

I felt sick for ever having admired Manchester, but there was no time—either I gave up the plan or the men at the edge of the alcove would die.

"We're trying to get a tracking dart in the beast!" I had to yell to be heard over the din. "Then I'm going to blind it with holy powder to cover our escape. These"—I gestured at the prayer flags on the shrine behind us—"signal that this is a holy place, and the beast cannot tread here. Now get out of the way! You're wasting our chance."

Manchester thought hard and then stepped aside to let his men pass. Remarkably, they were all able to fit after all. Everything was going as I'd planned until Manchester made a swift movement and kicked one of his men out into the canyon.

"What the hell?" I screamed.

"Well, the plan doesn't work without bait, does it? Don't waste your chance." Manchester stepped aside giving me a clear line of sight to the stunned man clutching his ribs in the middle of the canyon.

The booming of the yeti's footsteps shook the walls around us. "You're a real bastard," I said, barreling past Manchester to the opening. The dart was preloaded in the rifle, and I shouldered it to fire.

The man sitting in the middle of the canyon was frozen in fear, staring at his oncoming doom.

I'm a good shot, and I intended to get him out of there. The sack of holy powder was hanging on my right side, ready to blind the creature as soon as the dart was fired. From out of my peripheral there came a roar so strong that it blew the man's hair back. He tried to back away, but a massive form of white fur and taut muscle lumbered into view.

Without hesitation, I pulled the trigger. The dart shot out with a quiet hiss, barely audible over the commotion, and stuck between the yeti's shoulder blades. I reached for the holy powder, but it was too late.

The beast showed no mercy, and swiped at the man with five razor-sharp claws. It tore the man clean in half, sending his confused torso spinning into the opposite wall. Hot red blood coated the frosted ground, sending up tendrils of steam wherever it landed. I pulled my arm back to throw the bag of holy powder, but a pair of strong hands stopped me. My face felt numb as I watched the grizzled claws rip through what remained of the man on the ground.

"It's too late," Lopsang whispered quietly in my ear. "We may need that later. Save it."

Nothing could be done. It was clear as day, but still, I wanted to fight. The creature made short work of its prey, and Lopsang dragged me backward to the safety of the alcove.

The yeti lifted its head and turned as though it had heard us. I found myself unable to look away, staring straight into its eyes. They were black and glassy, with even darker irises at the center that were barely visible. Tough, cracked, gray skin protruded wherever fur didn't cover. The creature's lips pulled back in a snarl, revealing a jaw full of large, dull teeth covered in bits of what had seconds ago been a man.

For a moment, there was only silence and the wind. The

creature's breathing was steady, as if the attack had required no exertion whatsoever. It just stared at me, transfixed. Then, as if knowing that it could not approach us, the creature opened its jaws, roared, and ran off into the night. Its footsteps echoed through the cavern, booming until there was nothing but the whisper of the wind through the canyon.

I found the cold fear in my heart quickly replaced by hot rage. "You son of a bitch," I fumed, my voice trembling with anger. "Why?" I turned to face Manchester, who was still recovering from the shock of seeing the yeti so close.

He merely gawped at the empty patch of canyon where the creature had been.

"That man did not have to die." I walked toward Manchester, fist raised, but Lopsang caught me again.

"It's not worth it." Lopsang's voice was calm and reassuring.

"If ever there was a time where violence was worth it, it's now. This man," I raged, wrenching a hand free of Lopsang's grip and pointing it at Manchester, "needs to finally get what's coming to him. He just took a human life like it was nothing." My heart pounded in my ears, and I was acutely aware of how many guns were at the ready around me. The alcove narrowed to a tunnel with Manchester at the end of it, dull red everywhere else.

"He's not going to get what he deserves if you attack him now," said Lopsang, pulling my fist back again. "Stay your hand. Now is not the time."

My hand fell to my side, and a cool wave washed over my body as the frigid mountain air made its way back into my awareness.

Even after watching one of their colleagues be brutally murdered, Manchester's men still stood at the ready, waiting for his command. He must have paid a lot for loyalty like that. Where did he find these people? The likely answer was the local villages, but much of the crew looked nothing like Sherpas. Most of them looked like caricatures of mercenaries come to life. Some bore piercings that served no purpose other than to be menacing, others had rolled-up sleeves to reveal grotesque tattoos that would likely be removed by frostbite. Not a bright bunch, but they did look trigger happy.

After examination, I once more came to the realization that we were not in a position of power.

"What do you want to do about this, Harvey?" I reveled once more in the momentary anger that crossed Manchester's face at the use of his first name. It was the one scrap of power I could still hold on to.

"I believe you've just succeeded in planting a tracking device on the yeti, have you not?" He raised his eyebrows. "You also seem to have more knowledge on how to avoid it than I do." He gestured to the prayer flags and stones in the alcove and smiled once more. "It looks like for the moment, the safest option is for us to partner up."

If there was humility in the concession, I didn't catch it. Both James and Lopsang looked revolted by the idea.

"Perhaps I did not make myself clear," Manchester said, enunciating as if every word were a gunshot. He turned to his men. "A little help?"

Every man turned to point their gun directly at my head.

"That's better. Now, to rephrase, we *will* be partnering up. Styg over there"—Manchester gestured to an especially mean-looking member of their crew—"is very good at making foul play look like a mountaineering accident."

The man cracked his knuckles and grinned at me.

"You really should stop that if you're expecting to climb with those hands," I quipped, unimpressed. I've seen more than my fair share of feats of brute strength and wasn't easily intimidated by them. In situations where I was squaring off with an alpha male, I always found it better to conceal my advantage until the last moment. The brutes may think they're in power, but the smarter man always wins out in the end.

The bigger man dropped his gun to his side and smashed his fists together with a loud smack.

"Ah, I see he's got an affinity for injuring himself in grand gestures. Not very bright, but I see the point you are trying to make, Harvey. However, what makes you think this"—I paused, unsure of what to call the man—"*thing* can take me?"

Manchester laughed at the absurdity of the question, then noticing I was serious, straightened up again. "Look at the size of him, Nick."

"Look at the size of this," I said, dropping my hand to our gear bag and pulling out one of the AK-47s we'd taken from the Herukas. All of the men yelled at me to drop it, but James and Lopsang had pulled their guns as well and pointed them at the mercenaries. James fumbled with his gun for a moment but eventually managed to train it on Styg. Mexican standoffs have never been my thing, but I had to admit that in the moment, it felt exciting.

"Well, then," said Manchester, seemingly tired of the situation. "It looks like we're at an impasse. Shall we all end up dead in this freezing hellhole, or will we cooperate and maybe make it out alive? Choice is yours, Nick. I'm ready to die if you are." He lifted the brim of his wide black hat to reveal a face full of sarcastic joy.

I pondered Manchester's proposition as if it had been serious. I wasn't exactly keen on dying in the snow, but I didn't like the idea of capitulation either.

"Fine," I conceded with a huff that sent a plume through the frigid air. "But let's iron out the details of this venture now so that no one feels cheated."

Manchester spread his arms wide. "By all means, name your terms," he said, knowing well that he held all the cards.

"You want to ride our coattails all the way to Shangri-La, and that's fine, but I don't want you dumping me off the side of the mountain when we get there." I thought on this condition for a moment and then added, "and them as well, I suppose." I gestured to Lopsang and James.

"I swear that no harm will come to any of you on this expedition."

I didn't believe it for a second but continued bargaining any-way. "And seventy-five percent of whatever loot we might find." I tried to sneak it in nonchalantly, but the negotiations hit a brick wall.

"Absolutely not."

"Sixty?" I asked with more of a pleading tone than I would have liked.

"You'll get twenty-five between the three of you, and that's more than generous," said Manchester, taking the tone of a parent once more. "My crew is three times as big as yours; the division is fair."

I didn't like it, but there was also no guarantee of treasure in the first place. The real prize would be the advertising from taking down a yeti. We'd have it made for years to come. "Fine, it's a deal."

"Splendid," said Manchester, with just a little too much of a friendly air. "I'll get my ledger, and we'll sign in blood."

I scowled. "No dice. You could toss that over a cliff if you wanted to. I'm not putting my life in the hands of an accountant's plaything."

Manchester sighed. "What do you have in mind?"

"The old ways are the best. James, get the charcoal. We're going to draw us a pentagram."

11.

THE PACT

I removed a set of five candles from my bag. For the pact to work correctly, I needed to be precise. Both Manchester and I took the matter very seriously and knew that while arduous, if done properly, the black magic would ensure true fealty. As a rule, I tried not to dabble in black magic. It was one of the easier dark arts, but it also carried heavy penalties for missteps.

All we had to do was repeat a series of incantations over and over, draw a pentagram from charcoal, and light five candles made from human essence. Most of the supplies needed were easy to come by, but the candles had taken some time to obtain—a few months, in fact, and a few experiences I would rather not remember. But the candles burned slowly, meaning I would not have to repeat the process for a few years. The only other requirement for the ritual to work properly was two willing parties, which we surprisingly possessed.

Lopsang wore an expression of utter confusion at the proceedings. Interesting how one country's mysticism looks like absolute madness to another. In general, I find people accept black magic without having to see much proof. Almost everyone has seen something they couldn't explain, and it was very easy to transfer that feeling to a belief in the dark arts. The harder thing for the public to come to grips with was that there were living, breathing monsters hiding in just about every shadow. I had seen more than one professor sent running into the woods, stumbling like a toddler and crying out for their mother at the sight of nothing more than a common rat king. No one ever ran from the idea of dealings with the Devil for power because they made too much sense.

Once we finished preparing the ritual site, I lit the candles and stepped into the pentagram. I spoke in a language that was long thought to be dead, or nonsense, depending on who you asked.

"Come, gather here, spirits, and bear witness, for on this night, a sacred pact is made. Two men enter the unholy circle and leave as one." The words were cheesy, and it took all of my will not to laugh. I had not chosen the words, but they had to be recited precisely and with the correct inflection.

"We who enter swear our allegiance before you, and all the others who lie beyond. Look upon us with hungry eyes, for if either is to break this sacred pact, you may run forth and return them to the realm in which it was made."

The mixture of confusion and fear on the faces of Manchester's crew was enough to keep me going. Even if it didn't work, they'd think I was a necromancer, which might buy us some time.

Meanwhile, James and Lopsang stood off in a corner of the alcove, looking on with more ridicule than fear. To people who did not understand the language of the dead, it sounded like a series of horrible gargles and moans. James looked like he couldn't tell if I was being profound or having a seizure.

"Is he all right?" he asked.

"Do not interrupt," hissed Manchester. "There are dangerous forces at play here."

I continued to gargle on. "I swear unto thee, that if I break my pact, you may take me to the very gates of Hell if it so pleases you." I didn't really believe in Hell, but it was a necessary flourish.

With no prompting needed, Manchester stepped into the circle across from me, his face deadly serious. The candles around the edges flickered.

"I swear the same. On this night, let it be known that I will do no harm to Nick Ventner for the duration of our mission. While we both still breathe and share this common goal, I will ally with him and his men. This I vow before the undying eyes of ye spirits and whatever else watches from the unknown."

I would have liked a little more time than "the duration of our mission," but it would have to do. It didn't leave us much time to escape if he decided to turn on us once the deed was done. There was no time for thought; the longer the ritual site remained active, the better chance that something unpleasant would come through.

I checked my footing on the pentagram and took the same oath Manchester had. Once I finished speaking, we moved to the edges of the site and knelt at two of the points. I pulled a small knife out of my pocket.

Manchester followed suit, producing a hunting knife that nearly ran the length of his forearm.

I looked at the long and jagged blade, wondering what he had it for and glad that he did not intend to do us harm anytime soon.

"Let the ritual conclude with the spilling of our blood onto these now hallowed grounds. Take this offering as a tacit agreement between us and the spirit world," I said with grandiosity. In my experience, the undead were very fond of showmanship, and I did not want to disappoint. "Bind us together until the conditions are met, and hold claim to us if our word is broken."

We slit our palms simultaneously, and steaming blood ran

down into the circle. In an instant, all the candles were snuffed out, and in the smoke that remained, the ghoulish visage of a man in a decrepit top hat and molding suit appeared. He grinned through a lopsided mouth that appeared to be in the process of falling off his face.

"It is agreed," whispered the smoke in a gravelly voice that dispersed just as quickly as it had materialized.

As the smoke faded away, there was a cacophony of other-worldly moaning and shrieking. It was the sound of the undead basking in their newfound power. Two souls were worth quite a lot in the Land of the Dead, and the potential to obtain them was cause for celebration. I knew that those who had passed on always relished a chance to meddle with the affairs of the living. It was part of the reason black magic was so easy to perform. The difficulty came in controlling it. The dead are always looking for company.

I wondered how many more times I could stray onto the left-hand path. They were a miserable bunch.

---------------▼---------------

"Now I know you must be joking," spluttered Winston. "*Real* black magic? That's just a rumor passed down for far too long." He sat up in his chair as if offended by the idiocy of it all.

"Much like a story about a yeti when you think about it." Nick's head was beginning to clear, and he found himself wanting to leave. Despite trying to convince himself otherwise with drink and fantasies about beer and money, he still didn't want to tell the story.

"Yes, I suppose you're right there," admitted Winston. "But black magic? The yeti is hard enough to believe."

"I'm not here to convince you," snapped Nick, with more curtness than he intended.

Winston looked wounded. "If I've offended you, I am deeply sorry." He tried to look apologetic, but Nick could tell that it was less than genuine.

"No, no, I'm sorry," said Nick, noticing his glass had been refilled. He took a swig and found that it continued to numb him less with each cup. "I understand. Really, I do, but you and I both know there are many things to this world that aren't as they seem."

Winston nodded at this. "So you really know how to connect to the world below?" His voice was interested, slightly apprehensive.

Nick could not resist the opportunity and regained his casual air. "Oh yeah, it's not that hard. The veil between their world and ours is one of the easiest to break through. There's no group who wants to communicate more with the living than the dead. We're a sentimental bunch as humans, always leaving behind unfinished business."

Nick looked around the room ominously, eyeing the portraits of the long since departed on the walls. It was all an act, but Nick felt like taking a break from the story and perturbing Winston in the process. He did his best to look uneasy as he scanned the room. "Did any of these men have unfinished business?" Nick whispered.

"These men have been dead for years," Winston said matter-of-factly. "I wouldn't have a clue."

Tough sell, eh? "That's odd. This one seems to know your name," mused Nick, pointing to the picture of an army general. "There is a very strange presence from beyond surrounding this portrait."

A flicker of nervous tension crossed Winston's face.

"General Lazenby, is it?"

Winston cocked a suspicious eye. "Yes, it is."

One point for being observant. Nick had seen the name on a book below the portrait when he walked in the door. "Ah, yes, good old Lazenby. He's very angry," Nick said darkly. "Very angry, indeed. Any idea why he might be so angry, Winston?" Nick let his eyes roll into the back of his head. It was nothing more than a party trick he had learned to cure the spins that came with heavy drinking, but it added to the effect.

"I don't have the faintest idea what—"

"What did you do to this man?" Nick yelled. He conjured the fiery demeanor of a born-again mother who's just found out her daughter experimented with sex.

"I didn't do anything," roared Winston, affronted, but also clearly beginning to feel fear. A few beads of sweat ran down the sides of his face.

"That's not what he's saying," Nick countered, beginning to rock back and forth.

"I never met him, how could he know me?" A note of urgency had crept into his voice.

"Don't lie to me, Winston." Nick let his voice sink back in his throat, making it sound almost demonic.

"Dr. Ventner, do not bring about angry spirits in my parlor!" Winston shouted with more fear than he wanted to show.

Nick relaxed and let his eyes come back to face Winston. He grinned, satisfied with his trick. "The only spirits here are in in my glass." Nick swirled the drink.

Winston looked less than pleased. "I'd prefer it if we stuck to the story rather than amusing yourself with parlor tricks."

"I'm sorry. I was just having a little fun," Nick said, knowing that he might have overstepped his bounds.

"Quite all right," Winston said with a grunt. "I suppose it comes with the profession."

Not sure what he means by that, but sure, monster hunters do tend to have a sense of humor. "Suppose it does. Seeing the world's seedy underbelly necessitates a few jokes here and there to lighten things up."

Winston nodded, said nothing.

"All right," Nick said, feeling awkward. "Where was I? Yes, we had just made the pact." Nick did not think it was the proper time to tell Winston that the pact had also been greatly exaggerated. He could have actually performed the rite, but they were on a dangerous mountain in the freezing cold. In reality, a handshake had sufficed. "We decided that it would be better to camp together for the night and leave the shrine in the morning when it was safe …"

12.

CAMPOUT

Our two teams were cramped together that night. Initially, Manchester pushed for us to start the journey right away, but I quickly shot the idea down with a simple argument of: "It mostly comes at night ... Mostly."

Without further discussion, we pitched our tents to camp in the small alcove. Unfortunately for Lopsang, James, and myself, our second tent had been destroyed by the yeti, leaving us to share the remaining one. Some of the braver mercenaries moved to camp in the canyon beyond.

"Did you see the way Manchester just pushed him into the canyon?" asked James in a whisper that was far too loud for my liking.

"Yes, we were all there, but be quiet. He's right over there." I said the last words so they were barely audible and pointed with my middle finger toward one of the adjacent tents. Trying to forget the carnage we had just witnessed, I pulled out a small gray box that was paired to the tracking dart I had shot. "Time to see if it was all worth it."

Lopsang moved over to watch with great interest.

I flipped open the device's lid, revealing a dark green screen with a light green coordinate grid on it. For a moment, there was nothing but silence, but just as I was beginning to feel it had all been in vain, a light blinked to life on the screen.

"Hallelujah!" I exclaimed, unable to contain my excitement. Somewhere in a far-off tent, a mercenary grumbled about being unable to sleep, so I dropped my voice back to a whisper. "It's not that far off." I passed the tracker to James.

"Northeast," murmured James, disappointed. "It's heading straight up the mountain."

I'd figured we would have such luck. "Nobody said this was going to be easy."

The general rule of thumb at higher altitudes on the mountain was to wait one day for every 1,000 feet climbed. I knew this because Lopsang had chided us the entire ascent about how we were ignoring this rule. The main problem was that we were unlikely to find a marker every thousand feet to keep us safe, and no one knew how long the gates would remain open.

"We need time," argued Lopsang. "No one is going to climb the Vikram Wall without proper acclimatization."

"No one climbed the Spine before either," I pointed out cheerfully.

Lopsang's face darkened. "The ice wall is different. It sits right beneath the death zone, only a thousand feet below the mountain's summit. The air there is too thin to move quickly. One false step and you die." He sat back in his sleeping bag as if the matter was settled.

I was not so easily swayed. "So we rest at the base of the wall, then. Take a day to acclimatize and then make our bid. That's where we have to go." I tapped the screen where the green light was still blinking on and off." To me, Shangri-La was such a tempting find that even days of rigorous physical exertion did not seem like too much of an obstacle.

"Ascent this late is incredibly dangerous. We have the oxygen, but there's no guarantee of a marker once we make it above the Vikram Wall."

"They've been guiding teams to the summit for years, haven't they?" asked James.

"The villagers have, but the shamans did not often guide," said Lopsang. "But even they feared staying in the high altitude for too long. If any of them took the time to properly protect a site, they likely died doing it."

It was frustrating. We'd just risked life and limb to put a tracker on this beast, and now he didn't even want to follow it? "A man died to plant that dart, Lopsang. If you want to let him die in vain, that's fine, but I for one am trying to go up."

Lopsang faltered, taken aback.

"I haven't had a gun to your head since The Black Market. If you don't want to continue, no one is forcing you."

"Asshole," muttered James.

James was probably right, but it didn't change the facts. Lopsang had joined us forcefully at first but had plenty of opportunities to leave. The mountain winds whistled through the canyon, providing the only sound other than the snoring of a few of Manchester's men.

It was a while before Lopsang broke the silence. "You chose to turn back and face this problem. That, while stupid, is admirable. My father would never forgive me if I let you die on the mountain from my own cowardice."

I softened at this. "You know as well as I do that we have to finish what we've started."

"I know." Lopsang's eyes had gone far off again, as if he were lost in a different world. "I am just afraid of what we might lose on the way."

"It's a gamble we're going to have to make together. We'll break the news to Manchester and his team in the morning about acclimatization. He'll put up a stink, but so be it. Let's get some rest while we can."

Lopsang and James murmured in agreement and fell back in their sleeping bags. The hard ground would have been difficult for most to sleep on, but in our exhaustion, it might as well have been a feather bed. I fought it for a while, trying to avoid sleep and thinking of the journey ahead, but I soon began to fade as well. I told myself that Shangri-La had better be worth it, and Manchester better not slow us down. Then I sank into the inky blackness of deep sleep.

We woke early to pale blue light streaming through the top of the canyon above and Manchester barking orders at his team.

"Christ, can't anyone get some sleep around here?" I groaned, shaking the nightmares I had endured from my head. I'd wished desperately to dream of sandy beaches and fruity drinks, but no such luck. Reluctantly, I unzipped my sleeping bag and crawled out of the small tent into the freezing cold of dawn.

"You survived the night," said Manchester. "Looks like we'll be honoring this pact after all." He had a jovial air that did not belong anywhere near the early morning.

"Surprised you even need warmth with all that ice in your veins," I said, fumbling around for the camping stove to make coffee.

"Don't bother unpacking, we've got a long day's journey ahead. Best to get a move on." Manchester was already donning his climbing gear.

I looked at him with resolute anger. "Someone is going to die if I don't get a cup of coffee before we leave." My tone was final and I started looking for the grounds.

Manchester considered the proposition, then decided that although he would be safe, it was better not to argue. "All right, fifteen minutes, then."

"Always generous." I winced at the dull headache that was

forming in my temples. Was it altitude sickness or caffeine with-drawal? I did not want to know the answer.

I found the coffee grounds and brewed a small pot. The smell of it roused James and Lopsang from the tent.

Fifteen minutes later, we were packed up and preparing to move. The soreness in my legs had not abated, making me wince slightly with each step. Whoever said physical exertion is worth a damn should be shot. If Manchester hadn't lorded over us like a hawk, I might have put some booze in my coffee, but then again, it would have made the mercenaries want a sip, and I knew better than to allow mercenaries a drink on the job.

Ahead, Manchester stopped, halting the line to turn and face everyone. "Well, now that we've all shaken the sleep from our eyes, it's time for the morning debrief."

I tried to think about anything other than Manchester, who was likely to trip over his own power if he wasn't careful.

"Today's trek will be a long one." There were some grumbles at this, to which Manchester just flashed a deadly scowl and made them fall silent. "We're going to hike to the base of the Vikram Wall and scale it."

Lopsang shot a glance at me. "We are not finishing that climb today. There has to be a day to rest," he whispered.

"Yes, that means we're going to be camping just below the fabled 'death zone,'" Manchester droned on, addressing the ex-hausted group before him.

"All right, I'll deal with it," I said to Lopsang and stepped out of line.

Manchester stopped talking and stared at me. "We don't usually break line during the morning debrief, Mr. Ventner."

"Oh," I gasped, feigning surprise, "my sincerest apologies." I gave a little curtsy.

Manchester was about to start talking again when I cut him off. "The real problem is that we can't climb the wall without spending a day to acclimatize." I looked back briefly to Lopsang, who gave me a subtle thumbs-up. "It may not be ideal to lose a day off the pace, but it's better than dying from nitrogen bubbles in your blood." I added the last bit as a flourish based on a documentary I had seen about scuba diving. Same principle, right?

"I can assure you that you will have plenty of time to acclimatize once we have reached the top," snapped Manchester, as if he were dealing with a petulant child.

"There are likely no markers once we get above the wall," I said, "meaning that we will be both tired and completely unprotected. There's a chance that we will not be able to rest from that point on. No marker, no time to rest, and we're dead, simple as that." My point was a rational one, so I stood my ground in the warm morning air, trying to keep eye contact through the light of the sun.

It was clear that beneath the brim of his black hat, Manchester was thinking. While it's never a good practice to show weakness through capitulation in front of guns for hire, leading them on a suicide mission—one that they knew about, no less—was equal folly.

Eventually his face slackened, as he failed to find an alternative. "Fine, show us to the marker at the base of the wall, and we will ascend at first light."

The thought of putting off the climb for another day was nearly enough to bring me to joyous tears. I hadn't said there was a marker at the bottom of the wall, but we'd cross that bridge when we got there.

"But, Mr. Ventner, do not break rank again. I may have sworn to do no harm, but this journey does not have to be pleasant."

Manchester's eyes narrowed, and while I'm ashamed to admit it, I found the look frightening. Regardless, I kept my composure. "Understood."

"Wonderful," boomed Manchester, resuming his speech with the air of a man captaining a brand-new vessel. "Now that we're all on the same page, I'd say it's about time we set off. We will not ascend the Vikram Wall today, but that does not mean we will slow down. Now, my guides tell me that we must cross an ice field today and that it will be no easy feat."

I stopped listening and stepped back in line by Lopsang and James.

"The Vikram Wall is dangerous, but the ice field before it is equally so," whispered Lopsang. "The ice shifts by feet per day, opening crevasses that are impossibly deep. We will all need to be very careful."

The nearest mercenary showed a flicker of unease, and I smelled dissent in the air. "I guess we're lucky to be last in line," I said in an intentionally loud whisper, taking note as one of the mercenaries visibly processed the insinuation.

Manchester finished his debriefing, and the line slowly began to move out. The path ahead was no more difficult than the path to base camp, but that would soon change. Rather than moving through the canyon, which led west, we were headed for the icy plains to the east. I, for one, was happy to be in the sunshine again.

"So all we have to do is avoid the big cracks in the ground and we should be fine, right?" James asked, sounding a little nervous.

I wanted to make fun of him, but the same question had been on my mind a moment earlier. Crevasses didn't seem all that hard to avoid.

"There's no avoiding them," said Lopsang with no air of dissatisfaction. "The real trick is crossing them."

"How exactly are we going to do that?" asked James.

"Oh, you'll see. We're nearly there."

As we crested a small ridge, a massive field of large debris spread out before us. Chunks of ice and snow had cleared a path down the mountain, and we had to pick our way across it. The field itself seemed to stretch on for an impossible distance both up and down the mountain. A loud crack echoed across the expanse, followed by rumbling as one of the larger ice chunks dislodged and tumbled down the mountain.

"Piece of cake, right?" James laughed nervously.

"Should be fun," I said.

"Not all of us will make it," said Lopsang.

"Great pep talk, coach." I slapped Lopsang on the back and broke line once more to talk to Manchester. The mercenaries stared at me as I approached, but I did my best to ignore them.

Manchester stood at the front of the line, surveying the land through a pair of binoculars that probably cost more than all of my gear.

"I thought I told you not to break the line, Mr. Ventner." His voice was icy, distracted.

"Apologies again, Harvey, but I thought now would be a good time to talk about this plan of yours."

"What plan?" He continued to survey the field.

"The plan for getting us across this maze of death."

Manchester chuckled. "Oh, my dear boy, that's where you come in."

13.

THE ICE FIELD

Hours later, I was cursing at the front of the line with Lopsang and James. We stood on a large angular block of ice, flanked on all sides by equally large chunks of rubble. Before us was a twenty-foot crevasse, dark blue and sinking infinitely deep into the mountain. Behind lay half a day's trekking and the dozen crevasses we had already managed to cross.

Death surrounded us on all sides. I felt a constant tension in my chest, as though I were walking a high wire. It wasn't all that far from the truth. To cross the crevasses, we'd had to crawl on metal ladders, strung together for length, and hope to God that none of the ice broke loose. Every creak and moan of the shifting ice in the midday sun sent hot blood pumping through my veins. Even when I wasn't the one crossing, my heart hammered.

Lopsang, though, while not optimistic about our outcome, did not seem bothered. He always knew the path, even when the rest of the mountain was blocked from view by the ice field. He may have seemed grim about the proposition of ascending the mountain, but every so often I caught what looked like a glimmer of excitement in the Sherpa's eyes.

James, on the other hand, was miserable and content to criticize. "You just had to run your mouth, didn't you?" he said for about the fiftieth time since Manchester had sent us to the front of the line.

"You know, most of my apprentices—"

"Any smart man would have put us in front, regardless of Nick's fat mouth," said Lopsang. He carefully lashed two ladders together and stood them upright. They swayed a little in the breeze, but held. Slowly, he lowered the ladders down and over the deep, blue chasm. "Without a guide, the team wouldn't have made it ten feet into the ice field."

It was true. Almost immediately after we had started our journey across, Manchester nearly fell through what only appeared to be solid ice. Luckily—or unluckily depending on who was looking on—Lopsang saved him at the last second. The ice field was deceptive, with every path looking stable, but most of them being brittle facades disguising death. I wondered just how deep into the mountain the cracks went and what lay at the bottom. Scientists would say nothing existed below, but I knew better. There's no such thing as uninhabited territory.

The clack of the metal ladder landing on the other side of the crevasse brought me back to the present. A wave of nausea and stomach pain gripped me as I looked across. It hadn't gotten any easier throughout the day. In fact, each crossing brought us closer to the Vikram Wall, and that alone was enough to scare me. Heights had never really troubled me, but there was something about the cracks in the mountain that made me uneasy.

"Don't worry, friend, it's safe," said Lopsang, sensing my unease. He put a boot on the ladder and stomped up and down. The ladder shook but did not falter.

I wished he hadn't. If the ladder was stable, it wasn't now.

"Thanks," I said a little shakily, and I walked over to the edge of the crevasse. I looked down through the metal rungs and saw nothing I liked. The light blue of surface ice quickly gave way to pitch darkness, making it impossible to tell just how far down the crack went. Not wanting to spend any more time than I had to, I aligned my boots with the grooves in the ladder and began to climb.

Hand over hand, I moved across, slowly and safely. The ladder shuddered with each step I made, and the ice at both ends made uncomfortable grating sounds. Though I knew it was better to look ahead, my eyes kept wandering to the dark below. The lack of light caused shapes to shift and play tricks on my mind.

"Anything live in these crevasses?" I hoped that the answer was no. One shouldn't ask questions you don't want the answers to.

Lopsang's response was a bitter laugh. "The only thing that's down there is those who have long since passed."

The thought didn't make me feel any easier. "The dead are never restful," I muttered.

"Keep going, Mr. Ventner, almost across," said Manchester from safety. He had made a habit of talking to me right as I was in the middle of my crossings, perhaps hoping that through distraction he could aid an unfortunate accident. He had sworn to do no harm, but never promised anything about mild annoyance.

I wanted to give him some snappy retort but found I could not spare any thought. Instead, I told myself that if we made it out of there, I'd never go near a mountain again. So far, I had seen nothing to convince me that mountain climbing was a hobby worth pursuing. Anyone who did it for fun was clearly an idiot. Just listening to Lopsang talk about the ascent had been exhausting. Unfortunately, the climbing itself was much worse.

Halfway across the ladder, I paused, my hands trembling slightly from fear and exhaustion. Movement only became harder the higher we climbed. I told myself I could do it.

"Don't look down," whispered a voice that sounded as if it had come from directly below me.

"Very funny, James," I stammered.

"I didn't say anything," he called back.

I looked back to see if I could spot any trickery, but James looked genuinely concerned. Of all the places to run into an evil entity, this had to be the worst. I slowly turned back toward the front of the ladder, trying to avoid looking directly at the chasm, but a flash of movement caught my eye, causing me to stumble. I lost my footing and fell flat, gripping the metal sides with both hands. The ladder buckled under the sudden weight, and my blood froze. I held tight, waiting for the ladder to stop moving, staring into the darkness below.

The ladder held, and I pushed myself back up. I continued, faster than before. Climbing the ladder, while not steep, was still a feat of strength. My hands shook. My lungs burned. My vision wavered. I told myself my mind was just playing tricks, nothing more. There was a feeling in the pit of my stomach that said otherwise, but I tried my best to ignore it.

There were only five or so feet left to the other side when the voice called out again. "Better climbers than *you* have fallen here. Just relax. Join us." The voice sounded raspy and dry.

I looked down and saw a flash of orange quickly fade into the dark. I couldn't be sure, but I felt like someone –or something– was watching me from below. Fuck this mountain, I thought, and sped up my ascent. It took all my energy to keep moving and all of my concentration not to look back to where I had seen the orange flash. In a matter of seconds, I was off the ladder and on the other side of the chasm, panting in the warm afternoon light. The chill I felt on the ladder quickly melted as the sun bathed me in light.

I sprawled onto the bright white surface of a large piece of ice, feeling like a man who had just run a marathon. Looking back across, everyone seemed much closer than they should have been.

The mercenaries were laughing at me, but Lopsang and James looked perturbed. Only a few hundred feet away, the ice field ended, giving way to a smooth slope leading up to a steep face made of glacier and rock. The Vikram Wall. I shivered at the sight.

"Everything all right, Nick?" called James.

I thought back to the flash of orange and the voice in the crevasse. "Yeah," I said unconvincingly. "Just ... don't look down." I wasn't sure what kind of entity was in the crevasse, but when in doubt, avoiding eye contact seemed to be a safe course of action.

"Thanks for the cliché," James said, beginning to climb. The previous ladders had given him no trouble, but something was different this time.

His movements were stiff, slower than before. Could it be the altitude getting to him? No, that wasn't it.

"James, I'm serious, don't look down."

"You're not help—" He froze mid-sentence, his gaze inadvertently drifting between the rungs of the ladder and down to the crevasse. A rigid stillness took over his body, and his eyes glazed over. Something was moving in the darkness below him. Two pale pinpoints illuminated, and a voice began to speak.

"Help me," it whispered. "My team left me for dead, but I can still make it home." There was deep sorrow in the voice.

It cut to James's core; I could see it on his face—he could feel the climber's sadness. "There's someone down there," he said, dazed.

"James, don't listen to it, just climb!" I yelled.

James ignored me as his right arm drifted away from the ladder and hung down toward the darkness below. "Lopsang, get me some rope. We can reach him," he called. "We should help." There was a faraway urgency in his voice.

"Someone get up there, he's suffering from altitude sickness," commanded Manchester.

Lopsang stepped in front of the mercenary attempting to carry out the order. "Don't set foot on that ladder. Any more weight and it will fall." His voice was calm, but I could see worry in the Sherpa's face. If none of them could reach James, then it was up to me.

The mercenary stepped back, affronted.

Lopsang turned to James. "Don't listen to it. There is nothing down there but death. Look straight ahead and keep climbing."

James remained still, continuing to gaze into the crevasse. "It's a climber, I can see him." He reached his hand farther into the crevasse. "I can almost reach him."

"This is no time for childish pranks," spat Manchester. "We are wasting precious time."

I shot him a murderous look and turned my attention to James. "Come on, James, snap out of it." I was growing desperate. The longer James looked down, the worse the situation was likely to get. James did not move. "I'm taking a percentage for every second of my time you waste!"

James said nothing and leaned over the ladder to get a better look below.

"Worthless apprentices, always getting themselves killed!"

James barely seemed to hear me, but at the word "apprentices" he jerked away, just as some creature below tried to grab him. Surprise melted away the fear just long enough for him to turn away. With stiff limbs, he pulled himself across the ladder, fighting every urge to look down. In less than a minute, he had crossed, falling onto the cold but solid ice, out of breath.

"How's your day going, James?" I was pleased that we weren't going to leave him behind as a frozen corpse, but had no intention of showing it.

"There's something down there," panted James, ignoring the sarcasm.

"Yeah, I saw it, too. But"—I turned away and spoke in a low tone—"there's a chance it'll kill Manchester. This might work out after all." Genuine excitement crept into my voice.

James was not pleased.

"Oh, you're no fun. The other good news is we're almost out of here." I motioned to the Vikram Wall. It felt like a silent sentinel, guarding the mountain and laughing at our trouble on its slopes. I didn't have much time to think about it as a voice from behind startled me.

"Are you two all right?" In the space of a minute, Lopsang had crossed the ladder with ease.

We looked at him, confused.

"Nick was right. The trick was to not look down." Lopsang gave a broad smile as if all their troubles were over and the wall did not still lie ahead.

"What the hell *was* that?" I asked.

"A bad sign." Lopsang hung his head. "Many climbers have lost their lives in these crevasses. The mountain stops them from resting peacefully."

"A mountain of the undead. Wonderful." I should have splurged for a few more shotgun rounds. While equally as effective against the undead as other weapons, shotguns gave a more satisfying splatter.

"Not exactly. Normally the souls can't cross over, so they lay dormant, unable to leave but also unable to do any damage. It's like a dreamless sleep, but ..."

"But they're not sleeping anymore, are they?" I asked.

"It doesn't seem so." Lopsang's voice had grown dark again. "What did you see down there?"

"Nothing but an orange flash. I couldn't get a good look."

"I saw him," said James.

"Him?" asked Lopsang.

"Yeah, it was a man, or what used to be a man. His face was black with frostbite and his hands were rotted, but I could tell it was a climber."

Lopsang uttered what sounded like a curse in his native tongue. "Then the gates really are open. We need to get to the next marker now. If the dead are up and walking, we have more than one reason to get there by nightfall. The closer we come to the summit, the more we will find."

"Do people just leave them here?" James sounded appalled.

Lopsang shrugged. "It's too dangerous to take them down. Just below the summit is the Rainbow Trail."

"Let me guess, sounds nice, isn't nice," I said, knowing the answer.

"Correct," Lopsang said. "It is so named because of the colorful hiking jackets that still poke out of the snow. We will be fine during the day, but come nightfall, we don't want to be unprotected."

"Well, then, I'd say it's time to get moving." The sun was still bright but was quickly descending toward the mountain.

"Everything all right up there?" asked Manchester, annoyed.

"Sure is, Harvey," I called. "Come on over, and don't look into the crevasse. There's an undead hiker down there, and he's looking for some friends." I turned to Lopsang and smiled. "Let's get the next crossing set up. I'm feeling lucky."

14.

THE VIKRAM WALL

It had taken the team over two hours to cross the remaining crevasses, and by the time they came to the base of the Vikram Wall, everyone was content to make camp in silence. The night passed uneventfully, and to my surprise, sleep overtook me with a rapidity that I thought impossible in the face of such imminent danger. Before we knew it, the first blue light was creeping into the sky and it was time to resume our ascent.

I unzipped our tent flap to the cold face of the Vikram Wall. Just looking at it carried great weight, as if it were trying to impress its severity on me. The previous day, I had asked Lopsang about the ascent and what he told me was troubling.

The Vikram Wall was named in 1944 after the first explorer who managed to scale it without dying. Many had tried before him, most had died. The ones who came back were usually half mad or frostbitten beyond recognition. The terrain was some of the steepest on the mountain, and the ascent was deceptively simple. The main trouble was scaling a thick sheet of ice nearly five hundred feet straight up, with the air growing thinner the whole way. Like all of the glaciers on the mountain, the wall also shifted continuously, occasionally dropping sheets of ice at deadly speed without warning. Many explorers said that to climb the Vikram was to put your life in the hands of the mountain.

I stepped out onto the packed snow beneath just as the first rays of light touched the wall's icy surface. Loud creaks and moans filled the morning air. I told myself it was just the ice expanding, that it happens every day. My stomach was tied into knots at the thought of trying to find a clear path up.

"Well, I hope you've got a way to kill it, Mr. Ventner," came Manchester's voice from just over my shoulder.

I jumped, but tried to act as if nothing had happened. The man was like a damned ninja. "So do I. If we have to make a hasty descent down that"—I motioned to the wall—"we're dead."

"Once we've scaled the wall, there's no running," said Manchester.

We stood in a rare moment of silence, staring up at the wall. The sun's rays brought warmth, but neither of us felt it. All that pushed us forward was the cold determination to climb and finish what we'd started. I tapped the vial in my pocket, hoping the old man hadn't screwed us over.

"Well, I'm game if you are," I said, trying to muster up a jovial tone. "I'd say we've got a fifty-fifty shot." The real odds were much worse, but I'd never been any good at statistical calculations.

"No sense in wasting time, then. Pack up and get ready. We're moving out in ten," ordered Manchester, loudly enough that I thought the wall might have crumbled from the echo. Behind us, the mercenaries scrambled from their tents and began breaking down camp.

James emerged as well, rubbing sleep from his eyes and looking generally displeased at the wake-up call. He looked the wall up and down, then shrugged. "Doesn't look so bad from down here."

I couldn't help but laugh. I began packing up our gear and breaking down the tent. In a matter of minutes, one of Manchester's men had already begun scaling the wall and putting up guide ropes. Lopsang, who had been up long before the rest of us, looked on from the bottom of the wall, displeased.

I finished stuffing the tent into my pack and walked over to Lopsang. "What's the matter?"

"I don't trust their abilities. They don't look like mountain climbers."

"Don't you know the old saying? Never judge a book by its cover?"

"We have one like that. If it doesn't look like a goat, it's probably not one."

Yes, finally a joke from the demigod. "Couldn't you use your powers to get us up there somehow?"

Lopsang tilted his head angrily. "I have climbed this mountain for years without ever once using my abilities. They are not cheap party tricks. I made a deal long ago to only use them when absolutely necessary, and I've never broken it."

"Jeez, take it easy, it's early." I grimaced, a headache beginning to set in. "What do you suggest we do about this, then?" I motioned to the climbers.

Lopsang looked up at them thoughtfully, responding in a low tone. "Just make sure Manchester and his team go first. I'll climb after them and check all the guides to make sure that they're safe."

I grinned. It wasn't a bad plan for someone who claimed to have a moral compass. "Fine by me. I promised to do no harm. Never said anything about letting harm do its own work."

As the mercenary crew prepared the trail for us, we looked on, awestruck. The light glinted off the mountain summit, making it look almost attainable. I was starting to understand the drive climbers felt to continue through such adversity. It would be one hell of a view up there. Maybe that was something worth dying for. I shrugged off the thought, chalking it up to altitude sickness.

We sat and waited, conserving our strength for the task ahead. Climbing was not easy at high altitude, and I was well out of shape. Since our first day, my muscles had never stopped burning with soreness. The ascent might not have been as bad at a lower altitude, but at the base of the wall, it took all my effort just to catch a breath. A dull throb invaded my head, reminding me that I was not getting enough oxygen. I longed for the moment when we'd be allowed to use our O2 tanks, even if only for momentary relief.

An hour or so later, the ropes were set, and Manchester's team was high up on the face. Lopsang had insisted that we wait to space ourselves out, telling Manchester it was due to James needing more time to acclimatize. When we finally clipped ourselves onto the guidelines, the sun had already come up a quarter of the way through the sky. Lopsang climbed first, checking each of the pitons as he went, then motioned for me and James to follow.

The first few handholds were simple, and before I knew it, I was far off the ground. In the early morning chill, I almost felt exhilaration. Very few people got to visit that place in their lifetimes, and I was grateful for a moment, but the feeling did not last long. Soon, I felt the all-too-familiar burn in my limbs and the sluggish movement of my brain. The exertion was getting to me. When I looked down, I was dismayed to find that we were not even halfway up the face. Embarrassed, I halted, panting.

Lopsang climbed down so that we were almost level with one another. "Are you all right?"

Sweat stung my eyes; my arms shook as I tried to hold on to the mountain in front of me. "I don't think I can do it. It's too much." My breathing was ragged and harsh. Lack of mountaineering training or physical activity was taking its toll.

"Without you, there is no expedition, Dr. Ventner," said

Lopsang, speaking as if we were at a bar, not clinging to the side of a mountain. "If you want to chicken out and go back, that's fine. We'll all go together."

My pride burned in my chest, trying its hardest to match the fire in my muscles.

"You can do this," said Lopsang. "From this point on, it's all mental." He grabbed my harness. "Let go. Rest for a minute."

I did not argue and let my hands fall off the mountainside. I hung there, off the side of the wall, limp and completely at Lopsang's mercy. Looking out over the terrain below, I saw the field of ice we had crossed the day before, and the Spine the day before that. We'd come too far to turn back now. Through the haze of ache and pain, I once more found motivation.

"I've changed my mind," I said. "I think I'll come with you after all." I managed to catch half a breath.

"That's the spirit, Dr. Ventner. Now come on, we're almost there."

We were nowhere near almost there, but I nodded my head anyway. Slowly, I turned the heat of my burning limbs into motion and began moving once more. Hand over hand, I told myself I could do it. Just like the Spine, I stared at nothing but the rock in front of me and continued climbing. The ice cracked around us constantly but never fell. It was our one lucky break.

As the day wore on, I felt the paradoxical heat that came with climbing one of the world's tallest mountains. Outside my suit, the air was cold enough to bite, but inside it felt like a sauna. The irony was not lost on me that I would likely soon be begging for that warmth when the sun went down. I stopped to sip from my canteen, feeling the cool liquid slide icily down my throat. It was almost better than a proper drink.

I lost track of time. After what could have been minutes or

hours, I pulled myself over a ledge, and a pair of strong arms lifted me up. Rolling onto my back, I stared up at the darkening sky.

"It's early for it to be going dark," I murmured to no one in particular, and then it dawned on me. I couldn't see. The sky was not growing dark; my vision was narrowing to a pinpoint. I thought of James, hoping he made it up, and then I sank into blackness.

When I came to, there was an oxygen mask on my face and the air was warm. I tried to sit up but found the act too dizzying and immediately fell backward. Lopsang's smiling face swam into view.

"What are you so giddy about?" I asked, dazed but still annoyed. Each word was muffled through the mask and made me feel weaker.

"We found a marker. We can rest here tonight." I rolled over and saw that we were inside a tent. The canvas flapped around from the wind outside. Lopsang unzipped the flap to reveal a small stone obelisk.

"No flags?" I murmured weakly.

"Not here. The wind would have long ago blown them away. It's the incantations surrounding the site that matter."

"Oh, good," I said, my vision swimming once more. Darkness closed in around the edges of the tent.

"Dr. Ventner, you need to drink." Lopsang gingerly lifted me to a sitting position.

At first I felt nothing but nausea and the overwhelming feeling that I was going to black out again, but I slowly steadied. The bright orange interior of the tent came into view, and I saw James resting in the corner, clutching a cup of something hot.

"Fortune and glory, right?" James laughed. It quickly turned into a cough, but he kept his grin.

I tried to laugh as well, but the wheezing of air through my lungs hurt. A kettle drum beat in my head, constantly pounding at what had to be fragments of my skull.

Lopsang handed me a steaming cup of sweet-smelling broth. "Drink this. It'll help with your headache and nourish you."

I tilted the cup back without question and savored the warming sensation that ran through my aching limbs. A great wave of calm swept over me as the steam rose into my nostrils. We can do this, I thought. A week ago I would not have believed we could get as far as we had. The Vikram Wall was a feat for professional climbers, but we had managed it just the same. Luck had likely played a part in it, but we'd still done it.

There was no howling that night, other than the strong wind. We were the only people for miles, and far enough away from civilization that we could see nothing else but the snowy mountain above and below. As I fought off frostbite and the urge to sleep, I watched the tiny green dot on the tracking screen. The light blinked slowly, on and off, indicating that the creature had not moved.

"How long until we go after it?" asked James.

"We'll head out in the morning, just before first light," I said, looking to Lopsang hopefully.

"Yes," Lopsang agreed. "The creature is just above us on the other side of the mountain face. The route is not well traveled and will take more time to traverse."

"Sounds like a party." I laughed, but my laughter quickly turned to coughing through the oxygen mask. "All right, then, rest up. If we find that creature tomorrow, it's likely to be one of the longest days of our lives."

15.

THE DEATH ZONE

The air was what woke me. I was gasping for it. It was dark outside, and I could hear the sounds of the team preparing for the ascent.

Lopsang gently shook me. "It's time. Gear up, my friend."

"Five more minutes," I whined as I slowly pulled myself into a sitting position. Thankfully, the world did not waver as it had before, and I actually felt rested. The oxygen mask had been removed sometime during the night.

"We leave in fifteen," said Lopsang. He exited the tent, letting a frigid blast of mountain air in behind him.

Five minutes later, I was standing in the pitch darkness of early morning, looking through the tunnel of my headlamp over the edge of the Vikram Wall. Somewhere above us was the summit of the mountain, but in the low light, I could not see it. Sufficiently scared and freezing, I began to unpack what passed as climbing gear on a monster-hunting expedition.

I always carried a slew of weaponry with me, but attacking the yeti was a different type of challenge. The bags had been unmercifully heavy on the way up, but they would come in handy now that we were close. I reached into my bag and pulled out the bottle of slow-moving liquid we had obtained at The Black Market.

James crawled out of the tent and walked groggily toward me.

"What's the plan, boss?" It came out quiet and raspy, with each breath taking great effort. Lopsang joined us as well.

"Our best bet is to pierce its hide with something high powered and sharp." I pulled a great bundle of metal rods, sheets, and cords out of the bag.

"What are those?" asked Lopsang.

I smiled, flung my arm out to one side, and watched the Sherpa's wondrous look as the collapsible weapon assembled itself. In less than five seconds, my hand was wrapped around the middle of a sturdy, fully automatic crossbow, complete with hollow bolts.

"Highly illegal, but you have to admire the ingenuity," I said, expanding the other pieces of scrap metal in the bag with incredible speed.

When I was finished, there were two completely functional crossbows and a large harpoon gun neatly laid out on the snow. I handed them to James and Lopsang. "These are for you." I took the harpoon gun for myself, slinging it over my shoulder. It carried less ammunition and took longer to reload, which forced me to be patient with my shots.

Lopsang pointed to the harpoon gun. "You sure that's going to be enough?"

"Oh, this?" I hefted the weapon and pointed it up the mountain. "This little beauty got me out of a scrape with a couple of cannibalistic mermaids that were after my heart." God, I hated underwater jobs. "Only needed three shots, got two of them in the chest, one in the leg—"

"And left the rest of them for the sharks," James said dryly, finishing my sentence. "It's best not to ask, Lopsang. That story's been told in every bar from Boston to Shanghai."

"If we ever end up in one of the Atlantean cities," I said, "remind me to feed you to the Minotaur."

"If we ever end up in Atlantis, I'll buy you a bottle of that scotch you're always eyeing."

Challenge accepted. "Fair bet, Lopsang?"

Lopsang shrugged. "Sure. Now, what about the poison?"

"Ah yes, of course," I said, pulling out a small syringe. I delicately punctured the top of the vial and dipped the needle into the liquid, drawing it out slowly. Each harpoon was hollow, able to hold a small amount of poison and inject it upon impact. I filled my ammunition and then passed the remainder of the poison to James. "All of your bolts have a small hollow chamber just below the tip. Load them with the poison, or you'll just be wasting ammo."

James and Lopsang followed suit. When we'd finished, Lopsang proceeded to unpack and help me and James into our climbing gear. By the time we were done, I felt a bit like an astronaut, strapped inside of a large suit to protect me from the harsh world outside. The final touch was an oxygen tank to assist with the thinning air on our ascent. We wouldn't turn it on until midway through the day's climb, but I still felt one tank was too little. I walked over to Manchester's group, who had been preparing as well, and gave the thumbs-up.

"Glad to see you pulled through," said Manchester, his voice muffled by his mask. "Would have been a shame to take all the glory without you."

I changed my thumbs-up to a middle finger and turned around to rejoin Lopsang and James. The altitude was making me angry, and I was ready to be done with my partnership with Manchester. There was also the fact that something felt off about the morning. All our gear was prepped, and everything had gone according to plan, but somewhere in my numbed brain, there was fear. I strapped on a pair of orange-tinted goggles and adjusted my head lamp. There was no sense in delaying; we were almost there.

The last obstacle that stood in our way before reaching the altitude of the creature's signal was a technical ridge covered in blue ice, followed by a short trek off the map. The ridge was steep, but not as bad as the other terrain we had crossed. The real issue, aside from the air above the Vikram Wall being extremely thin, was the off-the-map section. There was a reason climbers used only one route when ascending the mountain, a lesson I had already learned once with the Spine, and wasn't keen on repeating.

With ragged breath and aching limbs, we began to move up the mountain at a crawl. The ice beneath our feet made constant brittle noises, punctuating the silence. There was no wind and the sky was clear. Above, a sea of dazzling colored stars moved slowly in the early morning sky. As we moved farther up the mountain, I noticed a set of large imprints running parallel to the trail, but I was tethered to the men in front of me and could not stop to get a better look.

"James, look at these." I pointed to the tracks. "Think it's our guy?" My voice was muffled, and my stupid grin was blocked by the gear covering my face.

"Unless there's another mythical creature up here, I'd bet on it," said James, panting. There was no room for sarcasm between breaths.

We made it to the top of the ridge without incident, just as the sun began to poke out over the valley below. When everyone had made it to the top, we prepared to do something no one had ever done.

"Are you sure that's where it is?" Manchester asked curtly, pointing away from the main climbing trail.

I pulled out the tracker to be sure—there was no point in engaging in a suicide mission if our prey wasn't even there. The green light blinked on and off, indicating that the creature was stationary. Why hadn't it moved? I grew nervous.

"It's there, all right."

Lopsang looked at the tracker and stepped forward. "This section of the trail has likely never been traveled," he warned. The certainty in his voice made me shiver. "If you want to live, let me go first and set the ropes." There was no animosity to it, just cold, hard truth.

Manchester chewed the thought over for a minute. "It's probably for the best. Go ahead, then. We don't have all day."

The path sloped up a narrow ridge, leading to the mountain summit. It was likely no more than a few hours away for an experienced climber. Just beyond where we stood was the Rainbow Trail, an area I had no intention of entering. I'd had enough encounters with the undead for one expedition.

The path we had to take wasn't really a path at all, as around the back of the mountain face was uncharted territory. When planning the journey to the creature's lair, Lopsang and I had operated on a simple principle: The yeti couldn't climb straight up, meaning that there was likely a way to follow it. But now, facing the unmarked trail, I felt nervous about our assumption.

"Everyone switch on your O2," commanded Manchester as Lopsang began to scout the path. We had been saving the tanks for when we really needed it, and the time had finally come.

I turned the knob that increased the flow of oxygen and inhaled greedily. It was the first time I was able to catch a full breath in days. The feeling was electrifying. Almost instantly, my vision began to clear, and the familiar alertness of standard altitude returned. A confidence I had not felt since our first night on the mountain possessed me. I followed Lopsang off the trail and into the unknown.

The lazy route that wound up the summit was far more difficult than it appeared. The path that Lopsang was on—if it could even be called a path—made no such illusions. Immediately after moving off the main trail, the space of walkable land grew narrow. Above us was the sheer face of the mountain extending beyond our vision, and below was the sharp drop to the fields of snow and ice.

"Still think it's worth it?" I called to Manchester, muffled through my mask.

"All truly amazing things are. We are on the edge of history here."

Edge of a cliff, maybe. I fell in line behind Lopsang. Even with the oxygen, each step was difficult. My body felt like it was made of lead, but I pushed forward like a doomed solider; the excitement I had felt after putting the oxygen mask on quickly dwindled.

Up ahead, Lopsang was humming the same tune as when we had been climbing the Spine.

"What is making you so cheery?" I asked.

"Oh, nothing," Lopsang said flippantly. He possessed no fear as he climbed forward. "It's just likely no one has seen this side of the mountain before." He smiled to himself. "Every step we take, we're discovering something new."

This heartened me a little as well. I had never felt like much of an explorer, but it seemed preferable to gun for hire. In the end, we were exploring the unknown to kill the unknown. Until then, I was content to enjoy the thrill of discovery. On my back, the harpoon rattled against the mountain, knocking off little flakes of ice. It would dull the blade, but I didn't dare adjust it when there was so little room for movement. One moment of dull scraping wasn't going to change our odds.

"Stop!" yelled Lopsang. He held up his fist. I nearly ran into him, and the line behind me threatened to buckle. A slight tremor ran through the ground beneath us, causing loose bits of ice to dance nervously on the ground. "We're too high for an avalanche," Lopsang said nervously. At the top of the mountain, powder didn't stick, it merely blew off to lower altitudes.

The rumbling continued as if the very mountain was about to split open. We all waited, holding our breath, trying not to move. After a few seconds more, the rumbling stopped, leaving us in silence. The wind whipped along the edge of the mountain briefly, then died. My heart beat steadily. Slowly, I pulled the tracking device from my jacket pocket and opened it. The little green dot flashed but did not move.

One of the mercenaries spoke up. "Can we get moving? I'm freezing my—"

A hunk of ice sprayed down the mountain above us, sweeping the man off the side, leaving no evidence that he had ever been there. We heard nothing other than the cracking and crumbling of the ice as it tumbled down the mountain. The roar of the debris picked up more snow as it went, faded quickly, and left silence in its wake.

I gripped the device in terror. The light blinked on and off, but when it reappeared, it was in a slightly different position. "Oh shit," I whispered.

"What is it?" asked James.

"It's moving."

"What do you mean it's moving?" yelled Manchester.

"Exactly what I said, dipshit. The creature—it's moving." Even with my venom, the words "it's moving" still felt foreign in my mouth. It was broad daylight, yet the creature was moving and we couldn't see it. The soft blinking of the light reminded me that danger did not stop just because the situation was confusing. We were too far along the edge of the mountain to turn back, but I didn't know what else to do.

"Then we better get moving, too!" yelled James, snapping me out of my dream state. "Move your ass now, Nick!"

Lopsang had already started securing ropes on the route ahead. Adrenaline pumped through my veins, and I moved as fast as possible while still holding on to the guide rope. I panted and heaved but continued forward, knowing that the second I stopped, death would come for me. I had to keep moving. If I didn't keep up, everyone behind me was going to die, too. Being at the front of the line served to motivate me. Otherwise I might have given in to the tired sluggishness I felt and taken a seat to wait for death.

My heartbeat slowed. Each beat was a punch from the inside of my chest trying to break through my rib cage. I could not shake the nagging feeling that no matter what I did, this was going to be the end. A proximity alarm began to blare on the tracker, making me speed up even further.

Suddenly the thin path before me gave way to a rocky plateau, and I stumbled forward onto it. I tried to grasp for the tracking device as I fell forward, but it slipped between my fingers. It fell to the ground, skittered across the ice, and flew over the edge of the mountain, its proximity alarm beeping the whole way. I stood like a man in a dream, not entirely sure of where I was but certain I was in extreme danger.

James, Manchester, and his team stumbled onto the plateau. For a moment, I couldn't believe it. We were all alive. As I looked around, I saw that we were standing in a circle of stones flanked by large boulders ringing off the edge of the plateau. Manchester stood just in front of me, wide eyed.

"What?" I demanded.

"The gates are open," stammered Manchester, shaking and pointing a finger behind me.

16.

THE DEVIL AT THE GATE

Just beyond the plateau was a large cave, tucked away beneath an overhang of broken ice. Past the threshold, a pulsating gold light streamed through a crack between two dark wooden doors adorned with scenes of blood and massacre, depicting the war between gods and their creations. The woodwork seemed to go on forever, twisting and turning its way to smooth edges. Even in the cold mountain air, I felt a warm gust blow from within, enticing me forward.

The hanging ice gave it the appearance of a snowy maw. What lay past the gates was unclear, but we would soon find out.

"I can't believe it," I said, stunned. "It's real." Relief swept through me in graceful waves, calming the nagging voice that had been telling me for days: "There's nothing up there." Warmth spread through my limbs.

Then the feeling was washed away and replaced by the cold terror I had become so familiar with. A large rock hurtled over the edge of the mountain above us, struck one of Manchester's men in the chest, and sent him over the edge in a matter of seconds. The only sound was the crack as his bones broke, followed by the distant tumbling of rock on rock.

To my astonishment, I had briefly forgotten about our pursuer. "Defensive positions, everyone!" I yelled, and I pulled at the harpoon gun on my back. The tip caught on my oxygen tank, and

I struggled with it as the loud booming of the creature's footsteps echoed off the stones. That was it, I thought, trying to steel myself for the events to come.

James rushed up behind me, helped unstick the harpoon gun, and thrust it into my hands. At the same time, he brought his crossbow to bear on the exact location the boulder came from.

He spared me a nervous glance. "How many of your apprentices have died horribly?"

"Oh, not that many." I made a gesture of counting my fingers. "Last one went into a volcano, very quick. Barely made more than a gurgle. You should be so lucky." I steadied the harpoon gun and laughed.

James would have laughed, too, but it was cut off by a mighty roar, followed by a loud crash. A blur of snow, ice, and fur leapt in between us and the gates, debris showering from the ledge above. White mist billowed out from where it landed, temporarily blinding us. Before I could get a good look at the beast, my attention was diverted by a mercenary's arm spinning through the air and spraying blood as it sailed past.

I had the odd hope that Manchester would at least give the family of the unfortunate victim some money. Did mercenaries have families? The thought was interrupted by the beating of worn flesh against stone. The creature shook the very earth beneath us, and it was a miracle the plateau held.

The white mist surrounding the yeti cleared, and I found myself staring the creature dead in the eyes. Long white fur hung tangled and matted down the length of its body. Snow clung to the edges, giving the beast the look of a walking frost giant. Its black eyes stared out from beneath heavy eyebrows, searching for prey. Its powerful jaw gnashed with anticipation as drool dripped in massive steaming gobs to the ground.

The image paralyzed me. It did not help that the creature let out a ear-splitting roar, directed right at me. Sinewy muscle shook down the length of its body in a show of brute strength. Long scars ran across the creature's body, leading to patches of skin with no fur. It was a survivor. This wasn't going to be easy. I raised my harpoon gun and thumbed off the safety with a click that was all too loud.

The yeti's head cocked to the side as if it had heard something interesting. Our eyes locked and we took a long moment to stare down one another. Its white fur rippled in the growing gale.

I tried hard to keep the creature's gaze. "Get on with it, you big ugly brute," I said, taunting the beast. "I don't have all day."

The creature obliged, its muscles rippling as it charged. Its knuckles scraped the ground, breaking ice as if it were no more than sugar glass. I waited until the beast was close enough to give a guaranteed shot and pulled the trigger. The quiet hiss of the harpoon leaving the chamber was barely audible. The yeti swung its paw in a mighty arc, missing me as I slid out of the way, but severing the hose for my oxygen tank. I listened in dismay as the air leaked out. In the last seconds before the oxygen was gone, I took the deepest breath I could.

The yeti stumbled into the ring of stones, sending them flying in all directions and causing the crew to take evasive action. Then it turned, looking for more targets. Chaos broke out.

It was as if all of Manchester's team remembered they had guns at the exact same time and started firing in unison. The bullets made heavy thumps as they hit the yeti's hide, but the creature swatted them away as though they were mere flies. I seized upon the opportunity to escape. As I ran, I noticed the harpoon stuck in the yeti's chest and briefly felt hope. Until it fell out and clacked sadly onto the ground moments later.

It hadn't even left a wound. I ducked behind a boulder, out of breath. The lifesaving oxygen that had been coursing through my veins was gone, and I was stuck with what little remained on top of the mountain. The cavern entrance was a cacophonous medley of death and destruction. Manchester's men continued to fire their guns to no avail, and one by one, the yeti picked them off with ruthless efficiency.

"Someone stop the beast!" yelled one of the mercenaries just before the yeti's mighty fist crashed down on his leg, shattering the bone. Then the creature took its other fist and beat the man's head into the ground, pounding it until there was nothing left but a grisly red swath of flesh and blood.

I looked at the creature and recognized pure rage. Fresh gore coated its white fur and fell onto the rocks below. It was angry, all right. I looked around and saw James and Lopsang firing their crossbows to no effect. The worst-case scenario had come. We had marched all this way up the mountain, and none of the weapons we brought with us left so much as a scratch.

Splinters of broken arrows and bent, hot pieces of metal littered the ground. I had almost gotten used to the rat-tat-tatting of the guns when they abruptly stopped. The first clip of ammunition had run dry, and the men had nothing to show for it. The beast stood to its full height, looking confused by the lack of noise as its nostrils flared in the cold mountain air.

"Get through the gates!" yelled Manchester. "It's our only chance!"

He ran past the distracted yeti into the glowing light beyond the door. There was no pop or sizzle as he passed through the dazzling light, just the silence that meant he was either somewhere else or dead. It also meant the yeti had one less target to focus on.

Behind us, the sun had slowly begun to rise, painting the plateau in a grisly deep red light.

Delirious from lack of oxygen, I pulled out the bag of holy powder I had planned to use in the canyon. "James, Lopsang, run now!"

Barely thinking, I stepped out from hiding and chucked the entire bag at the yeti. I watched in slow motion as the bag spun through the air and hit the creature square in the face. White hot light erupted from the point of impact. I ran, blind, toward the gates.

The creature roared, and everyone else seized the opportunity, jumping through the warm light, not knowing what they would find on the other side. I passed through the doorway and immediately tried to close the gates behind me but found a stone wall that had not been there a moment earlier. I listened for the thuds of the creature trying to get through but heard nothing.

I took deep breaths to calm myself, and a sense of clarity came over me. It took me a moment to realize it, but they were full breaths, and as I inhaled deeply, I felt no need to gasp. My lungs did not burn; in fact, they drank the air up. I removed what remained of the ragged rubber oxygen hosing from my gear and threw it on the ground.

"Looks like we don't need these in here." I managed wearily.

As I stood up, I took in the state of the team. Almost everyone had bits of what remained of other team members clinging to them, but for the most part, those who had made it through were unscathed. There was one exception—a man who had caught the yeti's ire just as he went through the gates. I did not think him long for the world. It was unfortunate, but judging by the amount of blood coming from his leg, the creature had nicked a major artery. Poor bastard had only a few minutes left, max.

"Show some respect, Nick. A man is gravely injured over here," snapped Manchester.

Hypocritical for a man who uses workers as bait, but I let it pass, as Manchester was currently covered in the man's blood. I went to check on Lopsang and James.

Both men were brushing themselves off and staring up at the large stone wall now blocking the doorway we had come through. Lopsang was speaking in hushed tones.

"All these years, I have dwelled in the shadow of the mountain, and now I know. The stories were true. This gate has been the only thing keeping us safe all these years."

James was wearing the same stunned look on his face that he had the first time we were attacked. "The bolts didn't even graze him," he murmured. "We can't kill it. There's no way."

"Maybe not with the weapons we brought," I said, trying to avoid the sinking feeling of defeat in my chest. "Old Faithful here may have finally let me down"—I patted the harpoon on my back—"but everything can be killed."

On the inside, I was trying to calm the beginnings of panic. The yeti would find a way to get to us eventually, and once we escaped, I would be out of oxygen. I shot a sideways glance at the dying man. That was one problem solved. The man's leg was in pieces, but his oxygen tank was intact.

I inhaled deeply, trying to induce a sense of calm within myself, and smelled the pungent aroma of tropical flowers. The source of the smell were exotic flowers that hung in impossibly long chains from the ceiling of the cave. Each set of blooms was attached to a solitary vine at the bottom, and a wooden tag hung down with characters scrawled in various languages.

At the far end of the room, opposite from where we had entered, was a large stone archway with natural light streaming through it. On either side were massive stone statues of gods with their arms outstretched. Both stared at a wide circle etched in the floor just before the entrance. In its center was a dazzling diamond inlaid into the floor that radiated powerful blue light. Between each of the gods' legs was an ornate stone tablet with assorted characters carved into it.

"Lopsang, what are those?"

Lopsang looked in the direction of the archway and gasped. "Those are the guardians of Shangri-La." Almost immediately after saying it, he dropped to his knees and said a quick prayer. "They have been depicted in many ways, but this has to be them. In every tale, their arms are outstretched to welcome weary travelers, and they carry a warning to outsiders." Lopsang paused for a moment, mulling it all over. "What we just passed through has to be the outer wall. That is the real gate," he said, pointing to the circle in the floor.

I could not help but be humbled by the gods' omnipotent stares. "What do those say?" I pointed to the tablets. I didn't like the look of the stone circle in the floor. It had "trap" written all over it, and I had been stung by too many poison darts to go galivanting past it without understanding the rules.

"I'm a bit rusty in this language," Lopsang admitted sheepishly.

"You don't speak it?" I only spoke one language well, while my knowledge of others was mostly relegated to curse words and the phrase "Don't shoot, I'm a geologist." I found that the last bit didn't work as well when I was carrying a weapon, but it had saved me a few times.

"Well, I didn't exactly have any other demigods to practice with," Lopsang said dryly. "I believe it says: Welcome to all who would enter this kingdom, but heed our warning. This is a place of peace and can only be entered as such."

"Not bad for 'rusty,'" I said. "But I thought Shangri-La had been mired in war for centuries?"

"If you believe the stories, it was at one point a refuge for Buddhist monks during times of trouble. The problems began when, out of boredom, the gods started creating new life. Divine power brought divine consequences."

I did not want to think about the sort of unholy abominations that were born out of a deity's boredom and pushed the thought from my mind. "What's the other tablet say?"

"It refers to the door we just passed through. The door opens at the rise of the sun and the rise of the moon. However, once through, it remains shut until the moon rises again." Lopsang looked confused.

"Does it make any mention of the yeti?" Prickles ran up and down my spine at the mention of the creature.

"No, just the two messages about the doors."

"What about on this?" Manchester called from the far end of the room. He was bent over, examining the base of a large carving just like the one we had seen at the top of the Spine. Once again, the yeti was depicted as snarling, with red wax flowing from its eyes and mouth. Beneath it was a large pile of offerings ranging from small pieces of gold to bones.

"Even the gods make offerings?" I asked. That wasn't good.

Lopsang hurried over to where Manchester was standing and ran his hands over the statue's base. "This one is easier to read. 'Remember this, our greatest folly: We have created death and banished it.'"

The pieces began to fall together in my mind. "The yeti isn't a divine being; it was just created by them." It made the idea of killing the creature even less plausible.

"Why would they make such a thing?" James walked over to look at the carving.

Lopsang continued reading. "Death is our sentinel, guarding the gate through the end of time. In exchange, death walks freely on the mountain, through the realm of men, unbidden in the winter snow."

"That's one hell of a bargain," I said with an aggravated sigh. "They get a guard dog, and the only expense is the realm of men. I knew there was a reason I didn't like gods." I looked to the ceiling, fearing that I might get struck by lightning, but no divine intervention came.

"Well, gentlemen, the guard dog is out," stated Manchester, shouldering his pack. "Let's get through the gates before it comes back."

"Hiking trip to a place even gods describe as war torn?" I smiled sarcastically. "I think I'll pass."

"Even if it's your only chance at survival?" Manchester's temper was rising once more.

"I don't believe in absolutes." My tone was cheery, as it often became in times of absolute despair. "By all means, Harvey, take what's left of your team and go through. As far as I'm concerned, our venture is done."

I made a sweeping gesture toward the large stone statues. Secretly, I had every intention of passing through the gate, I just had no desire to be the first one to do so. I cast a wary glance at the diamond on the floor. It was some sort of trap, I knew it.

"All right, Nick, have it your way." Manchester pulled out his gun and leveled it at James's head.

Part III:

Shangri-La

1.

THROUGH THE GATE

"You mean to tell me that you stood at the gates of Shangri-La and did not want to enter?" asked Winston, shocked.

"Two stone gods standing guard on either side of an ancient entrance, I knew better." Nick started on another drink and realized that it tasted like water. He was about to complain about the service when he noticed the liquid in his cup was still dark.

Ah, so I'm at that stage now. Nick found that when he could no longer taste the drink, it was time to ease off. That thought aside, he took another sip.

"So it was cowardice, then?" Winston seemed genuinely upset by this revelation.

"Sure was." Nick had never understood the bad reputation that cowardice had. In most situations, cowardice could be used as a path to survival. "That's why he pulled the gun. He knew just as well as I did that entering the gate was no easy feat. I just wish we'd all had the good sense to turn around."

"Why did you go in, then?"

Nick flashed Winston a winning smile. "Treasure tends to blind people to their senses, myself included."

"You're standing at the entrance to the gates of a godly realm and all you thought about was treasure?"

"It's like you don't know me at all," Nick said, trying to sound wounded. "Truth is, I've never had any desire to meet a god.

Lopsang was the closest I'd ever come to liking one. In general, they're a miserable, superior bunch who are content to sit in their ivory towers and think of creative ways to kill us. Do you know what ended the paradise that was Shangri-La?" Nick's temper was rising slowly at the thought of it.

Winston shook his head, confused about the direction Nick was taking.

"It was boredom. The gods had their perfect world, and it was boring, so they filled it with monsters just to add a little spice." Nick made a gesture like he was sprinkling seasoning over the carpet and grimaced. "Most people are content to pray to something they've never seen before in their life. Well, I've seen them, and rather than getting all starry-eyed, I spit at their feet and ask, 'Why?'"

Nick's heart rate had risen. *Might have gotten a little over-zealous there.* He tended to talk at great length about the follies of divine power when drinking.

Winston crossed himself.

Like that does anything. Nick couldn't help but sneer. "There hasn't been a zombie or a vampire here in ten years. I'd say your safe." The statement was not entirely true; there were vampires just about everywhere, and zombies only needed a crack in the crypt, but Winston didn't know that. *He didn't even say the words to give it power.*

"As much as this diatribe about religion is interesting, I'd prefer to get back to the matter at hand." Winston shifted uncomfortably in his seat, as if such blasphemy was too much for him. "What happened when you passed through the gates?" The words came out slowly, and Nick couldn't tell if Winston was being patronizing or if the drinks had slowed down time. Both were equal possibilities.

Throwing back his arms, Nick stretched over the chair and let out an extended yawn. "I'm not entirely sure you're going to believe this next part."

"I've stayed with you this far, have I not?" Creases at the edges of Winston's eyes let Nick know that his drunkenness was beginning to become an annoyance.

"It gets weirder, trust me. Some secrets of the world are just better left under the rug." He paused, questioning the metaphor, but let it die. "But ... you're paying me quite a bit, and that butler makes a fine drink, so I'll tell you. Let's see, when I left off, I believe Manchester had a gun to James's head ..."

———————— ▼ ————————

"What are you doing, Harvey? We swore not to harm each other's teams," I said, putting my hands out as though I was calming a wild animal. Both the crossbows and the harpoon gun were too far away to be of any use, meaning I had to rely on my utter lack of diplomacy with a madman.

"Until the end of common cause. Moments ago, you said it was at an end—the pact is broken." Manchester's face split into a sly grin. "Look, Nick, I don't want to harm him."

Anger bubbled up from within, but I couldn't let it show. "Oh, fantastic, you should try not pointing a gun at him, then."

"Let me finish. I don't want to harm him, but right now we have only one option, and that is to pass through the gate. You're coming with me one way or another."

"Why? If you're so sure you can make it on your own, why do you need us?"

"Well, I'm certainly not going to be the first one to pass over that seal," Manchester said, gesturing to the glowing diamond in the floor. "My team is looking thin enough as it is."

The five mercenaries that remained huddled in various corners of the cavern, not paying much attention to the standoff. Morale was at an all-time low.

"All right, I'll go through, then, just put the gun down." The seal was almost certainly a trap, but I wasn't going to let James die for my cowardice.

"Nice try, Mr. Ventner, but I can't let you go through alone. What if you set a trap for us on the other side?" Manchester tutted his tongue in a way that never ceased to infuriate me. "No, I think we'll send the boy instead. He ensures that you'll behave while I get my men through the entrance."

Through my fury, I heard Lopsang's quiet voice whisper behind me. "Don't worry, James will be fine." There was no doubt in his voice, only certainty.

Unfortunately, it was not subtle enough to escape Manchester's notice. "What's he saying?" he demanded, shaking the gun as he spoke.

"That I should turn you into red mist," I said, deadpan. "Lucky for you, I'm a man of honor."

"Funny how honor is always the virtue of a man at a disadvantage. By my mark, I'd cut you and the boy down before you'd get even five paces." Manchester's eyes flicked around the room, as if reassessing the odds. "But if you're willing to give it a try ..."

"The second this is over, I'm coming for you."

"Ahh. What would life be without your constant pursuit?"

"Just watch your back," I fumed, white hot anger coming off of me in waves.

"I've got men to do that for me," said Manchester, his smile saccharine. None of the mercenaries got up to join him. "Well, we've no time to waste. It's time you got going." He motioned toward the gates and pushed James out in front of him. "Start walking."

James stumbled forward apprehensively, but then stood up straight, seemingly unafraid. "My threat still stands if I die here, Nick," James warned with a dull resoluteness. "If there's an afterlife"—he looked at the gate—"and I'm pretty sure there is, I'm going to haunt you to the end of your days."

I laughed and stepped to James, patting him on the shoulder. Manchester shook his pistol at us, but I ignored it.

"I'll be right behind you," I said, "and remember: assholes like that"—I pointed to Manchester and made sure to say it loudly—"always get their comeuppance in the end."

The truth was, I put no stake in karma, but I was sure that somewhere down the line, Manchester would be on the wrong end of Old Faithful, and that gave me heart.

"Cute, Nick, but I think we all know that's not the way the world works. Men with power rule, and the rest of society shambles on beneath them."

"Spoken like a true megalomaniac," I said as I stepped away from James.

"Petty squabbles aside, let's get back to the expedition so we can put all this bloody business behind us." Manchester's tone had softened slightly, as if he felt there might be a way of going back to working together after holding James hostage. There were probably a whole cadre of psychologists that would pay to study his ego.

I returned my attention to James, who had begun to walk toward the gate. The sweet smell of flowers betrayed the true danger we were in. The large statues did almost seem welcoming, but I thought I saw past the kind gesture. Certain aspects, like the hollows of the eyes, were angular and meant to inspire fear. No one puts massive stone idols in front of a pair of gates without judgment in mind.

James stopped just short of the diamond seal. "Do I just walk through?" he asked timidly.

I shrugged. "Worth a shot."

James sighed with the enthusiasm of an inmate on death row and stepped toward the diamond. As soon as he passed, green and blue light shot upward to the ceiling, reflecting down like bright fire from a disco ball. The eyes of the statues lit up in blazing color and steamed with heat. From somewhere around us, a deep voice rumbled in a pitch too low to understand.

The stone archway began to glow red, radiating heat and filling the cave with light. As it grew hotter, the stone texture faded away and was replaced by the brilliance of solid gold. In the space between the arches, a tall door materialized and opened slightly. A cool blue mist seeped onto the floor.

"One small step for man …" muttered James.

Without another word, he walked through the door and vanished. A second later, the gold door popped out of existence, and the gold arch cooled slowly, returning to stone. Above, the flowers rustled as a breeze circled the top of the cavern. The sweet smell grew stronger, then everything was still once more.

"Did he make it?" I asked Lopsang.

"We'd know if he didn't."

I chuckled. "Always straightforward. Well, Harvey, you've got the gun. Who's next?"

"That will be me," he said haughtily. "Two of my men will follow." He pointed to the meanest-looking mercenaries on his team. "Then you and the Sherpa."

"All right." I sighed wearily. All of my effort was concentrated on not launching a useless attack against Manchester. I kept thinking, if I could just land one punch, it would all be worth it. But then I remembered James. I had to keep my cool for him. Manchester's time would come.

"We're about to make history here, Nick. Try to look happy about it."

I laughed. "James already made history. He's the first person in Shangri-La, so get off your high horse and get walking before he discovers it all."

Manchester bristled with anger, holstered his pistol, and walked toward the gate. "Someday I'm very much going to enjoy killing you, Nick." He stepped up to the diamond.

"Same to you." I imagined the moment in vivid detail.

With that, Manchester walked past the seal without hesitation. All was fine for a moment, but then Manchester froze and slowly rose as if held up by invisible hands to float a few inches above the floor. His body floated backward to a point just above the center of the diamond.

"What's happening?" he barked, annoyed.

I thought I sensed a tremor of terror in Manchester's voice.

"The gods have judged you unfit to enter," Lopsang said. His voice held no tone of righteousness.

"Unfit to enter?" Manchester let out a panicked laugh.

Before him, the eyes of the statues grew bright red, the previously neutral faces becoming grimaces as deepening red light cast long shadows over them. The stone eyes widened, revealing fire, roiling and searching for escape.

"Don't just stand there, you idiots, do something!" yelled Manchester to the mercenaries. "What do I pay you for?" The muscles in Manchester's neck were tight as he struggled against the unseen force.

The mercenaries looked on and made no move to assist him. Never put your trust in money.

Manchester's movement slackened as he turned his attention to the stone idols. "Just let me through." He was pleading. "This is my dream. I have worked so hard to get here. It's only a few more steps!" Tears welled in the corners of Manchester's eyes as he began to realize the truth: He was never going to set foot in Shangri-La.

"Is there anything we can do to help him?" I asked Lopsang in a whisper. The bastard may have betrayed us, but he didn't deserve that.

"No," replied Lopsang. "They have already chosen his fate. Intervening now would only mean our death."

"This was supposed to be my destiny!" yelled Manchester, his voice cracking.

Red light began to spill forth from the stone eyes, sending gobs of molten liquid spilling down their faces.

Manchester stopped struggling. "This was going to be my great adventure," he whispered.

Hot beams of fire shot forth from the gods' eyes, striking Manchester in the chest and setting him ablaze. The characteristic wide-rimmed black hat he had worn on every journey flew off in the hot wind and fell at the opposite end of the cave. He was only able to scream for a second before the fire consumed him whole.

I could do nothing but stare, my eyes rooted to the burning form of my greatest rival. In that moment, I took no pleasure in the man's demise, and I felt only a hollow, sinking feeling of helplessness. It was all over in a matter of seconds, and there was nothing left but a small gray pile of ash where the Great Manchester had once stood.

Above, the flowers shook and swirled once more as the cave was filled with wind. A vine dropped from the ceiling, and large black flowers bloomed from it, tinged with bright white stripes. As the petals opened, a small wooden tag lowered, attached to a line of string.

On it were the words: Harvey Manchester.

2.

ONE SMALL STEP

I stood rooted to the ground, staring up at the stone idols. I had often fantasized about getting Manchester killed, but now that it had happened, I felt strangely empty.

Manchester's last pleading moments had been painful to watch, and I was at a loss for words. "What just happened?"

"He got his comeuppance," Lopsang said without emotion. "To enter Shangri-La in peace, it's a safe bet one shouldn't bring weapons."

"Ah." I unstrapped the knife and pistol from my sides and let them fall to the floor. Without any sort of weapon, I felt naked, but it was better than burning to death. "What about you lot?" I turned to the mercenaries examining Manchester's smoldering hat in the corner of the cave. They hadn't said much, and I wasn't even sure they spoke English, but I harbored no ill will about their previous allegiances.

The group muttered amongst themselves for a moment. "We'll stay here, thanks," replied a tall, lean man with a sun-washed face. His voice was soft and intelligent, which surprised me. "I've got one too many sins on my conscience to pass the judgment of a god for some treasure." The mercenary began unfolding a large bipod and then placed his machine gun on it.

"What's that for?" I asked, knowing full well the answer.

"Well, we're not getting down the mountain without him."

The man pointed to Lopsang. "We'll wait here for you, hold off the beast, and then we can all head down together."

Despite his gentle voice, the man seemed perfectly at home behind a turret, unfazed by the fact that his leader had just been burned alive in front of him.

I sighed. "All right, then." I was sure the mercenaries would be dead by the time we returned. "After you, Lopsang."

"Uh," Lopsang said uncomfortably. "There's one thing I forgot to mention."

"No," I said, with more sadness than anger.

"I can't go through. As a half-breed, the gods would see right through me and strip me of what they feel to be unholy."

"Leave it to the gods." My hatred of the divine continued to grow.

"They view the times that gods come to Earth as mistakes. I am not going to die today, even if it means not seeing what lies beyond the gates."

"The gods are a bunch of bastards." I winced defensively when I said it, but the stone statues looked almost smug in the light, as if saying: "We know."

"So you're going to chuck it in with this lot, then?" I gestured to the mercenaries, who looked as though they were preparing for a full-scale invasion. How did they even fit that many weapons in their packs?

"Yes, we'll wait for the gate to open and give the creature hell until you get back. Just be sure to make it a quick visit." Lopsang smiled half-heartedly. "Something tells me once that gate opens, we're not going to last long."

"You'll make a monster hunter yet." We laughed before lapsing into an awkward silence. "Use the last of the potion we have left. Maybe this time you'll get lucky." It was a long shot, but better than nothing.

"You're a good man, Dr. Ventner, despite how hard you try to be otherwise." Lopsang patted him on the shoulder. "Now go. James is waiting on the other side, and he won't be safe for long."

With a final smile, Lopsang turned toward the mercenaries to help with their preparations.

I couldn't say anything. A demigod had just said I was a good man. I was flabbergasted. Without another word, I started walking toward the gates, and with hesitation, stepped past the diamond seal. A cold sensation started at the top of my skull, ran down my spine, and filled my body as if I had been dunked in ice water.

Oh shit, I'm going to die, I thought, and I waited for my limbs to freeze in the vice grips of the stone gods.

My limbs remained mercifully unfrozen, and the diamond once again glowed blue and green, showering the chamber with tiny motes of light. The gate appeared before me, the gold door opening slightly. I stepped into it, passing through the blue mist. The sounds of the cavern disappeared immediately, replaced by a heavy silence. There was nothing but the cool sensation of water droplets clinging to my skin. The air smelled crisp, and as I walked forward, the sound of a roaring waterfall cut through the air.

I walked blindly until, in an instant, the mist was gone. However, the clarity that followed was equally blinding. I closed my eyes, allowing them to adjust. As I reopened them cautiously, my vision cleared and the landscape of Shangri-La materialized before me.

I was once more in a cave, but this time a beautiful blue waterfall covered the entrance. Beyond it, verdant hills stretched past the horizon, giving rise to brightly colored flowers and plants. The vivid nature of it all almost gave me a headache. I didn't realize it at the time, but the world was in an entirely new spectrum of color. Strange chirping lizards with red and green stripes running down their backs scuttled up the damp stone wall behind me, making their way up to the lush vegetation growing above.

"It's real," I murmured, unable to contain the shock. The waterfall subtly began to change colors from royal blue to a deep purple. I watched the changing color, unable to comprehend it, until the sound of military boots on stone caught my attention. Just on the edge of the waterfall was a small stone path leading out of the cave and to the greenery beyond. At the end stood James, flanked on either side by impossibly tall men dressed in flowing robes adorned with strange bones and metals.

"On your knees, intruder," one of them ordered, pointing at me with his spear.

"I thought this was supposed to be a peaceful—"

Something heavy thudded against the back of my head, and my vision went black.

Waking moments were like flashbulbs in a world that had otherwise gone fuzzy. Through my half-woken state, I was vaguely aware that I was being carried over the back of a tall man like a sack of grain. The scenery that bobbed past my lopsided viewpoint was difficult to make sense of. The horizon, if there was one, was a wash of blooming colors that occasionally shifted to match the ground below.

Thoroughly confused, much like I imagined Alice was in Wonderland, I tried to search for some point of context in the ever-shifting world, and the best indicator turned out to be the road we were walking on. Rather than the constantly changing sky, the road stayed the same, sparkling in the odd twilight. The material was smooth and looked almost like it would be soft to the touch. Gold, I thought dimly. The entire road was made of solid gold. Even through my massive headache, I began to calculate how much I could get if I sold it brick by brick.

After this became boring, which didn't take long, I looked around for James again and found him being prodded along by another tall man with a spear. He was sporting a wicked black eye. Note to self: don't mouth off to the gods. I could only assume James had picked another poor battle to fight, but I admired the fact that he had any fight left at all.

Through teeth stained with blood, James gave me a half-hearted grin. "We made it," he mouthed, receiving a sharp rap with the flat end of the guard's spear for doing so.

The guard looked at me. "This one is awake. Lift him." His voice was deep and resonating, as if being played through a bass drum.

The world turned around me as I was dropped hard onto my feet, nearly falling over.

"I suppose being carried the whole way would have been too much to ask?" I favored the guard with a smile, who returned the expression and slapped me on the head with the flat end of his spear. A non-existent chorus of bells rang loudly through my head, causing pain to shoot through my skull and down the rest of my body.

The man who had been carrying me walked into view, looked me up and down. He had eyes that yellowed around the edges and came to bright points in the center that resembled molten gold. Metal rods had been twisted and inserted beneath his skin and poked out painfully. I supposed they were there for intimidation—it was working.

In the calm breeze, the man's robes billowed, completing the godly appearance. "This time, you will walk or you will not wake up. Is that understood?"

When I did not respond immediately, the man pulled a dagger from his belt, held it to my throat, and spoke louder. "Do you understand?"

Jesus, gods were touchy. "Yes, I understand."

Even with the knife pressed to my throat, I had to restrain the urge to rebut. Being held prisoner by a god was an odd feeling, and I was still unable to reconcile my dislike for the divine. It took all of my willpower not to question the violent nature of a land that was supposed to be akin to the Garden of Eden. However, climbing a mountain only to get killed just before we got to the treasure felt anti-climactic, and so I kept my mouth shut.

Slowly, the god removed the knife from my throat and sheathed it. From off in the distance, we heard the tortured roar of a strange, and no doubt dangerous, creature. Even the gods that held us bristled, muttering amongst themselves in another language. Soon they were silent and moving along the road once more.

If it frightened a god, I wanted no part in it. I distracted myself by examining our captors and listening to the soft clapping of my boots on the gold pavement beneath us. The gods were taller than any man I had ever seen. They wore bright robes that shifted with the surrounding landscape. Two of them carried long spears with fat heads that curved to a small point, like a scorpion's stinger. One had a bow strapped to his back and a quiver of thin arrows. The others carried nothing but daggers, like the one that had been held to my throat.

The environment around us continued in a constant state of flux, changing colors and shapes at random. I found that if I looked to the hills and back at the guards, their robes would have slightly changed tint. The trees around us weren't predisposed to stay in any given shape, and I couldn't be positive, but I thought some of the rocks were following us. There was a good chance we were still in the mountain lodge and drank the wrong tea, I thought.

The hillside rose around us, and we descended into a deep valley. The cries of odd creatures I could not see echoed off the walls. I saw a strange, spindly shadow flapping lazily through the air in the distance, but it paid us no attention and continued on. If the guards were bothered by it, they said nothing.

After a while, the valley stopped abruptly at a steep rock face, and I had an eerie feeling that I had been there before. I looked around and noticed that while everything looked different, the valley had the same fundamental shape as where we had been captured by the cultists. Déjà vu swept over me in waves. It was all the same, only the guns had been swapped for spears.

Sure enough, as we got closer, I saw a massive temple carved into the cliff face at the end of the valley. I looked over to James, who shared my sentiment of stunned confusion. Luckily for us, this entrance was not adorned with depictions of death and dismemberment, but life and growth. As we approached the end of the valley, we began to see jewels wrought into the very rocks around us, glowing brightly from the many colors of the sky.

"Not a bad place you have here," I said casually to one of the guards.

The guard looked at me, and before I could even wince, he slashed shallowly across my back with his spear. "No talking."

Fire lit up from anywhere the spear touched. A trickle of warm blood oozed from the long cut into my parka. Good to know the gods had some self-control and a firm grasp on two-word sentences. What if they had telepathy? What if they are listening right now? I started thinking the lyrics to Come Sail Away as loud as I could. I'd never dealt with mind control, but it was worth a try.

One of the guards next to me winced, and I felt a moment of fear before a calming voice spoke. "They can't hear your thoughts."

A woman stepped out from a recessed door hidden between

two boulders. She was tall, just like the men, and carried the same lean muscle tone. Her long robe was a pale green, blending with the emeralds in the boulders behind her. "But I can. Whatever it is you're thinking, please stop. It's giving me a headache."

The gods didn't like Styx. Now there was a review. "Sorry," I said, regretting that I had not gotten to finish the chorus. The woman carried no weapons, and I had a feeling there was a reason for it.

"I don't carry weapons because I don't need to," she said in the same calming voice. "If you so much as made a move toward me, I'd disassemble you with my mind and leave you as no more than a sentient puddle on the road."

My eyes widened.

"Kidding," she said through a laugh. "Well, I think they've behaved themselves well enough." The woman motioned to the guards, who filed away into unseen doorways. She returned her attention to James and I. "Come. You've traveled a long way, and there is much to discuss."

With a wave of her hand, a large door materialized in the bejeweled rock wall before us and opened to reveal a dark tunnel.

James looked hesitant to step in.

"Don't worry, boy." The woman's tone was almost sweet. "If we were going to execute you, I would have had them do it far away from the palace. I don't like blood on my floors." She stepped forward into the tunnel and motioned for us to follow.

I turned to James, shrugged, and then stepped into the darkness.

3.

DOWN THE RABBIT HOLE

As we entered the gloom of the tunnel, the rocks closed shut behind us, and we were enveloped in complete darkness. I heard the woman's footsteps clacking forward as though she didn't need light to find her way. Almost as an afterthought, she snapped her fingers, and small paper lanterns lit up all around us. Some were attached to the tunnel walls, which seemed to widen with every step, while others simply floated, bobbing up and down as if on an invisible string.

We walked on, dumbfounded, as the sides of what had initially appeared to be a narrow tunnel soon widened to where we could no longer see them. Above, the ceiling grew so high that soon there was nothing but the twinkling of thousands, maybe millions, of paper lanterns. They were all manner of colors, reminding me of staring up at the stars on an especially clear night. Even my inner desire to be caustic and make sarcastic remarks was stayed by the beauty.

James did not seem as mesmerized. He kept his eyes on the floor, no doubt considering the multitude of ways we could die at the hands of an unfriendly deity. Despite the goddess's charming nature, good fortune never lasted for long. At least, it didn't when he was with me.

"Don't look so glum," I said, giving James a pat on the shoulder. "She said they weren't going to kill us."

James remained silent, his eyes glazed over.

The goddess laughed. "Your friend is right. Try to relax." She lifted her hand to the lanterns above us. "Take in the view. Not many people get to see the inside of this palace and live to tell the tale." She considered it for a moment, and then with a mischievous look I could not help but admire, said, "Actually, you'd be the first."

"He felt ... uncomfortable." The thought of what the gods might do to a demigod made me wince.

"Traveling with a demigod?" asked the goddess slyly.

James jumped.

"Whoa, demigod?" I said nonchalantly. "Who said demigod?" I laughed uneasily. I had to keep my thoughts blank and not think about Lopsang. She'd probably kill us if she found out. Shit!

The goddess stopped and turned to face me. "While the other gods might tout the benefits of pure bloodlines, I can assure you that I am not so narrow-minded. Now, if you could begin by trusting the person who saved your skins from feeding time at the resurrection pit ...."

I flushed with color. It was only then that I realized I was still wearing my outer parka, and the air of the tunnel had become uncomfortably warm. It had been hours since we'd had water, and the walk wasn't helping.

"My apologies," I said, and felt a sudden wave of dizziness overtake me. That could not be good. "We meant no offense." I steadied myself and took a few deep breaths.

"Good. Now let's continue on. We're almost there." She didn't have to read James's mind to see that he would be compliant.

As we walked through the ever-growing darkness, the effort required caused my vision to swim. The paper lanterns blurred and swirled. Before I knew it, the darkness was closing in, and I fell forward. I rolled onto my back and looked up at the multicolored lights swirling into the darkness. I suppose it wasn't the worst way to die. At least I wasn't burning at the feet of judgmental stone gods. My vision narrowed to a pinpoint until all I could see was one lantern, floating far above me.

I heard muted voices speaking about something, but they were far too faint to make out. A cool hand touched my forehead, and I had never felt anything so pleasant in the entire world. From the moment of contact, relief swept down my body, invigorating my limbs and filling me with life. My thirst was quenched, and the pinpoint widened, revealing the tunnel in vivid detail.

James helped me to a sitting position and removed my outer coat.

"Are you all right?" asked James, removing his own coat so that he, too, wouldn't pass out.

"Never better," I said. It was not in my nature to be soothed by apprentices, but I couldn't help but feel thankful James was there. "Thanks." I let James help me back to a standing position. "What was that?" I made a gesture to the goddess's hands.

"One of the many powers that come with being divine." She smiled. "Doesn't help much for me, but for a mortal it must feel quite nice."

"Indeed." I wondered what the woman was the goddess of.

She favored me with a wink, and we continued walking. I found my thoughts drifting back to Lopsang and the mercenaries. I knew the woman would hear them, but I had given up on trying to shut her out. If she was listening, she said nothing.

I wondered how long we had until sunset. I pictured Lopsang setting up with the mercenaries, pointing their guns at the door and trying futilely to destroy the creature once more. I told myself we'd get back in time. I wasn't sure if it was true, but the thought was reassuring.

In the distance, more lights appeared. As we approached, they expanded to reveal a structure made of latticed wood, with paper walls bearing intricate drawings. The edges had been trimmed with flaking gold, making the building look as though it had just melted into existence. Bridges and paths ran down from the entrance like an Escher painting, all circling a bright rainbow pool that occasionally shot shafts of light into the surrounding darkness.

Our path led directly to a golden bridge that crossed a chasm of empty, dark air. As we walked over it, I heard the hollow whistling that came with a valley of unfathomable depth. After crossing, we stepped onto a stone path leading around the pond. The sound of monkeys and birds hiding in lush green foliage echoed through the still air, and the far side of the building was saturated in dense greenery. In the distance, I could see what might have been other floating structures, but they were too far away to clearly distinguish.

The fresh smell of the tunnel left us and was replaced with the succulent aroma of fruits and tropical flowers. Every inch of the garden and the structure it surrounded exuded calm. The goddess led us through a maze of terraced walkways, leading us all over the gardens and below. I felt the urge to explore, but above us, a large golden door hung open, and I knew we were meant to enter.

Together, the three of us walked up stone steps, through the door, and into a room sparsely furnished with dark wood. It was a stark comparison to the bright colors and opulence outside. In one corner, a tea kettle stood with a wisp of steam coming from its stem, and around it three plush cushions had been arranged.

The goddess took the cushion closest to the kettle, sat, and turned to face us. "So, a drunk, an apprentice, and a demigod hunting one of the most dangerous creatures ever created. It sounds like we have a lot to talk about."

"Well, we don't want to be rude," I said to James. I sat down on one of the cushions opposite the goddess and felt immediate relief coursing through my limbs. James, still silent, also sat, and I heard a relaxing sigh from him, even though he tried his best to conceal it.

The goddess poured steaming tea into a set of mugs and handed them to me and James. I took mine graciously and smelled the pungent aroma from within. Tea of the gods had to be good. I wondered if there was any chance we might sample their liquor as well.

James sipped his tea politely, but I saw an air of unease below the surface. Finally, he cracked.

"Who are you?" he blurted, his face reddening immediately after asking.

"Come on, James, don't be rude," I said, taking another sip from my tea. The truth was, I wanted to know the answer as well, but I hadn't the courage to ask.

"That's quite all right," said the goddess. "I am Siana, goddess of mischief, interrogation, and gardening."

I tried and failed to stifle a laugh.

Siana raised an eyebrow at me. "Something wrong with your tea?" Her voice had some bite to it this time.

"No." I tried to regain my composure. "Three things, though … That's quite a lot for a god, isn't it?"

"Monster hunter, drunk, and political science dropout. That's a lot of things for a mortal, isn't it? And I prefer goddess."

"I'd ask how you knew all that, but the first two are easy, and I'm going to chalk the last one up to divine power." I tried to hide my surprise. I couln't tell if she had read my mind, or if I was just that easy to figure out. "Why be the god–er, god*dess*–of those three things?"

On one hand, I felt bad for offending the deity who had saved our lives, but on the other, I felt an unrelenting drive to question the divine.

"The same way mortals choose hobbies, I suppose." She waved her hand as if it were a simple manner, and one that was quite boring. "But enough about me. I didn't bring you here to talk about myself." The light air dropped from her tone. "How is it that you were able to find Shangri-La?"

"*That* is a long story." I wasn't sure if it really was, but after having just lived through it, I wasn't inclined to recount it. Somewhere around seeing the third man cut in half, I had decided to lock those memories far away, where they couldn't be revisited. It was the best trick I had for ignoring some of the darker parts of my life.

"I've got time," Siana mused.

"Our friends don't," cut in James. "Once sunset rolls around, the yeti—"

The lights flickered, and an evil wind blew through the room. I swore I heard the roar of the creature, but I wasn't sure if it was just my imagination.

"Kindly don't say its name," Siana said. James may have momentarily ruffled her, but she quickly regained her composure.

"Right," James said. "But our friends—"

"Will be fine. Time does not move in the same way in Shangri-La. When you return—and you will if you satisfy my curiosity—it will be as if you never left."

"How do you suppose—"

This time it was me who cut him off. "Just chalk it up to divine intervention, James, and relax. If a god—"

"Goddess," corrected Siana.

"Right, goddess," I said, peeved. "If she says they'll be fine, then they'll be fine." I had never known a divine being to keep their word, but we didn't have much of a choice other than to trust her.

"For once, your friend is the voice of reason. Now, if you can, tell me how two"—she paused, trying to find the right word—"amateur hunters were able to find Shangri-La in less than a week."

I hadn't thought much about it, but hearing it out loud, the prospect was insane.

"I suppose you could call it a classic case of failing upward," I said, unsure of where to start. In the end, I told her every detail of our journey, down to the fight at The Black Market. There were no requisite "oohs" or "ahhs" on Siana's part, only quiet listening. When I came to the parts about the yeti mercilessly disemboweling Manchester's team, a slight grimace flickered across her face, but she quickly hid it. Finally, I told her of how Manchester was unable to pass through the gate and was burned alive.

When I had finished, she let out a long sigh. "That's quite the story. You've had a long journey in a short amount of time."

That summed it up about perfectly. "Yes, we have." Just recounting the events exhausted me. "Now that I've told you our tale, I've got some questions." With the tea warming my body, and my brain slowly working its way back to full capacity, I was feeling bold. It was the ultimate challenge for an atheist: question the gods even as they are staring you right in the face.

"I suppose you've earned that," conceded Siana, as if the proposition of answering a mortal's questions was tiring.

"Who made the yeti and why?" It was blunt, but really the only question worth asking. From the moment I'd learned such a beast was the power of divine creation, I only wanted to know why. Thoughts of treasure and fame were lost. A part of me knew there was no way we were going to get very much of a reward down the mountain with such a small team. The only way to make the journey less than a total loss was to get the truth from a god.

Siana's eyes looked lost, as if she were thinking about somewhere very far away. Their color shifted from molten gold to a deep green, growing darker toward the center.

"That was back when there were no rules, and we were free to make what we wanted, when we wanted."

"And that's what led this place into ruin, right?" I remembered the story Lopsang told me.

"Yes …" She paused for a long silence. "Unfettered creation is one of the most dangerous concepts in this universe. With it, our heart's delight can just as easily become another's terror." Her face took on a distant, faraway look. It was the look of someone who had done terrible things.

"Who made the creature?" I knew the answer as soon as I asked.

Siana looked up and stared straight into my eyes. "I did, and I have been living with that mistake for more lifetimes than you can imagine." Her tone was cold, like one scolding a child, but beneath it I could hear a deep remorse. "It is not the worst of our creatures, and in fact, it might have even lived peacefully in our world …"

This time, it was James who spoke up. "But it *didn't* stay in your world."

"No, it didn't."

"So what? Did it escape?" James had also crossed the threshold of politeness, and I did nothing to chastise him for it.

"No, the worst of the gods thought it could be best used to

protect us and keep the realm of mortals in check. The beast I created was watchful. And intelligent. But somewhere along the way, that purpose was changed. All it takes is one person with ill will to turn something of wonder into a weapon, and that's exactly what happened. The creature was released into your world by a militant group of gods who believed the mortals were getting too close to discovering Shangri-La. It was meant to ensure that the gates would never be found."

Silence fell over the room, and I could feel Siana's sorrow. I understood her pain, but it wasn't enough.

"If you gave it life, then you have to know how to take it away." I wasn't sure this was true, but it felt like the creator had to have some power. "This creature is roaming the slopes and killing innocent people. It's your responsibility."

Siana looked me in the eyes again. "I know what my responsibilities are."

"Then why haven't you gone to stop it?" My voice had risen to nearly a shout. "You created this creature that is terrorizing our world, and you have to stop it."

"It's not that simple, Mr. Ventner."

"You're a goddess." I sighed with exasperation. "It is exactly that simple!"

"The creature was meant to protect our people and wouldn't have done a very good job if it was easy to kill."

"It's done a fine job of that." I stood and gestured to myself and James. "Your 'protector' may have slaughtered over half our team, but we're still here."

"Humans never understand."

"*Gods* never understand. As far as you're concerned, mortals are just a science project. Real people are dying just beyond that door, and you're doing nothing about it but sitting here in your

castle, drinking tea." I finished this last point with particular vitriol, then fell back onto my cushion.

"It's quite good tea," Siana murmured with a trace of hurt and
an undercurrent of sarcasm.

"It *is* damned good tea," I admitted, holding out my cup for
more.

Siana picked up the pot and filled my cup.

"That's it?" James turned to me. "All that anger, and you're
going to let it go for tea?"

I savored the look of frustration on James's face, as well as the
deep calm from the tea. "I think I've made my point, don't you?"

"But nothing's changed!"

In every argument, there comes a point when shouting
doesn't serve any purpose other than to damage hearing. There
was a time and a place for anger, and sometimes it worked, but it
was important to know when to let it go.

"Hasn't it?" This time, I turned to Siana.

The goddess was in deep thought and looked pained. Together, the three of us sat in silence as she rubbed her temples and
thought the matter over. Once, James tried to speak, but I silenced
him with a kick. "Shut up and drink your tea," I mouthed. James
may have been angry, but he listened.

Eventually Siana broke the silence. "We put the gate in one
of the most inhospitable places on Earth. How many hints do
mortals need not to come here?"

I laughed. "Apparently a few more."

Siana looked at James. "I'm trying to help you. No weapon of
your mortal plane can harm my creature. The only way to get rid
of it is to banish it."

"Banish it where?" asked James. "Some other realm where it
can wreak havoc?"

"No." Frustration was clear in her voice. "There is a void in the space between worlds where it can be held. It can stay there with no pain, in a dream-like state, but there's a catch."

"There always is," I muttered.

"A human has to be the one to do it."

4.

UNDERSTANDING THE VOID

"A human's voice carries a different weight than that of a god. As we are the ones who created the creature, we cannot subsequently banish it on a whim." Siana was explaining the concept as if it were nothing more than basic arithmetic. "Think of it as a system of checks and balances."

Because that tends to work well, I thought bitterly.

"I heard that," she said.

I was starting to get peeved about having my every thought read by the goddess. There was only one solution for that; I began thinking of Come Sail Away once more. Truth be told, I didn't like the song very much, but when it was in my head, it became hard to think of much else.

Siana's face grew momentarily pained, but she continued unabated. "For the most part, it does actually work well. The rule makes everyone think very hard about what they're creating before they do it. It's only in select cases—"

"You mean where someone builds an unstoppable killing machine and sets it loose on an innocent realm?" James said, doing nothing to disguise his contempt. Despite the danger and the strange situation, he seemed to be enjoying the process of questioning a goddess.

A fire had built behind his eyes, and I took a liking to it. It's difficult to be a hunter without questioning all that is holy. Good on him. When it came to confronting the omnipotent, shouting "Why?" at an unresponsive sky could be cathartic, but it got nothing done. Questioning the divine in person, while more difficult, was satisfying, and it produced results.

All the same, I knew we were at Siana's mercy, and I didn't want to piss her off too much. "I think we all understand at this point that the yeti was a mistake. No need to throw any more salt on that wound."

James didn't seem happy about it, but eventually he nodded. In the moment, he had forgotten that he was at the goddess's mercy, and upon remembering, managed to look humbled.

"You're probably right," he admitted. "My mistake."

If Siana was peeved, she did not show it. "To do this task, a great deal of danger is involved."

"I don't think we've got a lot of options." I had tried to think of a way out that didn't involve us coming face-to-face with the beast again, but I couldn't. "The creature is blocking our exit, and I don't like our odds of descending the mountain with that thing on our tail."

"I could just take you to the portal that leads to the bottom," Siana remarked flippantly.

I perked up momentarily.

James noticed and gave me a not-so-gentle jab with his elbow. "Lopsang is in the cave, remember?"

For a moment, I'd forgotten. The thought of a warm drink and leaving the mountain behind forever sounded like heaven. I sighed heavily. "He's right. Our friend would still be trapped up here. We can't leave him behind."

"And the whole point of this godforsaken journey—" James stopped, remembering their company. "No offense."

"None taken," said Siana.

"The point was to get rid of the beast once and for all."

I stopped myself from thinking about treasure before Siana could pick up on it. "Yes, of course. We can't leave the mountain if the beast is still roaming the slopes." I couldn't even convince myself. "We have a reputation to uphold," I added. At least that part was true.

Siana cocked an eyebrow at me. "Are you sure? The chances of you surviving are slim." There was no jab in the way she said it, only the same matter-of-fact tone that Lopsang often used.

I knew she was only stating the facts; they were the facts we had always known, albeit ignored, when we embarked on our journey.

"We just climbed one of the world's highest mountains, watched our team get dismembered by a mythical beast no one thought actually existed, and I'm pretty sure had an encounter with the restless dead. We know the dangers. Just tell us how to get rid of it."

"If you are set on it, I will not stop you." Siana stood from her cushion and smoothed her robes. "Follow me."

She walked over to the farthest wall of the room and touched a palm to the surface. The delicate paneling split down the middle, revealing a sliding door. She stepped through, and we followed without question.

The room we entered was exactly like the one we'd just left. Again, there was minimal decoration, only this time the walls were painted dark blue. When the sliding door shut behind us, tiny motes of light illuminated in the darkness. It looked like a star field, giving the impression that the room stretched much farther than it actually did. In the center of the room, the floor opened, and a pedestal rose out. On top of it was a heavy-looking leather-bound book.

At the sight of it, I felt a pang for my master's journal sitting on the other side of the gates. While the man had been a drunk and not much help, the book still held immense value to me. I could only hope Lopsang would stop those mercenaries, should they get any bright ideas about literacy and burn it.

Siana walked toward the pedestal, and as we followed, the room grew noticeably cooler. It was nothing compared to the chill of the mountain, but still enough to make my skin prickle.

"*This* is one of the most precious books our civilization has ever created. It is the Book of All." Siana paused, as if trying to let the title sink in.

"Creative title," I said, trying not to laugh and failing miserably. James coughed in an attempt to hide his own laughter.

"This is a sacred book," snapped Siana.

"Sure. I mean, look at it." The book was leather bound, embossed with what appeared to be flowing liquid gold. On the front were intricate scenes that changed between depictions of peace and war at a whim. It might have depicted the history of Shangri-La, but with a title like the Book of All, I really couldn't be sure. "Certainly the decoration implies a degree of ceremony, it's just … a bit confusing, you know?"

"It is called the Book of All because it is a book containing all things."

"Must have taken forever to write," I muttered.

"The book is never complete. We are constantly adding more to it. Now, if you are done questioning the minute details of the tome that is likely going to save your life …"

"Yes, sorry." I tried my best to take on a humbler tone. "Sometimes I get away from myself." It was true. Life or death situations didn't always provoke my most helpful side.

Siana motioned for me to come closer.

I obliged and watched as the cover shifted into a scene depicting a burning castle, which then became a roaring ocean. The constant change was beginning to give me a headache.

"You may very well be the only mortal to read this book." There was something about her voice that sounded almost condescending. "But I suppose there's a first time for everything. Why don't you take a look?"

With some hesitance, and a touch of anger about the way Siana phrased the word "mortal," I stepped up to the pedestal and ran my hand over the cover. There was a static charge in the air as I made contact, as if great power was surrounding it. The hairs on my arms stood on end as the gold on the cover began to glow. It felt heavy, as if each page was made of dense stone. With some difficulty, I opened the book to the first page.

"Each passage carries the weight of its contents," said Siana, noticing my struggle. "If I hadn't imbued you with power just now, you wouldn't have been able to open it."

"It's heavier than *this*?" I asked.

"Each word contains the weight of the emotion that was felt by the writer, so yes, it's heavier than that. The weight gives the book meaning and energy beyond what can be contained within the simple written word."

I stared down at what appeared to be a series of dots and squiggly lines scrawled across the page. "Great, a book that's too heavy to lift, in a language I can't read. Some plan this is."

"If you will listen for a minute without opening your mouth, I can teach you how to read it." Her words came out with a smile, but I saw frustration in her expression.

I was about to protest getting a school lesson, but Siana held up a hand, silencing me.

"The sight needed to read this language comes with a

price. To read it, you must understand the context in which it was written."

"What does that mean?" It didn't sound that bad, but the tone of Siana's voice told me whatever it was would be unpleasant. Just once, I wanted the solution to the problem to be drinking. Not every time, just once.

"In a way, you're in luck." Siana reached down to the side of the pedestal and opened an inlaid cabinet. From it, she produced a shallow wooden basin and a jug of liquid. With a flick of her wrist, a set of pillows appeared on the floor. "This *is* going to involve drinking."

"Could you please stop doing that?" It was maddening not to have a single thought to himself. Imagine the damage that would have done in grade school.

"I'm sorry, if I had a choice, I would. Your thoughts aren't all that interesting anyway. Booze, fortune, and more booze. Very repetitive, don't you think?"

I reddened with both shame and anger. "Can we move on?"

"These pages are not for the faint of heart. If you think you can handle it, have a seat." The sarcastic charm was still there, but a darkness flowed beneath it.

"I've seen quite a bit," I said, staving off bitter flashes of corpses returning to life, monsters beyond imagine, and a bloody trailhead far away. "What's one more unpleasant memory to add to the pile?"

I wasn't sure what was in the jug, but I was willing to chance it if there was any possibility it was alcoholic.

Siana set the basin down between the cushions and poured clear liquid from the jug. "Sorry to disappoint."

"Figures."

Siana smiled, reached behind her back, and pulled out a long blade.

I tensed. "What are you doing?"

Siana looked me in the eye. "Relax, it's for me." With a smooth motion, she drew the knife across her palm, spilling a small trickle of blood into the basin. The water swirled, clouding to a muddy red. "Now, here's the first unpleasant bit: You're going to have to drink that."

"You're joking."

"I wish I was."

"Blood-borne diseases of the gods it is, then. This is one hell of a toast." I grimaced. "You sure there's no liquor cabinet around here to take the edge off?"

"We can't dilute it any further. You'd be amazed what can be accomplished with a clear head. Now, drink."

5.

THE WORDS' INTENT

I looked down at the pale muddy liquid swirling in the bowl before me. My only thought was "no way in hell." Then, ignoring the sentiment, I tipped the bowl backward and swallowed the liquid in two quick gulps. Thankfully, it was mostly tasteless.

"For blood of the gods, it sure is bland." I coughed, stifling what was sure to be an unpleasant belch.

James and Siana stared at me, motionless.

"Oh, come on, don't tell me this was some sort of sick prank," I stammered nervously. My voice reverberated through the air in a hollow way, echoing back as if it had traveled some distance. Oh shit, I thought, trying to move my hands and finding that they were rooted to the ground.

James wore a blank expression, as if he were staring straight through me. His pupils had grown to the size of dinner plates and were continuing to widen.

"What did we say about drugs on the job?" I said, but the chastisement fell flat. Something was very wrong.

James's pupils continued to widen until they filled the edges of his eyes with darkness. I almost thought it was blood, but the color was pitch black. It began to spill forth from his eyes, dripping down his chest like some macabre candle wax, making its way to the floor.

"*What the hell did you have me drink?*" I yelled, turning to

Siana. I recoiled in horror, as black liquid poured from her as well. As it touched the floor, it formed a pitch-black layer. It was like staring into the dark recesses of space. I tried to back away from it, but the liquid closed in on all sides. Just as it was about to touch my feet, the entire room went dark.

The darkness that enveloped me was so complete that I wondered if I was still alive. There was no sound, no sight, and as far as I could tell, nothing to touch. It was the perfect void. Classic deity move, tricking me into drinking poison. James was probably getting gutted. Poor bastard. I never should have trusted her.

Then the world sprang into being so intensely that it was like being struck by lightning. Where there had been blackness a moment earlier, there came shimmering light in the form of a vibrant garden. Wild, exotic birds with four wings apiece fluttered gently on a sweet-smelling breeze not unlike what I had experienced at the gates. It was paradise; I'd made it to heaven! I was wrong, of course.

The laughter of children broke this illusion. Two young girls ran past, trying to catch one of the four-winged birds. The sky above shifted and swirled. I was still in Shangri-La. The thought of paradise was an immense relief. I'd always feared what came in the moments after death, mostly because of an ill-advised wager with a minor demon, but also because the afterlife had plenty of potential to be unpleasant for those who fought its denizens.

Brushing these thoughts aside, I looked around and turned to see Siana sitting right next to me on a colorful blanket that changed to match the vivid sky. In her lap was a white crystal ball with swirling light contained within. Siana was so transfixed by it that she didn't seem to notice the beauty around her. Her eyes flickered with the movement of the light, and she seemed distant.

"What the hell was in that drink you gave me?" I demanded.

As before, Siana did not hear me, and instead continued gazing into the crystal ball.

"Siana, come. Play with your children," called a man striding into the garden.

Not wanting Siana to be interrupted, I rose to greet him myself. "Hi, I'm sorry, I don't believe we've met." I stepped to shake the man's hand and felt an odd sensation as he passed right through me. Realization dawned on me. I was just along for the ride. Not wanting to have anyone pass through me again, I stepped off to the side to watch.

The man was solid muscle and stood a full foot taller than me. He looked different compared to the other guards. His black hair flowed long behind him, catching the summer breeze and blowing wildly.

"Siana?" he said.

Siana muttered something into the ball, and a look of pain flashed across the man's face.

"Can you not stop for a moment to look at the creation you have already wrought?" he pleaded, subtle anger rising in his voice. Two children approached, and I saw Siana's face clearly in them. "Whatever it is, I hope it's worth it." The man turned and put a hand on each of his girls' shoulders. "She's busy right now. We'll come back later."

If Siana had heard or seen them, she showed no sign. Instead, she continued to mutter at the crystal ball. I moved in to get a closer look and saw that within the light, intricate shapes were beginning to form. The bands of brightness closed into a tight sphere and darkened. A brow began to form, and I felt a flash of recognition. White fur sprouted around it, and I heard the distant sound of a piercing roar. The light quickly shifted, obscuring the formed pieces from view, but it was unmistakable.

The garden slowly dimmed until everything was black once more. In place of the garden, a small room formed, with a window looking out on a cloudless night sky. In the corner, barely lit by the flickering of the crystal ball, was Siana. She sat on the wooden floor, uttering incantations and instructions to the writhing power at her fingertips without rest.

If seeing the first form of the yeti had made me uneasy, this new scene made matters worse. I could not place why, but there was something intensely wrong. The shafts of moonlight coming through the window felt like daggers waiting to impale unsuspecting victims, and there was a painful silence punctuated by sharp mutterings from Siana. The very air itself was waiting on what she was going to create.

The weight of it all made me nervous, and it suddenly felt as if I was being stabbed in the gut. The scene blurred and swirled until I was sitting midair, looking down on a small town. A white light came from a window below, and I guessed that's where Siana was. I checked my stomach for the source of pain but found nothing.

I looked down at the world, trying to understand just what had gone so wrong. The village didn't look that different from somewhere in the real world. The houses were simple—timber frames, shingle roofs. The scene was quaint, almost peaceful. And yet why did it feel so wrong? I watched, then I understood.

Tiny lights moved throughout the village, silent and sparking fire as they went. For a while, only small embers burned, bright orange light in the otherwise silent darkness. It wasn't until the first ember matured into a real flame that the screaming started. I watched as the flame licked its way up the side of a wooden house and engulfed it faster than I would have imagined.

The illusion of calm was shattered in an instant. A man and two children came rushing out of the burning house, staring in horror as their home burned to the ground. They didn't have long to do so. A few seconds after they exited, muskets went off, dropping their bodies to the ground. As more people came out of their homes to see what the commotion was about, they were greeted with lead.

From the trees that surrounded the village, a veritable army emerged and formed ten distinct groups. Each had been spread out to a different angle of entry on the village. They were military in their precision.

The slaughter played out before me as if it were no more than a child's diorama. The house with the light in the window caught fire, and that was when I felt the pain again. The stabbing in my gut was mixed with emotions of terror and extreme anger. Not long after the flames reached the window, I heard a piercing, all-too-familiar roar. The houses shook, and the musket fire momentarily stopped.

I watched the burning house intently as the white light that came from the window went dark. Seconds later, the flaming wall surrounding it exploded outward. Splinters and ash flew out in all directions, striking several of the attackers and leaving them with grievous wounds. In the firelight, the massive hulk of the creature emerged, brushing bits of the house off as if they were no more than twigs.

The attackers ceased their fire; the villagers did not move. They might not have known what was happening, but they knew it was bad. The creature sniffed at the air, searching for prey. It did not take long to find some. Just to the south of the house, one of the groups stood silent, pointing their weapons at the creature. While most of the attackers seemed content to be silent and let the beast go about its business, one of them had an itchy trigger finger. A single musket shot rang out in the night air, and the lead ball within hurtled toward the yeti. The shot struck true, hitting the creature on its brow, but bounced off as if it were nothing more than a child's toy.

The yeti charged forward with amazing speed. More muskets fired, but most of the men were cut down before they could even get their finger on the trigger. It reminded me of the initial attack on Manchester's camp, only this time there was no fog to obscure it. The beast only needed one swipe to kill a man, but even so, it struck repeatedly, roaring its anger to the night sky. Its claws tore their armor in half as their bodies tumbled away in pieces.

Sadness welled from within me, unbidden and strong. The carnage slowly began to fade away, and before I knew it, I was sitting in the burned-out remnants of a house. Siana knelt in one corner over a pile of debris, weeping and covered in soot but completely unharmed. Tears rolled down her cheeks, wiping clean lines from her soot-stained face.

I moved forward, then felt sick. The bodies of her family lay before her, covered in ash and debris. As she mourned, emotions coursed through me. First, hot rage, followed by unending sadness reverberating from my very core, and finally, a cold determination to seek revenge on those who had done me wrong.

From the corner of the room, the small crystal ball lit up, bright red this time. Unable to look at Siana's grief any longer, I walked over to the orb and gazed in. Rather than vague shapes and floating light, I saw the bloodstained faces of the attackers as they ran from the beast.

The ball pulled me forward, closer and closer, until I was finally in the eyes of the beast. The room disappeared, and I could feel the beast's powerful limbs pulling itself across the landscape.

The world was red, lit up by bright spikes of light where the mercenaries ran. The hatred and grief that I felt from Siana fueled the creature, driving it forward, ripping and tearing anything in its path.

It was through this lens that I got my first good look at the attackers. They weren't gods, and then it began to make sense. Their clothes were modern, providing little to no camouflage in an environment that was constantly shifting. They ran from the town, dropping their weapons and heading for the trees they had come from. A bright insignia flashed in the darkness off one of the attacker's armor. They were English soldiers. Someone believed in *Lost Horizon* after all.

I was trapped inside the creature's head, helpless and along for the ride. The rampage lasted for three days as the beast relentlessly hunted down the attackers. One by one, their hiding places were exposed, and one by one they fell. The hills of Shangri-La ran red, and afterward, there was nothing for the beast to do. Its primary purpose had been conceived out of rage, the objective now gone. I shared a great confusion as the landscape swam before my eyes. The creature made its way high up into the hills, where it found a cave and sat, breathing heavily, retracing the first few days of its existence.

My vision shifted once more. I was still behind the creature's eyes, but a cold wind snapped at my face. We were back on the mountain. Loneliness tinged the scene as the beast looked over the snowy landscape. From the top of the mountain, there was truly nothing. Icy crags, snow, and rock stretched out as far as the eye could see. The creature sniffed at the air and found nothing but the stale taste that came with a lack of oxygen.

With a primal growl, the creature once more made its way down the mountain. Its movements were swift and heavy, cracking the icy surface as it went. In no time at all, it swung down onto an outcropping, looking in at a familiar cave. The wooden doors swung open of their own volition, and the creature stepped through the portal between them. Warm air and the succulent aroma of flowers greeted the beast. There was a pang of what might have been nostalgia, but it was quickly extinguished.

Slowly, the creature lumbered over to a corner, sat, and waited. The portal to the mountain remained open for a second, but then it disappeared, leaving nothing but rock. Below the wall, a stone hourglass rose from the floor, dripping grains of sand to the bottom at a snail's pace. The creature closed its eyes and prepared to wait for the following winter, when it could roam free once more.

6.

A DAMN FINE CUP OF COFFEE

I awoke with a jolt on the floor, covered in sweat. I couldn't think of anything to say. It all made perfect sense. At the moment of the creature's inception, Siana had been filled with rage and thoughts of revenge. The rest was history. I had a hard time feeling bad about the many deaths that followed. Conquerors ought to know: the conquered never stay that way for long. The images of the slaughter swam before me as though they were still happening. One particularly gruesome image of a man being crushed in his armor stuck. But they'd deserved it, right?

"What happened?" asked James, bringing me back to the present. "What did you see?"

For a moment, I just watched the dark ceiling. "Nothing good," I replied, pushing myself to a sitting position. Siana was staring at me intently, waiting for a response, but I could not find anything to say.

"As you probably assume, those men were from your world."

"Yeah, that part I guessed." Gods probably didn't have much use for muskets. "But I don't understand. Why didn't the other gods fight back? I saw a demigod take apart forty men with automatics in less than a minute. Surely gods could have handled a militia of musketeers."

"In short, we were unprepared. Before that day, we visited

your realm often, bringing gifts, imparting wisdom. The attack was an eventuality that we had never even considered."

"The human race is never content with peace," I sighed, embarrassed and ashamed. "But even still, I wouldn't have thought the gods to be so vulnerable to mortal weapons."

"In your realm maybe. But in ours we are just as vulnerable as you. Hence the hostility when you arrived."

"And the anti-demigod sentiment," I added.

Siana nodded. "After the attack, we held a council, and decided it was best for us to stick to our own realm, and keep others out."

"So you found the creature and sealed it on our side." I tried my best to sound angry. I wanted to think that it was unfair, and that the poor decisions of one group didn't justify the god's actions, but I couldn't. The yeti may have left some mortal bodies in its wake, but humans with both good and ill intentions had certainly left more.

"Yes. We closed the mountain passage and put guardians on the inner portal."

I recalled the image of Manchester burning. "Yeah, I remember."

If Siana felt sorry about this, she didn't mention it. "The outer gate was to open only in the winter months, when the mountain was thought to be impassable. In this way, we hoped to allow the creature some freedom, while not interfering with your world."

"And so the legends formed about climbing in the winter months." I thought back to Lopsang's story. I began to feel sick about my ambition of plundering. Partly because, so far, I hadn't seen anything that wasn't nailed down or embedded in rock, but mostly because of the parallels I drew between myself and the attackers.

We were one step away from ending up like them. The thought made me shudder. Without the guardians, Manchester would have come in here with his team and tried to colonize the place. In hindsight, burning the man alive didn't seem that extreme. It certainly did the trick of keeping people away. "This place should remain hidden."

"Perhaps now you understand why we've tried so hard to keep it so." Her eyes were fixed on mine. There was a deep sorrow within them, and I understood it. I had lived it, after all, and the nature of my world sickened me. At last, Siana broke off. "I think that's enough for tonight. Both of you have certainly earned some rest."

I yawned, feeling the exhaustion of one who had lived many lives in a short time. "I'm not going to argue with that. But what are we going to do after?"

The fact had not escaped me that when we left Shangri-La, we'd still be tasked with facing the beast once more if we wanted to get home.

"My creation has caused enough harm. Tomorrow, we will fix my mistake and close the gates for good." Siana stood and took the basin that I had drunk from back to the hidden panel in the wall. "I have rooms prepared for you." She motioned for us to follow, leading the way up a small flight of stairs.

One floor up, I was presented with an image of immense beauty. Siana opened a door to a bedroom with two thick mattresses and so many pillows that I could drown in them. She left us without another word, and I fell onto the bed with the weight of a dead man. The mattress enveloped me, wrapping me in the soft sensations of home, and before I knew it, the drowsiness of a week of sleepless nights was upon me.

I turned to look at James, who had fallen face-down on the opposite bed. The kid had embraced it as if it were his long-lost lover, and it didn't look like he would ever let go. If time wasn't passing at the same rate, then a little sleep wouldn't hurt us.

Before I could think any more on the subject, I had drifted off.

———————— ▼ ————————

I awoke to the same dim light that had been there since we arrived. It was hard to tell whether I had slept for an hour or a day. Stretching my arms above my head, I felt the soreness of climbing a mountain with little experience catching up to me again. However, without the constant threat from the mountain, the creature, and Manchester's mercenaries, I had been able to sleep undisturbed. That might have been the best sleep I'd had since childhood.

On the bed beside me, James stirred and sat up. The bags under his eyes had all but disappeared. He looked like a new man.

"Ready to banish a yeti?" James asked, with more pep than he had shown on the entire expedition. He let out a loud yawn, but he looked ready.

"Ready as I'll ever be," I said, still dreading what was to come. "How are you feeling?"

It had been a long and strange journey. In the end, James had handled himself quite well. As far as apprentices went, the kid had long outlived his predecessors and been far more useful. The thought of using him as a volcanic sacrifice had only occurred to me once, and by previous standards, that was nothing short of a miracle.

"I'll be honest, I feel like I could take on the world." James smiled. "Don't suppose they serve breakfast around here, do they?" His voice was hopeful, as if there might be a diner he missed on our initial trip in.

"I would kill for a cup of coffee," I moaned, feeling the start of another caffeine headache. "Double homicide for a bit of whiskey in it."

"That won't be necessary," said a voice from the doorway. Siana walked in carrying a steaming tray, filled with meats, bread, and small saucers of coffee. "We do have coffee, but unfortunately there hasn't been whiskey in the realm for ages. However, I think what we brew here will suffice." Her tone was playful once more, and the darkness behind her eyes had diminished.

"Someone got a little too creative on a bender?" I guessed.

"Something like that." Siana smiled and handed cups of coffee to us.

"You truly are a goddess," said James.

"Were you ever in doubt?" She set the tray of food between our beds. We slumped to the floor around it, preparing to attack the food like ravenous animals, but we waited. Siana joined us on the floor with a smile. "Go ahead, while it's hot."

The food was unlike anything I had ever tasted, though I wasn't sure I wanted to know where the meat had come from. I'd hoped it wasn't four-winged-bird sausage, but it was juicy and succulent. Either way, the flavor was too good to stop. Each bite was filled with spices I had never tasted, overwhelming my senses.

After stuffing my face with as much as I could handle, I turned my attention to the coffee. I lifted the small cup to my lips and felt a wholly unique sensation. It was as if I had never truly been alive up until that point. The liquid was smooth but strong, sending radiant energy coursing through my veins. The aches in my muscles disappeared, and I felt a raw energy that I had not possessed since my youth.

"That is a damn fine cup of coffee." The liquid filled me with a sense of awe.

"It should be. It was roasted by the gods," quipped Siana. On the morning of battle, she seemed positively pleased. "When you are finished eating, meet me back in the reading room. It's time to find out if what you saw last night was enough." She stood and left the room.

The food did not last long. We were both starving, and finished what we were given in minutes. I tried to savor the coffee down to the last drop, but even that was gone too soon.

"I don't think I'll ever have a cup of coffee that good again."

"Look on the bright side," said James, polishing off the last crumbs on his plate.

"There's a bright side?"

"Sure. We might be dead at the end of the day anyway." He laughed half-heartedly.

I laughed as well, apprehensive but confident about our mission. Truth be told, I hadn't felt that good about it since we had set out from The Black Market.

"With the power of a goddess, a demigod, and the Book of All, we might just stand a chance." Lopsang's demigod powers wouldn't help much against the yeti, but it sounded good.

James nodded in agreement. "We'll certainly stand a better chance than if we had gone it alone. I just hope whatever's in that book will be enough."

"It will be," I stated with confidence. I made one last attempt at getting a few more drops from my coffee cup, then gave up. "Let's see what the gods have in store for us today."

We grabbed what little we had and left the room. As we descended the staircase, I noticed the aesthetics on the first floor had changed slightly. Bright light shone down between the boards of the ceiling as if it were midday outside. A quick glance out the windows confirmed that it was still dark.

Siana was sitting on a cushion, holding the Book of All open before her as if it were just some light reading. At the sight of us, she closed the book and smiled. Her eyes sparkled in the dazzling light, drawing us in.

"Well, I suppose it's time to see if all that pain last night was worth it." Siana held the book out to me casually.

Gingerly, I took the book and sat down. The pages were still heavy as stone, but I suspected Siana was imbuing me with power again, because I was able to turn them. At first glance, it seemed as if nothing had changed. The lines were still written in the same squiggly characters, providing no more guidance than if they had been blank. Then the ink came to life, dancing across the page to form words.

"Well, I'll be damned."

"What does it say?" asked James.

"As the sun lowers toward the edge of the night—"

"No!" shouted Siana. She slammed the book closed, nearly smashing my fingers. "What are you thinking?"

I looked at her, stunned, knowing I had crossed a line, but unsure as to where it was. "What?" I asked, annoyed.

"*Really*?" she said incredulously. "I give you a book with omnipotent power and you just pick a passage at random to read?"

"Ah," I said, realizing my folly. "A little warning would have been—"

"That spell would have cast the entire realm into a pocket universe and raised an army of the undead to conquer the 'lifeless' planet you know as Venus."

I scrunched my face up. "Well, that's … oddly specific." What did they need that one for?

"There is powerful magic in this book. Read in your head, lest you free something more evil than the yeti." Siana's face was flushed with color, and she was breathing heavily.

"More evil than--"

"At least when I made the creature, it was not with evil intent. Imagine what someone could make if they wanted to do mass harm."

If the best intentions of deities had such foul consequences, I was not sure I wanted to know what the worst intentions could do.

"All right, I'm sorry. I'll be more careful."

Siana's face softened. "It's all right. We stopped you in time, but you can read the words. That was the point." She stood and walked over to a cabinet, pulling out a drawstring bag.

"What's that for?"

"If you can read the incantation, then there's no time to waste." Siana slid the book into the bag with great care, pulled the strings tight, and handed it to me. "By my count, it will take us three hours to get back to the gate. I'd suggest you do some reading on the way there."

7.

A STUDY IN DIVINITY

Rather than walking, we rode in a sturdy ornate carriage. It looked like a mix between a Victorian horse-drawn buggy and a World War II tank. All the windows were decorated with fine cloth curtains, but just above them were heavy metal slats that could be lowered to protect those inside. Sharp spikes adorned the front, presumably to discourage highway robbery.

"That's a hell of a ride," I said, whistling.

"One can never be too careful in a realm at war," Siana said darkly as she stepped inside.

I followed suit, and to my delight, a carafe of coffee sat steaming right next to one of the seats. The carriage was lined with plush cushions and intricate wood-carved paneling. It was meant to transport in style and safety, a combination I admired.

James stepped in after me with a look of pleasant surprise. "Never thought I'd ride in the limousine of a god."

"It sure beats walking at spearpoint," I joked.

"You can't blame us for being a little suspicious," Siana said.

"No, I can't." The thought of the last men to walk through the gates from my realm brought a coppery taste to my mouth. Conquerors were always ruining the world for the rest of us.

Siana shut the door and clapped her hands. The carriage began to roll along the golden path at an easy pace. Outside, the massive temple entrance carved into the canyon faded away, and the multicolored hills of Shangri-La took its place.

I poured myself a cup of coffee and got to reading. There were only two pages concerning the yeti, and the information provided was interesting but not exactly helpful. One page was dedicated entirely to the creature's taxonomy, which only served to hammer the point home that it was nigh indestructible. The second page was the incantation that would be needed to banish the creature. There was also a small biography of Siana, the creator, almost like what would be found on the back of a novel. That was it.

I could not help but laugh at the absurdity of it all. If James had not been there to share the adventure with me, I might have thought I was going insane. All the same, I read over the ritual repeatedly, hoping that when the time came to say it aloud, I could do it quickly and without error.

Sooner than I would have liked, the carriage rounded a corner, and the massive waterfall that hid the gate was looming before us. We came to a stop just at the edge of the rushing water. Siana unclasped the lock that held the carriage door shut and stepped outside. I took one last longing sip of my coffee, put the book back in its bag, and followed.

The smell of mist greeted me, and the cooling sensation flowing through the air was enough to calm my overcaffeinated nerves. Together, the three of us walked into the cave hidden behind the waterfall. The overwhelming sense of dread I felt previously on the mountain crept up my spine once more. As a distraction, I thought back to the first time I had been in the cave, and the spears that had greeted me. I wondered where they were.

Siana walked over to the back of the cave where a smooth stone wall ran up to the overhang. She placed her hand on the surface, muttered a few words, and stepped back. There was a loud cracking sound, and the wall slowly recessed, revealing an archway adorned on all sides with runes. At the top, just above the entrance, was a large stone globe depicting the Earth.

"All right, I'm beginning to feel illiterate. What do those say?" I motioned to the runes.

"Try not to feel too bad. You have to be a god to read that one," Siana said. "It says: Beyond this gate lies a barbaric place."

"Gods really don't care too much for mortals, do they?" James asked dryly.

"The ones who made this didn't," she said, gazing up at the gate. "They had one objective, stop people from coming here and avoid repeating the tragedy that took my family." The darkness was back in her eyes momentarily, but it went out almost as quickly as it had appeared, and she regained her graceful composure. "No one has used this gate in over two hundred years."

"With good reason," I added bitterly. "The creature isn't exactly the most welcoming host."

For a humorous moment, I imagined walking through the door to find the yeti waiting for us, bottle of champagne in one hand, mercenary entrails in the other. "Welcome to my home. Sorry about the mess," it would say. I laughed.

"There is something deeply sick about your mind," Siana said, as if noticing this for the first time.

"You and a long line of doctors with fancy couches would agree." I actually enjoyed talk therapy, but in my sessions, the doctor usually left the room in tears. Some people really can't handle thinking outside their box. "My mental state aside, is there anything we need to worry about with this door? Spikes that shoot out of the floor? Massive stone guardians that are going to challenge us to mortal combat?"

The last one, while almost certainly ending in our deaths, was an exciting prospect to me.

"There is nothing preventing you from leaving Shangri-La, only from entering."

I was a little disappointed in the lack of ceremony, but I didn't complain. I took a moment to steel myself for what was to come. From the moment we stepped through the doorway, we would be running out of time. Shangri-La had been a brief respite, and a part of me didn't want to leave.

"I don't suppose either one of you wants to go first?" I asked casually.

"Oh, no, after you," insisted James, making a polite gesture to the gate. "I believe it's your turn."

"Such a gentleman." I took one final look at the beautiful waterfall behind us and then walked through the gate without further hesitation. Within seconds, I could see nothing but impenetrable blue fog. Behind me, the pounding of the waterfall grew distant, until it was nothing but a faint murmur. Then, just as before, the fog cleared. In one disorienting instant, I found myself back in the cave.

The bright, shifting colors of Shangri-La were gone, replaced by the dim, muted stones that we had left. I looked hazily up at the flowers, trying to use their many colors to focus my eyes. Slowly, the cave came into view, and I saw Lopsang staring at me with a confused look. Behind him, the mercenaries looked up briefly, only mildly interested in my miraculous reappearance, and went back to cleaning their weapons.

"Dr. Ventner?" Lopsang stuttered slightly with the air of someone seeing something they could not believe. "Now is not the time to turn around. You have to go get James."

James strode through the gate. "He's already done that." He smiled at the stunned look on Lopsang's face.

I chuckled. The kid was finally learning how to make an entrance. "How long were we gone?"

"You just walked through the portal a second ago," stuttered Lopsang, still awestruck. "How in the—"

"Time is a little weird on the other side," James said.

"Righ—" Lopsang's voice caught in his throat as Siana stepped through the portal behind James. "And who is she?" Lopsang spoke like a man in a dream.

"*She* is the goddess Siana," she said. "You must be the demigod."

Lopsang recoiled at the revelation. "A true goddess? From Shangri-La?"

"I'm sure it's a lot to take in, but as I understand it, we're short on time." Her tone was friendly but clipped. "Suffice it to say, I think some of the ways the gods keep to are outdated. You have nothing to fear from me." She favored him with a smile, enjoying the further confusion spreading across his face.

Lopsang kept opening and closing his mouth, trying to think of something to say. He was trembling slightly.

"Oh, come on, Lopsang. You're half god anyway. Get over it. We've only got two hours until sunset, and there are a lot of preparations to be made."

Lopsang straightened up, brushing the dirt and grime from his coat. "Right, sorry. It's a pleasure to meet you, Siana." His voice wavered, but the sentiment was so genuine I could not find any room to make fun of him.

Siana winked at him, causing his face to go beet red. Unable to keep eye contact with her, Lopsang instead turned his attention to me. "So you've been to the other side and back. What's the plan?"

I pulled the Book of All from my bag and held it up. "The plan is a very simple one. We're going to read the beasty a bedtime story."

8.

CANDLES, INCANTATIONS, AND ROPE

"A bedtime story?" Lopsang asked skeptically.

"Well, it's going to be a hell of a story," I said. "This is the Book of All. Contains all knowledge written by gods, for gods. The usual fare."

Lopsang tried to interject with a question, but I held my hand up.

In truth, I could have talked about the book at great length, but the sun was setting, and we'd soon have an angry yeti to contend with. There would be time to discuss it later.

"The point is, in these pages, there's a spell to banish the creature to the world between worlds and keep it out of our realm forever."

"Banish it? How do you know it will work?"

I looked at Siana, who gave me a slight nod.

"Long story short, she's the one who created it," I said.

Lopsang's mouth dropped open once more.

"I know. It's a lot to take in, but we've got bigger problems to solve. I can read the incantation, but it's going to take some time, and our friend"—I gestured to one of the stone yetis at the far end of the cave—"doesn't like to sit still."

"And how are we planning on getting around that? Our weapons didn't even scratch it last time."

Lopsang had quickly grown exasperated. It was clear that he

had been expecting something more from the realm of gods than a simple incantation and a lackluster plan.

I thought back to the liquid we purchased at The Black Market. The old man had seemed genuine, and he had warned us that we might not be able to pierce the hide. It couldn't be total bunk.

"We were scattered last time. If there's one thing I've learned in my travels, it's that every creature has a weak spot. We need to be tactical about this. If we can even get a drop of the poison in the creature's bloodstream, we can slow it down. That means one arrow or one bullet, and we're golden."

"Only one?" asked Lopsang.

"Well, preferably more, but even one should be enough to slow it down some." This was another fact I was unsure of, but I said it with confidence nonetheless.

"And then what?" This time it was James who spoke.

I wished they'd give me a break. After all, I was coming up with most of it on the fly.

"Then, we tie it down as best we can in the middle of a chalk circle and hope my speed reading has improved since grade school." I smiled broadly. It was a shit plan, but in the end we could have done a lot worse.

"Well, at least we've got plenty of rope," offered James, upending one of the gear bags and sending its contents spilling onto the ground. Sure enough, there were three coils of thick rope. Not much, but more than expected. "And this is just ours. I'm sure they have some as well." James motioned to the mercenaries still prepping in the corner. "Not sure if it'll hold it down, but it looks like the best option we've got."

I turned to Siana. "Don't suppose you know anything about keeping it still?"

Siana shrugged. "The only thing that might stop it is a meal.

The creature does not need to eat to survive, but it likely still feels the desire." She looked around the cave as if expecting a steak to materialize out of thin air. Must be hard not being able to summon anything you want.

"We don't have much," I said, anticipating her question. Our dried rations would last us down the mountain but likely wouldn't entice a beast used to hunting fresh meat.

"All we have are powdered eggs and soup pouches," reported Lopsang.

"That's not entirely true." I threw a sideways glance at the freshly deceased mercenary decomposing slowly on the floor. It wouldn't be the most proper of post-death rituals, but at least he'd be of some use.

James looked disgusted and began to protest.

I cut him off. "There's not much left of him, but it might be enough."

Giving up on the idea of fighting the use of a corpse as bait, James began laying out the ropes. "None of these will be enough to hold the beast on its own. We've already seen how strong it is." James held up a length of rope for us to see. "The only way this will work is if we somehow use their combined strength to hold it in place. A pulley system would be ideal, but—"

"Right, so we hold it down, fire everything we have at it while I read from the book, the creature gets banished, and everyone goes home happy." I smiled. "That just leaves one problem."

"You mean aside from the lack of a pulley system?" James asked.

I sighed. "Oh, come on, James, use your imagination a little. We're surrounded by climbing gear!"

"I suppose you're right," conceded James. "But what's the problem, then?"

"Assuming our divine friends over here"—I motioned to Lopsang and Siana—"are strong enough to hold it down, we're still going to need to get *them* to help." I jerked a thumb at the mercenaries.

They were standing around a mounted heavy machine gun, smoking and preparing for the battle to come. When it came to unwinnable fights, they seemed content to use the strategy of "if it doesn't work, just shoot it again."

After a moment's hesitation, I decided there was no time like the present. "Let me take care of this." I waltzed across the cave toward the mercenaries and gave them a winning smile. Up until that point, they had been content to avoid any action that wasn't cleaning and loading their firearms.

One man looked up from the grease rag he had been using to polish the machine gun, but the rest carried on with whatever they were doing.

"Hey there, friends," I said awkwardly. For most of the journey, these had been the people assigned to keep a gun pointed squarely at my backside, but we were in desperate need of allies. There was only two hours until sunset. Not much time.

The mercenaries continued to ignore my presence. One of them gave a non-committal grunt, but I didn't know if it was directed at me or not. As I stood, waiting for acknowledgment, I took a good look at what remained of Manchester's crew.

There were only four of them. The first was the man who had spoken to us briefly before, sharp-looking and smoking a cigar from behind the turret of the machine gun. The second, a lean woman with two high-caliber pistols strapped to her thighs, stared intently at a set of neatly arranged bullets. The third, a thick wall of muscle, polished the machine gun with all his might. He'd rubbed the spare grease on his face like war paint. The last was a lanky man bearing tattoos with names that had been crossed off up and down his forearms.

What did mercenaries want most? I almost kicked myself. The answer was too obvious. For the most part, it was what I wanted as well: *treasure*.

"I'm guessing most of your pay burned up with your dearly departed commander, Manchester."

This got their attention. Work ceased on the machine gun immediately, and four uncomfortable sets of eyes zeroed in on me. They were listening, but now I had to give them a reason not to kill me.

"What if I told you I could pay you?" That was a stupid thing to say, as I was currently only in possession of a few coins in the local currency, worth approximately a medium-sized lint ball, a couple bullets, and a book that Siana would not give up willingly. We'd cross that bridge later.

The woman stepped forward and looked me dead in the eye. "You're going to pay us either way." A knife was at my side before I even saw her move. "We lost friends out there, and you're right, our employer is dead now, but the way I see it, you're not in much of a bargaining position." She turned away and walked over to the machine gun, running a hand over it as if it were a precious child.

"This bad boy fires six thousand rounds per minute, and I count four of you." She pointed her finger at Lopsang, Siana, James, and then me in turn. "The cave may be big, but I'm guessing we're not going to miss that many times." She spit what I hoped was chewing tobacco at my feet.

I thought through my options. There was no way the bullets would reach us if either of our divine companions had anything to say about it, but threatening our only source of help was not the way to go. Instead, I relied on my charm and appealed to the mercenaries' shinier interests.

"You are absolutely correct," I said. "That machine gun will tear us to ribbons before we can even say 'ouch.'" I took a moment to let this sink in. "But your problem isn't with us—it's with the beast at the door and the mountain beyond it."

The enemy of my enemy is my friend. I repeated that in my mind, hoping it would inspire confidence. "You can kill us with ease, but the beast is going to come right through that door and rip you to shreds." I made a quick gesture of a claw swiping through the air and felt pleased when some of the mercenaries jumped slightly.

"When that beast comes back," the woman said, "we're going to give it hell or go to hell." The mercenaries behind her let up a spirited military "hoorah," then fell silent once more.

"Or, if I might be allowed to counter: We have a plan to kill the beast, and it might be more successful than just hurling bullets at it, which, so far, has only made it angrier." I didn't like having to bargain, but there weren't many options. Once more, I had their rapt attention. "While I admire your commitment to dying in battle, I don't think today is the day for it. Help us. We'll kill the beast together, and afterward, I'll see that you're fairly compensated."

There was a murmur of agreement from the mercenaries, and the woman looked back at them, slightly annoyed.

"What's the catch?" she said.

"Well ..." I said. "We're going to need your friend there." I gestured to the decomposing body.

9.

SHOWDOWN IN THE MOUNTAIN CAVE

Getting the mercenaries to part with their freshly deceased companion was no easy task, but in the end, the promise of shares in the loot sufficed. I neglected to mention to them that there was no treasure and that a share of zero was still zero, but I figured that was a minor detail to be discussed later.

Looking around the cave, I was amazed at the preparations we had managed in just a few short hours. Suspended from the ceiling by a host of makeshift pulleys was a net James had created from our spare gear, with weights haphazardly constructed from everything that wasn't a weapon. Even with the strength of a goddess, every extra pound counted. The end plan was a little close to the board game Mouse Trap for my comfort, but I didn't mention it. Lopsang, Siana, and James stood at three points around the net, next to ropes that would hopefully hold the creature down once we had it trapped.

"Five minutes, everyone," I called. The five minutes before a fight were always the slowest. Anticipation was much worse than actual pain. I checked my handiwork and saw the dead man sitting, propped up in the center of a crudely drawn chalk circle. If not for the smell and the flies buzzing around him, the man could have easily passed as sleeping. I found myself wondering where flies came from at that altitude. I shook my head, trying to bring myself back to focus.

The mercenaries had helped with preparations, and now they stood rooted behind their machine gun, ready to fight. I had given them some of the remaining poison, which had in turn been loaded into the heaviest caliber they had. It was all worth a shot in my mind, and it gave the mercenaries a confidence that I did not share.

Time ticked away. I checked the lines on the chalk circle once more. All was as it was supposed to be. The candles around the edges were ready to be lit, just as the book instructed, and I was ready to read.

"Sixty seconds, everyone," I stammered.

I reached into my pocket and fumbled with a matchstick I procured from one of the mercenaries. After a few tries and even more cursing, I got it to light. As quick as I could, I ran around the circle, igniting the candles. I then got into position, hiding behind a large boulder, and waited. Sweat beaded on my back, and I shivered as it dripped down my spine.

"Ten seconds, everyone," I said in close to a whisper.

Everyone else stood silently at their posts. James never let his eyes waver from the spot on the wall we had come through. A few near-death experiences in a couple of days had changed him, and I liked what I was seeing. If he kept that up, he might outlive me yet. That thought was interrupted by the silent flash of light that accompanied the portal opening. My throat tightened.

The stone wall gave way to the windy alcove of the mountain, white with fresh powder, covering the gruesome scene we had left. Snowflakes drifted through the portal, melting as soon as they touched the warm air of the cave. Tendrils of icy air tried to reach me, and I shook slightly. Even if we got the beast, the trip down was going to be no cakewalk.

For the first minute, we heard nothing. The red light of

sunset could be glimpsed just through the obscured portal. The roar came as its final rays touched the horizon. Beyond the portal came the sound of muted crashes, and the ground began to shake. This is it, I thought, and then in a single bone-chilling moment, it happened. The creature dropped onto the plateau, shaking fresh snow from its fur. It stood, staring at the portal. Anger was in its eyes, plain to see.

The candles flickered but did not go out as the creature lumbered forward. Pebbles hopped and skittered across the floor as it crossed the portal's threshold. It entered the cave, then stopped to sniff the air. The bastard needed to take the bait. Desecrating the corpse had been bad enough. If it turned out that it wasn't appetizing enough, it would all have been in vain.

The smell of the decaying mercenary wafted through the cave as the creature breathed steadily. I shook and held the rock tightly, telling myself to get it together. The cave trembled as the creature began to move forward once again. I could not see from behind the rock, but I could feel it getting closer. *Please, take the bait.*

To my immense relief, there was a sickening ripping noise as the yeti unceremoniously bit into the dead man's flesh. For a moment, there was nothing but the noise of the beast gorging on its meal. Everyone stood in silence, waiting for the signal. I told myself to move my ass. No one wants to live forever.

"Now!" I yelled as I jumped out from behind the rock. A sense of immediate regret washed over me as the cold, black eyes of the creature found mine. It might have been my imagination, but I thought I felt a flicker of recognition. The creature's lip curled into a sneer as it prepared to charge. Then the net dropped on top of it, and with a mighty crash, the creature was brought to the ground. Siana, James and Lopsang pulled hard on their ropes, doing their best to keep the creature pinned to the ground.

Its claws dug deep trenches into the cave floor as it tried to escape. The sound of its roar filled the cave, causing the flowers above to tremble. The creature's breath blew back my hair. I was both disgusted and terrified. The Book of All felt ten times heavier in my hands as I looked into the eyes of the beast. My limbs froze. I could not move. Sound began to take on the odd, muted quality of someone who had just been shelled by artillery. The cave fell quiet as I stared blankly into the creature's eyes.

Then, from the other end of the cave came the booming percussion of the machine gun firing. There were loud thumps as the bullets hit the yeti's back. The creature tried instinctively to reach back but found itself caught by the ropes. Most of the bullets bounced off harmlessly, tinkling to the floor and leaving nothing but squashed lead pellets, but then there was small splash of red blood as one miraculously found its mark. The beast heaved furiously, bringing James momentarily off the ground as he tried to hold his rope steady.

"Anytime now, Nick!" he yelled, straining against the creature's weight. Even with the help of two divine entities, holding the creature was difficult.

Sound came back to me immediately in a painful cacophony. The machine-gun fire was thundering and drove the stiffness from my limbs. I began to read. The words flowed like water from my lips, electrified and holding great power. The lights of the candles surrounding the beast dimmed, then turned bright blue.

"The days of your reaping are over on this plane. It is time now to rest and move on, for your cause has been called to another. Today, I beseech the world between worlds, open your doors, so that a new child may enter your embrace." The lines on the page glowed gold beneath my fingers as I read.

The yeti groaned uncomfortably, as if each word was causing

it pain. Then the creature's eyes once more met mine. Its movements were slowed, but the deadly power beneath the surface was still evident. The hatred and anger boiling inside the creature invaded my mind. My perception flashed rapidly between the creature's and my own, to the point where I was unsure whose eyes I was looking through. The creature flexed a massive arm beneath the ropes, and I felt its desire to eviscerate me.

"Don't stop now!" yelled Siana. "Remember the words' intent and finish the incantation!"

Sweat ran down her forehead from the exertion of holding the creature in place, but still she held on. Lopsang had closed his eyes, but his arms were trembling. James was almost crying from the strain.

With great difficulty, I broke the creature's gaze and returned my attention to the glowing words in the book.

"Follow these guides to the land beyond lands and be gone from ours forever."

Now was the hard part. I stepped forward, leaving behind the chance of escaping to cover, and crossed the outer border of the chalk circle. I knelt to the floor and placed my hand on the stone, mere feet from the yeti. The stone beneath grew warm, and the candles flickered.

The creature grunted and continued to stare at me. A feeling of primal rage invaded my mind again, tinting the entire room red. The creature's roar felt like it was within my very skull. I tried to regain control, but looked at the slowly heaving back of the creature and had a terrifying thought.

It was calm.

Fear and dizziness began to overwhelm me. With one violent motion, the creature lunged for me but was pulled back by the net. James was yanked off his feet once more, only this time he could not hold on to the rope. His body flew like a rag doll and landed sprawled out on the other side of the circle from me. The net around the yeti slackened only slightly, but it was enough. The creature gave another mighty heave, and the other two ropes snapped.

Time took an even slower edge in that moment. The yeti first looked at me, then at a stunned James. The mercenaries, who had finally reloaded, began to shoot at the beast once more. With little effort, the creature charged at the machine-gun nest and tore them apart in a matter of seconds.

I barely had time to see what had happened. There were splashes of red on the walls. Screams. A howl. The creature moved with incredible speed. Even sedated, it was too fast for us.

"James, move! Now!" I yelled.

The yeti finished its quick work of the mercenaries and turned back to face us. Blood dripped down its fur in dark red tendrils. It gnashed its teeth and made a low growl. My brain went numb with fear. It was all over before I was even two steps into a run. The creature lunged back to the circle with incredible speed.

James's face went pale with fear as the yeti towered over him. The creature raised a massive fist and brought it down, crushing James's leg and nearly severing it. James howled in pain, but it couldn't be heard over the roar of the yeti. Blood spilled from James's mutilated leg and into the chalk circle, filling in the lines I had drawn.

Directly above us, the flowers began to move restlessly, swaying to and fro. A low hum of static electricity filled the air, followed by several crackles of blue light. The yeti paused its dismemberment to look up. Confusion and anger crossed its face, and the flowers parted to reveal a swirling vortex of energy. Sparks danced in descent until they were only a few feet above the yeti's head.

I seized the opportunity and ran toward the beast with my knife drawn.

"Hold on, James!" I yelled. The candles ringing the circle grew to a conflagration and shot flames into the air. The force of the sudden flame knocked me onto my stomach and singed my back. A massive wave of heat joined the growing vortex above. My skin sizzled and popped. I tried to stand, but the pain in my back paralyzed me, and all I could do was watch through bleary eyes.

The beast's fur stood on end, and a strong wind whipped around it. It roared its displeasure, filling the cave with the awful sound.

James had grown very pale, but he was still awake. He just needed to hold on a few more seconds.

The wind around the yeti grew stronger, forming a suctioning force. I worried that James would be sucked in, too, but the wind seemed to affect only the beast.

"Your ride's here!" I shouted over the growing din, looking with pleasure at the growing realization in the creature's eyes. Despite the pain in my back, I grinned triumphantly. We had finally done it.

The yeti took one final look at me, realizing the end was near, and raised its clawed hand.

My heart raced as the creature's rage surged through me.

With a quick but brutal motion, the yeti slashed at James's stomach. James screamed, and the sound abruptly died in his throat. Fresh blood coated the yeti's already matted fur, and it roared a final roar. Then, as if the wind had finally become too much for it to resist, the beast was lifted off the ground and sucked into the portal, vanishing in an instant. The candles went out, and all was silent.

Lopsang and Siana both lay stunned on the floor, unmoving.

Where the mercenaries had stood, there was no more than gore and an ever-widening puddle of blood.

I rushed to James and bent down beside him. "Lopsang, get the med kit, quick!"

Upon hearing his name, Lopsang staggered to his feet and began searching for the pack that contained the med kit. It was likely buried somewhere beneath the bloody remnants of the mercenaries' last stand. Lopsang took one look at James and quietly quickened his search.

"Nick …" James muttered weakly. Deep gashes across his stomach oozed blood, and red mass trailed out from the holes in his jacket. He coughed violently, spitting up blood. "Did we get it?" James's eyes were glassy, already somewhere far away.

"Yeah, we did, but I'm going to need someone to split that reward with, kid, so hold on." I motioned again to Lopsang. "Lopsang, hurry up with that kit!" Somehow, amongst the carnage, Lopsang found our small red med kit and brought it over. By the time he was kneeling beside James, it was clear that it was far too late.

"I hear …" James whispered, his voice beginning to fade.

"What do you hear?"

"Music …" His voice grew fainter. "Spanish music …" James seized violently for a moment, then lay still. His eyes took on a glassy look, and a single droplet of blood ran out from the corner of his mouth. From the ceiling above, a large bright flower dropped down on a vine. Orange bursts of color flanked by blue streaks spread out from the center, and a small wooden tag hung down beneath it.

It read simply: James Schaefer.

EPILOGUE

"Spanish music?" said Winston. "If you're trying to pull a fast one—"

"Yes, it was god-damned Spanish music," said Nick. Talking about James's death had been no easy thing, and as at the end of most good stories, they had run out of booze. "The last thing the kid said to me was that he heard Spanish music." A dull throb crept into Nick's temples. It was a mixture of anger and agony at the memories he'd tried so hard to avoid.

"But, what on earth?"

"Trust me, I've been trying to figure out the same thing." Nick sighed. The last words had perplexed him for months on end, with very few real answers coming to light. When all other options had been exhausted, he had been forced to accept the only one that made any sense, no matter how improbable it was.

"What did you do?" Winston asked eagerly, his voice growing sharper than it had been all night.

Ah, you've got what you want now, don't you? "Siana snuck back through the portal while we mourned James. I'm guessing she couldn't take the sight of it. Lopsang and I buried the dead and headed back down the mountain. If you can believe it, there was nothing but clear skies the whole way down."

A bitter taste filled Nick's mouth. *James should be here with us.* He shook off the thought, one of many that had assailed him since James's death.

"We left James buried in the snow, just beneath the summit, in a place where he'll never be found. His family has a big empty mausoleum, of course, but I think he would have wanted to stay on the mountain."

"Yes, of course," stammered Winston, sounding a little impatient. "What happened to the demigod?"

Wouldn't you like to know? "Lopsang and I parted ways back at the village. Never saw each other again," I lied. "I don't think either of us could take the sight of one another after what we'd been through."

Winston's face drew into a long smile.

Knowing full well what was about to happen, Nick smiled back. "I suppose you're not going to pay me now."

He had told the story, through and through, but from the moment he'd set foot in the mansion, there had been only one thing Winston wanted.

"No, I don't suppose I will be."

Winston's bumbling act was dropped in an instant. The cold-blooded collector came to the forefront, and Nick saw where his sordid reputation had come from.

He is quite a good actor. The gun barrel pressing up against Nick's neck was no surprise. "Ah, you weren't just interested in my story, then …"

"No, I just wanted to know where the Sherpa was." His voice was smooth and calculated.

There was a click behind him as the gun was cocked. *Taking your sweet-ass time, Lopsang …*

Nick laughed.

"This is no joke, Mr. Ventner," spat Winston.

"Oh, I know. This gun could take my head off, but I'm just so damned slow sometimes." He looked at the suit of armor in the corner of the room and started laughing again. *Inside the suit of armor? Really?* "You just wanted to know where 'the Sherpa' is—"

Blue smoke erupted from the suit of armor, and the pressure from the gun barrel was gone. Nick stood up. "Thanks for that, Lopsang, but next time, maybe don't wait so long. This man's butler was about to turn me into paste."

"You said 'Wait to make it dramatic,'" Lopsang reminded him, shrugging.

"Well, not that long," said Nick. "I guess it worked out, so no harm done." Nick turned his attention back to Winston. "Winston, meet Lopsang. Lopsang, Winston."

"The demigod?" stammered Winston.

"The one and only," Nick said, beaming. "Now, I know you wanted to get information from me, but actually we need information from you."

Winston sat quietly.

Nick took the pistol from Lopsang and fired it once into the ceiling.

Winston nearly jumped out of his skin. "Fine! What do you want to know?"

Nick clapped his hands together and sat back down. "Couple of things, nothing much really, but why don't you start by telling us everything you know about the Land of the Dead."

Nick Ventner will return in *Downpour*…

SPECIAL THANKS TO:

The film crew for our crowdfunding video:

Producer - Robert Speewack Bojorquez
Director of Photography - Roxy Ewing
Location Audio - Dylan Mander

Our proofreaders:

Deborah Peters
Ethan Batson - King of Painful Puns

There's plenty more for you to experience

at Aberrant Literature

Visit our web site for new and exclusive stories and articles at AberrantLiterature.com, as well as news regarding upcoming and new releases.

Stay in touch with Aberrant Literature:
Facebook.com/AberrantLit
Twitter: @AberrantLit
AberrantLiterature.com

Stay in touch with Ashton Macaulay:
Facebook.com/RealMacAshton
Twitter: @RealMacAshton
Web: MacAshton.com